IT MUST BEE LOVE

LAURA SAKINE

D1496329

WWW.LAURASAKINE.COM

It Must Bee Love

Laura Sakine

For Dan

PROLOGUE

I SHIFT IN MY SPOT UNDER THE WILLOW TREE, FEELING full and drowsy from the picnic lunch. The Cove Girls must be feeling the same because no one's said a word for the last five minutes, all of us just sprawled out on the quilt I made earlier this summer. I sewed it together with pieces of our old clothes, mementos from our childhood, hoping that it would remind us of what our lives were like before we start high school next week. It's a comfort, for me, anyway, to have something tangible to hold on to, something that feels like *us* while I wait for this new chapter to begin. We haven't talked about it, but I know they feel it too; this overwhelming desire to be both older and younger, to grow up but for things to stay exactly the same.

There's a splash in the distance, laughter traveling across the water, drowning out the throbbing hum of the cicada bugs, one of the more familiar sounds of a New England summer. The girls keep on chatting about Taylor Swift and influencers and what we should wear on our first day, but I'm barely paying attention, my eyes growing heavy from the heat.

Another splash, this one sounding closer, but it's just

someone jumping off *The Monte,* the highest point on the rock structure across the water from us. Teenagers come to the Ranger Reservoir all summer with the intention of jumping from the top, but only the bravest really go through with it. We never venture over to that side of the woods, though, because we have our own spot, nick-named the *Willow Glen.* It's a special place, a place that has somehow remained ours throughout the years, or at least ours *and* the boys'. They are the ones who discovered it, after all.

Rochelle clears her throat, and my eyes flick back open, knowing she's about to ask a question. She's always filling the time with riddles or word games, and I can never resist playing, even if it's midnight, and I'm practically begging her to let me sleep.

She looks at Stacey, who is currently unwrapping a funfetti cupcake. She is the only person I know who eats her cupcake like a whoopie pie, splitting it in half and flipping the frosting, so it's smooshed together in the middle. When she has it the way she likes, she looks up at Rochelle expectantly.

"Ok... kiss, kill, marry," Rochelle says, "and you have to answer for real this time... Jonathan, Kyle, or that kid Brett from the coffee shop downtown."

I roll my eyes. My annoying brother, Kyle, almost always makes the list of boys to pick from. They are still holding onto their adolescent crushes on him. I thought for sure that would have changed this summer after seeing him in that *Suns Out Guns Out* tank top almost every day, but I guess some crushes stick around for a while. I would know that better than anyone - I've been in love with my brother's best friend, Adam, for as long as I can remember.

Stacey shifts, leaning her back against the base of the tree, her shoulders covering some of the carvings we've made over the years. Names, quotes, special dates - if it's important to us, it's there. We laugh here, cry here, have fights here, make-up here; we've grown up right here, under the willow tree.

"All right, I'd definitely kill Brett Jenkins," she says, and we laugh because it's a no brainer that she'd shut him down right away. He was her first kiss, back in June, and while she thought it was special, he'd gone on to tell his entire baseball team about it. She unfriended him from all of her accounts but not before she posted a selfie with a semi-cryptic caption that read, *live for what today has to offer, not for what yesterday has taken away.* "Kiss Jonathan and marry Kyle." She shoots me an apologetic smile. "Sorry, Bee."

I shrug, reaching into my bag to pull out my new journal. It was a gift from Mom; she woke me up early this morning, too excited to wait for breakfast, saying I need a fresh canvas for my thoughts since I'm about to embark upon a new journey next week. I'm grateful for the gift, but I wish she didn't use the word *journey*; it makes me feel more nervous about the uncertainty of what I'm about to face. I want to pretend like the idea of high school doesn't scare me; like I'm one of those cool girls you see in the movies, the ones who breeze by big transitions like it's nothing.

"Bee...kiss, kill, marry - Jonathan, Kraig with a K from Spanish One, or Adam."

No brainer. "Kill Jonathan, Kiss Kraig, and marry Adam."

"You'd kill Jonathan before Kraig?" Rochelle asks, reaching for a cupcake.

"Every time," I say, flipping open the journal to look over my list again. **Bucket List for My Freshman Year at Graves High School.** So far, what I have is pretty basic. *Go on a real date. Figure out how to add a layer of peplum to a dress. Get invited to an upperclassman party.* I could have started with a regular journal entry, describing what I've been up to this summer; *had my first kiss with Johnny K, almost* *died when I swallowed a spoonful of cinnamon,* but the kiss was slimy, and it was embarrassing that the most thrilling thing I did was swallow a spoonful of spice. I don't want future me to look back at this journal and think, *wow, I was really lame.*

"There's no point in playing with Bee, it's *always* Adam." Sara teases, finally sitting up to take a sip from one of the mason jars filled with Rochelle's special pink lemonade.

She's not wrong; I do always pick Adam to marry, even when he's everyone else's choice to kiss. I want to kiss him, sure, but it isn't just his lips that consume my thoughts; it's everything about him. It's the way his laugh seems to crack right through me and settle into my bones, or the way my heart pounds any time I'm lucky enough to be alone with him. I'm still reeling from that night earlier in the summer when I caught him eating Dad's chocolate ice cream right from the carton. Dad has always been very protective of his chocolate, even going as far as writing right on the carton in black Sharpe, *FOR DAD ONLY - IF YOU ARE NOT SOMEONE'S FATHER, DO NOT EAT THIS.*

But instead of acting caught, Adam dug the spoon back in, smiling mischievously before he lifted the spoon to my mouth to feed it to me. I could hardly breathe; we'd never done something so intimate before, and he acted like it was the most natural thing in the world, like he had no idea that I'd be replaying those seconds over and over again in my brain for the rest of my life. So, *no,* one kiss would never be enough; it's the little moments I'm after, and I want them all.

"What are you writing, anyway?" Sara asks when I don't respond.

"Just my hopes and dreams for freshman year," I say, pumping my eyebrows up and down at her like I'm hiding a big secret. We call Sara our third-eye because she's always at the center of all of our business. I know it's low-key killing her not to know what I'm writing about.

Stacey tosses a black olive into the air and catches it in her mouth - a lucky catch because she almost always misses. "Sooo, Rachel's older sister told her that we're going to get hazed next week. Apparently, the senior girls go around and smother peanut butter in our hair."

Sara scoffs, not buying it, but reaches back and grabs her ponytail, anyway, curling her fingers around the silky strands. "There's no way... that kind of thing doesn't happen in high school, and plus, Nina never said anything about it. She would have told me."

I swallow, my throat feeling tight. When it comes to school starting, I'm running out of things to be excited about. A longer lunch period isn't *that* cool when you are worried about peanut butter in your hair. But maybe Sara is right. Her older sister, Nina, is going into her junior year, same as Kyle and the boys, and she probably would have warned us about something like that.

"Maybe she's in on it," Rochelle says plainly. "Maybe it's like some weird rite of passage that we all have to experience."

Sara shakes her head, but she's still uncertain. "I'll ask her about it tonight and report back ASAP."

I'm about to write *don't get hazed* when we hear footsteps coming from the path. All of us, but especially the boys, feel a strong desire to keep our spot hidden from the rest of the world, as if it isn't just a patch of woods in Massachusetts but rather, a magical cave somewhere in the Mediterranean. It has stayed hidden thanks to some overgrown bushes and a sign the police department put up warning people not to swim in the reservoir, but the threat of discovery is always there.

I focus my eyes on the bushes, repeating the instructions Kyle has given us over and over again: *stay quiet and listen, don't give yourself away*. I always thought it was stupid advice - obviously, we wouldn't jump up and start singing, but I can't deny that my initial reaction was to scream.

The sounds -which are clearly footsteps- draw closer, and that's when I shift my eyes back to the girls, expecting to see similar expressions of panic on their faces. Instead, they all look like they'd rather die than let someone infiltrate our territory. Their intensity is ridiculous; I almost expect Stacey to suggest we climb up the trees and jump down on them. But before any of us can go *Guerrilla Warfare* on them, we hear an unwelcome sound.

"Babyyyy Bee, where are youuuu?" *Kyle.* I gave him strict orders to leave us alone today, but I should have known that he'd come anyway, especially after he realized I was packing for a picnic. He pops out from behind the bush, all smiles and flailing nostrils. "I smell food!"

The girls drop the *Commando* act and start giggling. *Traitors.*

The others follow him in - Andrew, Jimmy, Jonathan, Adam and Adam's girlfriend, Caroline, settling in around us. We are younger than them by two grades, but at the *Willow Glen,* age difference never matters. Besides Caroline, we've all been in each other's lives since we were little because we all live in *The Cove,* our close-knit neighborhood by *Kripp's Cove.*

I'm about to get back to my journal when Adam catches my eye. "Happy birthday, Bee!"

"Oh... thanks," I say, blushing, surprised and charmed that he remembered. The others look up, murmuring obligatory *happy birthdays,* but out of the corner of my eye, I can't help noticing that Adam is still looking at me.

"No plates?" Kyle asks as he places two cookies, a sandwich, and a fruit skewer so daintily on his lap, he could probably be mistaken for the queen of England.

I roll my eyes, more frustrated than I should be. "Will you just get out of here? You're ruining our picnic!" But even as I say it, I know it's pointless; Stacey's already handing him a cupcake while Rochelle pours him a cup of lemonade. At least Sara has the decency to look disappointed that our Cove Girls picnic is now officially over.

I busy myself with my journal, but every few moments, I find myself watching Adam and Caroline.

Two years into their relationship, yet the sight of them together still makes my stomach turn the same way it does every time I think of baked beans. It's not just that he had a girlfriend; I'm pretty sure I could find it in my heart to be happy for him if he was with someone who truly deserves him. But Caroline? She's about as nice as Cersei Lannister.

"Do freshman girls get hazed?" Stacey asks, snapping me out of my stare-fest.

Kyle looks at Jonathan, who looks at Andrew, who glances back at Adam, and in their weird secret boy language, I know they've just decided they're going to mess with us. The girls must sense it, too, because Sara turns to Caroline, the only soon-to-be upperclassman girl here, but surprise, surprise, she looks away, pretending like she didn't hear the question. She only speaks to us girls when parents are around. It's all *come here, Bee, let me braid your hair* in front of them, but when it's just us, she acts like we are the chewed-up gum you sometimes find underneath your desk at school.

"Who told you that?" Andrew asks.

Sara shakes her head. "Doesn't matter. Is it true?"

The boys look so excited, like this question could not have worked out better for them. Jonathan actually raises his hand, as if to say, *guys, I've got this one.* "Ladies, because you're all like the little sisters I never wanted, I'm going to give you a little tip... during the first month of school, you should definitely wear your hair braided. That or just cut it short."

"Ohmygod! It's true!" I yell, panicked.

The boys start laughing, looking pretty pleased with themselves, but it dies down when they see the real horror on our faces. And maybe it's because they can remember how weird this particular transition into high school feels, Andrew stops laughing and clears his throat. "If you're going to skip a class, use the doors by the gym. The security cameras don't work there."

"And don't take any of Mr. Underwood's science classes. The room always smells like beans," Jonathan adds.

Adam nods in agreement. "Have you heard about the pool?"

We shake our heads no, so he goes on. "There's an urban legend that there's a pool hidden somewhere in the building, but no one's ever been able to find it." He's been looking at Sara, but then he turns his head, so our eyes lock. "It would be the perfect place for skinny dipping."

Um, okay. I glance around the group, expecting everyone to be just as surprised as me, but they've already moved on to something about fake cheese from the cafeteria. How did no one else pick up on that innuendo? I know about innuendos now because Sara and I have gone through her Mom's selection of romance novels, titles like *The Duke's Last Dance* or *An Earl with a Swirl* - books that were chock-full of interesting insights that would definitely help us with boys.

I pick up my journal, tapping the back of the page with my purple gel pen before I write, *find the hidden pool and go skinny dipping.* I look up, hesitating to write the next part, but whatever - maybe future me will be impressed. I add *with Adam Stanson* before I can change my mind. *Find the hidden pool and go skinny dipping with Adam Stanson.*

When it seems like the boys are bored with all the school

talk, Sara suggests swimming, which is perfect because I've never needed to plunge myself into cold water more. First, he remembers my birthday, then he's looking at me all funny - it was making my head spin.

I stand, pulling off the black polka-dot cover-up that took me practically the whole summer to sew. It's only when I'm stripped to my bikini that it feels the most appropriate to look back over at Adam. And when I do, I get what I was hoping for - his eyes all over me.

I've caught him in that narrow window of time where he still hasn't realized that I'm watching him while he's watching me, and I think there's a pretty fair chance I'm going to bungle this thing by fainting. Or giggling. But wow, it feels good to be under his gaze like this. I want it to last forever, but at the same time, I'm desperate for him to meet my eyes because maybe it's there that I'll find an explanation for why the air suddenly feels so thick. Why it seems like something has just totally shifted between us.

And then it happens: our eyes do lock in an excruciating showdown, and for a moment, we're the only ones here. He doesn't look caught or embarrassed; on the contrary, he seems glad. Time freezes, and I realize that I was right; he *is* saying something with his eyes. Actually, he's saying *everything* with them. *You're sexy. I like you. Something is happening here.* But before things can get really juicy, Caroline calls to him, something about the debate team, but I hardly hear it as rush down to the water, confused and exhilarated in equal measure. *This can't be happening. Can it?*

I submerge myself into the water, and when I come back up, the facts are more clearly laid out for me. Adam has a girl-friend! And he's Kyle's best friend! He's been in my life since the very beginning; my first memories are blended together with my family and his, and there is just no way he's looking at me as anything other than a little sister.

And yet... somewhere else, deep inside me, something is screaming, *you don't look at your sister like that.*

But he doesn't come down to the water.

I ignore the heated game of *Marco Polo* happening around me, trying not to look up at him, *at them*, but it's impossible. I'm searching for clues that he's freaking out too, and while he doesn't seem like he's been struck by lightning, like me, there is something different about the way he's carrying himself. So, when Caroline walks away to Facetime someone, it's no real surprise that I find my body moving in his direction.

I stop just behind him, ready for anything at this point, but then I see what he has in his hands. My journal. I left it lying there on the blanket.

He jumps when he realizes it's me. "This fell out," he says, handing it over. "I just picked it up."

I take it, standing there for a long moment trying to decide what to do. I could call him out, ask if he was snooping, but do I even want to know? If he just read the words that are written on that page, I'd have about a million reasons to be mortified, and I can't go there, not right now when I'm feeling such unhinged adrenaline.

I walk by him, reaching into the cooler to pull out a jar of pickles. Everyone knows I'm obsessed with pickles, but only the Cove Girls know how far I'm willing to take that obsession. I find the fattest one and crunch into it, satisfied by the perfect snapping sound it makes against my teeth. On instinct, I raise the jar to my lips, peeking down at him to make sure he's not watching. Then I tilt the jar back and take a sip, wiping away the liquid that drips down onto my chin.

"Did you just drink that?" he asks, his expression both horri-fied and amused.

Great. Just when I'm feeling like a sex goddess, he catches me doing something that makes me look like a five-year-old. I've been meaning to break the habit; I've decided it's definitely something a highschooler shouldn't do, and here's my proof. "Um, yeah," I say, trying to play it cool.

He holds my gaze for a beat before he starts laughing. "You are the weirdest girl."

I know he's being funny, but *weird* isn't what I want to be called right now. It makes everything that just came before this seem unimportant. "Okay, Hot Shot, have you ever tried it?"

He shakes his head, breaking into another smile. "No... because I'm not a lunatic."

I look down at the water; the group has switched to a chicken fight, and Rochelle looks like she's about two seconds away from being knocked in. After a quick glance at Caroline, to make sure she's not looking, I turn back to him, whispering, "I dare you."

He's clearly surprised, but if I know anything about Adam Stanson, it's that he won't turn down a dare. He's got a scar on the palm of his left hand to prove it. "Fine," he says, snatching the jar and raising it to his mouth. Right before it touches his lips, he starts to laugh. "Why am I nervous?"

I shrug, nudging him on. "Because you're about to step over to the dark side," I say, startling myself with how flirtatious it came out. I guess I learned how to *use* innuendoes, too.

His eyes smile at me over the jar.

"You are not going to believe this," Caroline says, stomping over to us. I didn't hear her walking up - probably wouldn't have heard thunder, either, even if it was right over my head. She doesn't even notice me standing there, or if she does, it's of little importance to her.

He shoves the jar at me before neatly stepping away,

putting as much distance between us as possible. The best moment of my life is gone... in an instant.

I spend the rest of the day thinking only of him. Not that that's not how I spend most of my days, but now, it's different. It's the way he was looking at me, how his eyes seemed to be saying more than words ever could. When I open my journal again later, what I find isn't surprising at all.

Adam.

1

One year later

I WALK INTO MY HOUSE, MY EYES STILL SWOLLEN FROM crying. I didn't expect to be so attached to a summer job - it was just babysitting, but the girls, Hayden and Nell, had made their mark on me. We knew it wouldn't last forever, but that didn't make our last day any less hard. The girls were practically inconsolable as I was leaving; I put on a brave face and everything, promising to visit and babysit for date-nights, but as soon as I shut the door behind me, I burst into tears, sobbing as I walked the six blocks home.

The house is still empty, but the familiar sound of rubber against pavement echoes from the driveway, letting me know that Kyle is out there shooting hoops.

I walk through to the kitchen, grabbing one of Mom's blueberry muffins, but just as I go to take a bite, the pounding outside stops. The silence is suspicious; between our neighbors and the Cove Girls and Kyle's clan of unruly friends, it's never quiet in this house for long, which means Kyle might have already sniffed out my tears. He has ESP for that kind of thing, like a dog sniffing a bone. He always comes around when I'm vulnerable. I already know what he'd say: *only losers cry on their last day of work.*

I shove the muffin into my mouth and run upstairs to the bathroom.

What I really need is a shower. Dad takes one the second he gets home from work - he says he likes to wash the day away. Granted, he works in construction, so he literally needs to wash the day away, but still, I figure it will make me feel better.

I let the water run for a moment before stepping in, my breath hitching when I feel the cold pour over my body. Kyle says only psychopaths like cold showers, but what he doesn't know is that the most successful people in the world start their days like this. My favorite Instagrammer, Misty, says so, anyway. I'm pretty sure she went to some fancy Goop retreat, so she definitely knows what she's talking about.

When I finish rinsing the new coconut shampoo from my hair, I step out and wrap myself in my favorite bathrobe; the one with the lemons on it that the Cove Girls gave me for Christmas last year. I step into my room and pick up my phone to scroll through my accounts before I get ready for tonight.

The plan is to do something wild to close out summer but historically, we haven't been wild. The riskiest thing we've ever done was steal Mr. Braxton's garden gnome, and even then, we returned it an hour later with a note that said we were sorry.

We'd probably just end up getting an ice cream at the *Dream Cream* downtown like we have almost every other night for the past two months. But at least I've finally nailed down the best flavor combo: one scoop of chocolate brownie, one scoop of cookie dough, covered with chocolate sprinkles. Heaven, in a bite.

A new post from Stacey pops up on my feed, a tribute to

summer with an array of photos from the last couple of months. Beach days, the day trip we took into Boston, and an array of random snapshots. She ends the caption with *I can't believe we'll be #sophomores!,* and I really can't believe it, either, because our Freshman year was seemingly the slowest and fastest year of my life.

I consider picking up my journal just to jot down another list to start the year, but it would probably end up being a waste like the one from before. Actually, if I could go back, I would just write one thing: *survive.*

As it turns out, ninth graders in the social structure of high school are considered the lowest of the low. That should have been obvious, I know, but I was still surprised when we were treated like house flies: ignored unless someone was trying to squash us dead. You'd think that having a cool, older brother would have helped with that, but it didn't. Somehow, it made it worse. I'm still cringing from that horrifying night when the Cove Girls and I accidentally "stumbled" into an upper-classman party, only to have Caroline call us out in front of everyone and tell us to leave. It was humiliating.

But it wasn't all bad. I even had a boyfriend - for a little while, anyway. His name is Tyler, and he was really sweet. He would surprise me with fun-sized pieces of Almond Joy; I never had the heart to tell him it was my least favorite candy - the only one I would throw away when I used to trick-or-treat. I kept sticking them in the front pocket of my backpack, and on one of the warmer days, all the chocolate melted, making a huge mess. We decided we were better off as friends.

There's a knock at the door, and Mom steps in, her long, flowy skirt swaying as she makes her way to the bed. I make a mental note to borrow it later, so I can try to recreate it with the pale pink satin I bought on my last trip to the fabric store.

"Hey babe," she says, running a hand through her hair.

Even after working all day, she still looks so effortlessly beautiful. Dad always describes her as being a great beauty; people
say we look alike, but I don't see it. It's hard to see that kind of
thing. "How was your last day?"

"It was good," I reply. "Sad."

She leans in, inspecting my face. "You're burnt, Bee. You
have to be more careful." She sighs. "You're damaging your
skin."

"I know, I know." I toss my phone onto the other side of the
bed, stretching out next to her, signaling for her to start
scratching my head.

"So, the girls were upset?" she asks, taking the bait. I know
she's referencing the text I sent earlier asking for advice on how
to deal with two hysterical children. I didn't know what to do,
especially since I wanted to cry myself, but she walked me
through it using all her soothing words.

"Yeah, they were."

She leans down, squeezing me. "That sounds really hard,
but just think of how amazing you made their summer. They'll
cherish it forever."

I nod once against her neck but pull away fast, not wanting
to cry again. "Thanks, Mom."

She stands and walks over to look at the photo collage on
my wall. There are photos from the last two years - an evolution, if you will - where we go from scrapbook parties to
hanging out underneath the bleachers at school. Not that we
were doing anything sketchy under there, but it still felt rebel-
lious. "Dad and I are going to have dinner at the *Lobster Pot*.
Do you want to come?"

I push off the bed, glancing in the mirror. My cheeks are
a little red, but I wouldn't call them burnt. I grab my face
lotion and generously applying it to my cheeks in small,
circular motions like the beauty influencers say to do. "Sara

and Stacey are coming by. Not sure what we're doing yet, though."

"All right, well, shoot me a text when you know. We'll leave some cash downstairs so you can order something if you want," she says, leaning in to kiss my forehead.

When she's gone, I pull on a red cotton dress and go down into the kitchen. Kyle's playing ball again, the constant *thump, thump, thump* serving as a backdrop as I move around the kitchen.

I grab the blender first, then all the ingredients to my favorite smoothie: spinach, banana, mango, and oat milk. We call it a *Bee Plus*; it's definitely not as good as a milkshake, but it's a runner-up. I pour it into two cups and walk down to the basement to wait for Sara.

"Well, good for you, I guess you moved on really easily... You found a new girl, and it only took a couple weeks..." I sing the Olivia Rodrigo song as I glide down the stairs, hopping off the bottom step like I always do. But when I look up, Adam is sitting on one of the recliners. "Oh." I jump back. "You scared me!"

He glances up at me briefly before looking back down at his phone.

That was rude, I want to say, but instead, I stand there, rocking back and forth on my feet, unsure of what I should do. Normally, I would walk right back upstairs, but something is keeping me there; maybe just the fact that we hadn't seen much of each other this summer - he worked nights at the country club while I worked days.

Finally, he puts his phone down, looking up at me with a smile. "Sorry, Bee," he says, more welcoming now. "You have my attention."

Oh.

It should be a relief, but now I have to decide whether or

not to sit, and that requires the assumption that he wants me to. "Did you want to be alone?" I ask.

He smiles, in that heart-breaking way of his. I read about *Helen of Troy* in English last year, and I wanted to shout *but have you heard of Adam Stanson of Padstow?* I'd literally steer a canoe over the Atlantic Ocean to wage a war over him. In a heartbeat.

He leans back, running his hand through his thick, shiny, perfect hair. "It's your house, Bee... you don't have to ask if I need privacy." He pauses for a beat, clearly leaving the decision up to me.

I roll my eyes because it's such a typical boy thing to say. Evasive and mysterious, leaving me no-more-sure of what I should do. It's like answering a question with a question. Finally, I take a seat, and he asks me what's in the cups.

"Smoothies," I say, handing him one.

He looks inside. "Bee Plus?"

I nod, taking too big of a sip, and it instantly rushes to my head, paralyzing me with pain. I almost lift my hand to start pounding on my forehead - everyone knows that's the only way to cure a brain freeze - but to do that now would make me look like a child. And I really don't want to look like a child in front of him.

He looks at me over the cup. "Who was this really for?"

"Sara," I say, suppressing a laugh. She'll be furious when she finds out I gave her smoothie away, especially because the boys hardly ever share their food with us. But this is a special occasion. I'm almost never alone in the basement with Adam Stanson. "I'll make another one when she gets here."

"Mmm. I think this is my favorite smoothie," he says after he's had a sip. Then he sits back into the recliner and looks back over in my direction. "So, *Bee*, how was your summer? We didn't see much of each other, huh?"

I look up, taking him in. He's wearing his everyday uniform, basketball shorts and a tank top, but it takes me a moment to realize what's different about him: his arms. They're bigger, more defined. Maybe bussing tables at the country club made him buff? "It was good. I mostly just worked," I say, looking away. "How was yours?

"It was good... it went too fast. You were a mother's helper, right?"

I look away, trying to hide how happy it makes me that he knows what I've been up to all summer. It always catches me off guard to learn that he knows something personal about me, but it happens a lot, actually. Like when he said -in front of everyone- that I didn't like sweet and savory things, or when he brought back my favorite penny candy from the old-fashioned sweet shop after going fishing in New Hampshire. It reminds me that I'm not always the only one paying attention.

"Yeah, with the Johannsons. It was cool. I basically got paid to swim all summer. Today was my last day."

When I look back over, he holds my gaze for a moment too long, making his innocent smile feel like something more. It reminds me of last summer at the Willow Glen, when he seemed to be telling me all sorts of things with his eyes. I don't know what I thought would happen between us after that day, it's not like I expected that we'd ride off into the sunset together or anything, but I never thought he'd ghost me. I think I could count on one hand the amount of times we've spoken in the last year. He totally avoided me, and after a while, I started to avoid him, too. Kind of - I mean, I might have added fifteen seconds to my walk to PE on Tuesdays and Thursdays just so I could catch him coming out of geography, but I'd take that to my grave.

Before the moment can stretch into anything too intimate, he looks away, mumbling. "That's cool. I can tell you were outside a lot. You're so tan, I don't know that I've ever seen your skin so sun-kissed before."

My stomach drops - but in a good way. *Sun-kissed?* I look away, studying the bottom of my cup so intensely, I wouldn't be surprised if I burnt a hole right through it. But because I'm me and he's him, I look back up just in time to see him looking over my... *sun-kissed-ness,* his eyes slowly trailing down my neck, my arms, then lingering on my legs.

What. Is. Happening?

I clear my throat. "Yeah, I'm a little burnt....so... what did you do?" I ask, trying to change the subject. It's all well and good that he's checking me out, but the last thing I need is to get my hopes up again.

"I...um... I... worked at the country club, and we went to Colorado to visit my uncle. Did you know that?"

"Beaver Creek, right?" I say, knowing full well that he was gone ten days in July.

"Yeah, it was cool. We hiked a lot and swam in a natural spring. It's really different from here." He looks inside his cup, moving the straw up and down. "I want to go back."

"Lucky. Colorado's on my list."

"What list?"

"My travel list... I can't wait to see the world one day."

He smiles. "Ok. Let's hear it."

I sit up, excited because traveling is one of my favorite things to talk about. I've spent an unhealthy amount of time on *Pinterest* planning for my dream trips one day. "Ok... well, in the US, I really want to go to Sedona to hike the vortexes."

He rolls his eyes. He was there the night we watched a documentary on energy forces. Rochelle and I had been captivated, but the boys called us gullible. "Yeah, yeah I'm not surprised by that one. Where else?" he asks, leaning forward like he's really interested.

"Ok... I want to ski the Vail mountains in Colorado... road trip through Texas, eating my weight in BBQ, and tour Alcatraz in San Francisco. There's way more... that's just my short list. I'd go anywhere really."

He suddenly looks serious, like he's trying to decide whether he wants to share what's on his mind. That's Adam, though. He always seems like he is holding something back.

Only an over-observer like myself would notice, but I suspect there is more to him, more than what he allows people to see. "I want to travel more, too... I actually can't wait to get out of here."

"Really? That's surprising... your family is like Padstow royalty. I thought for sure you'd stay a townie."

He seems offended, so I look away. But if ever there was royalty in this town, his family would be it. The Stansons have lived here for generations; his dad, like mine, is a townie, but the difference between our families is money. I guess the classes never mixed back then and while Padstow isn't really like that anymore, they are still well-known enough to be considered the top-tier.

He waits until I look at him again before saying, "Maybe that's the reason I want to get out... My dad likes to remind me constantly that I have a responsibility as a Stanson, to show up and represent the family. Be a good student... excel in basketball... everything is about my image, about how I appear to everyone else."

"Oh, um..."

"One day, I'm going to get out of here and leave all of this behind. There is so much more to the world than this small town."

My breath hitches, realizing that it's kind of a big deal he just said that. He's being vulnerable and trusting me with something he doesn't share often - his truth. I'd be willing to bet he doesn't say these kinds of things to Caroline. You don't have to be a rocket scientist to see that she doesn't have a lot of depth. But if you're worried about your image, she's the perfect person to date. On paper, she's like a politician's wife: smart and pretty and her hair is always curled. Parents love her. But if you look beyond that, you'll find that she is a mean girl, through and through.

"Do you think that's weird?" he asks.

I shake my head, practically barking, "No, no. I'm totally with you. It's the reason I want to travel, too. I'm really happy that I grew up here and everything, but there's a burning in me to see more."

Our eyes lock. "A burning, huh?"

I search his eyes, trying to find the sarcasm, but his expression has softened, and I get the sense that he feels understood. This is way better than having him check me out. It feels like I just cracked open his soul.

A wild thought pops into my head. *He's going to come over here and kiss me.* But I push it away before it can take roots. Whatever this is, it's not *that*. We won't kiss, *can't* kiss, because that moment doesn't exist between us. "Have you decided where to apply to college yet?" I ask.

His eyebrows push together, confusion lacing his features. By asking about college, I've somehow catapulted us out of the strange little bubble we just found ourselves in. I guess that was the point, but now I wish I could call back the words and live in that moment for a little while longer. "Let's not talk about that. Tell me more about your list."

I let out a relieved breath, but just as I'm about to go on, I hear noises coming from upstairs. I know it's Sara by the sound of her movements: she stomps more than she steps. "Brooke, you down there?" she calls.

Instinctively, I jump up, which should have seemed aggressive, but out of the corner of my eye, I see him straighten, too.

"Yeah, I'm here." I call back, and then she's barreling down the stairs with Kyle and Caroline behind her. *Caroline.* How rude of her to show up right now, just when I'm acquainting myself with Adam's soul.

Sara sees the cups on the table, whining, "Ugh, you gave him my smoothie, didn't you?"

"I'll make you one right now." I try to pull myself together. No one seems suspicious of anything, which should be a relief, but it bothers me. It makes me feel like I'm making it all up in my head. Again.

Andrew comes down next and suggests doing a fire in the backyard.

Just before heading back up the stairs, I look over my shoulder to see if Adam's looking at me. He's not.

Later, we're sitting around the stone fire pit in my backyard, watching Kyle and his friends sneak sips from two rogue cans of *Coors Light.* Sara, Stacey, and I are huddled in the corner, like always. We can hang out when everyone is at our house, but we have to blend into the background, or else Kyle might banish us into the house. We know better than to try our luck; it has happened too many times to count.

Jimmy starts telling a ghost story, and it feels like the perfect opportunity to look over at Adam. Since coming out here, it has taken a tremendous amount of will-power on my part not to glance in his direction. Every morsel of my being is urging me to see if he's reeling like I am; I mean, for a moment there, things got pretty deep, and you don't just recover from that kind of thing.

I make a plan in my head. *Start slow, don't make it obvious. First, look at the grass, wait two seconds, then look up at the sky and intermittently lower your head down until you land on his face.* But in the end, it's all for nothing because when I get my chance, he's already looking at me.

I jerk my head away, embarrassed. I thought I was being so slick, and he probably saw right through my whole scheme. But the question still remains: *why was he looking at me?*

Just when Jimmy's about to get to the scary part, *something about a fisherman alone on eerily calm waters,* Andrew interrupts, holding up his phone like he's holding up a report card with straight As. "Party is on! Who's coming to the woods?"

The group stands, forgetting the story, and that's when the girls and I scooch our Adirondack chairs closer together. It's all fun and games until we feel the sting of being left behind.

But then Andrew walks over. "Wanna come?"

I look up, dumb-struck, wondering if I heard him correctly. We've never been invited to a party before. Not ever.

Sara shoots up. "Yes... we are. I mean... yes... we do!"

Kyle turns around, rushing back over. Out of the corner of my eye, I see Adam stop, too. "No, it's not a good idea," Kyle says, shaking his head.

Sara's face falls for half a second, until I recognize the determination in her eyes; nothing is going to stand between her and this party. Not even Kyle. "It's the *best* idea! You can't take back an invitation once it's been issued."

"This isn't like... a ball, Sara, it's a party... with drinking. It's too dangerous."

Sara laughs out loud. "Oh, come on. Dangerous how?"

Adam joins our small group, sitting on the arm of my chair, only inches away from me. If I turned the tiniest bit, our arms would be touching. It's a bold move, him sitting this close. He would have never done something like this last year. Maybe our basement conversation has opened up something between us. Maybe he trusts me now.

He looks down at me. "These parties always get broken up by the cops."

My excitement deflates. "And?"

He holds my gaze, even as Caroline comes up behind him and starts nudging him away. "What are you going to do if we get chased out?"

"Come on, guys," Andrew interrupts, "they'll be fine."

But Adam doesn't budge, still waiting for my answer. By now, Caroline looks pissed. I even think she mumbles *so annoying* under her breath.

"We'll run," I say, standing.

That seems to settle it.

Sara bites her lip, pulling Stacey up, and we try forcing more neutral expressions on our faces, downplaying that being invited to a party is the coolest thing to ever happen to us.

Twenty minutes later, after walking through the eighth hole of the St. Andrew's golf course, we arrive at *the spot*. It's just a regular patch of woods, but to us, it's so much more because there, in all of its glory, is a *real* party with half-dressed teenagers and red solo cups.

The group scatters, leaving me, Sara, and Stacey on our own. "What do we do now?" Stacey asks.

"The log is open over there." Sara points to a piece of driftwood near the fire. "Let's go sit." We inch forward like our bodies are attached, too nervous to move too far away from one another. We were in such a rush to get here, but now that we are, my stomach is twisted in knots.

Just as we sit, a group of senior girls walk by, Caroline leading the pack. "They practically begged to come." She glances over her shoulder. "It's so pathetic." The rest of them break into a fit of giggles.

"This feels weird." Stacey sighs, looking into the fire. "Maybe we should go."

"We're not exactly welcome," I point out, regretting this night already. Were other people looking over at us, thinking we were pathetic too? Was it so obvious that we didn't belong here?

I scan the crowd, not sure what I'm looking for until my eyes settle on Adam, who is - surprise, surprise - already looking at me. Did he hear what Caroline said? He's not oblivious to her taunting, and luckily, he's always stuck up for me. Maybe that's what irritates her the most.

I'm about to look away when he smiles, and after a long, agitated moment, I find myself smiling back.

Sara shrugs next to me. "Who cares? We'll people watch for a bit and then we'll traipse back through the wilderness and find our way out. Come on, *girls*, this is our first party! This is a big deal!"

I let out a breath, looking away from Adam. It *is* a big deal for us, one that we've been waiting a long time for. We've heard about enough upperclassman parties last year to be envious. It isn't about drinking; it's about being included. And maybe a little bit about status. "Yeah, you're right. Who cares!"

It figures that just when I decide to let my insecurities go, Tucker Williams walks up to us, smiling in that devilish way of his. If we were waiting on a sign to just let go and have some fun, this is it.

While I've never spoken to Tucker *per se*, it still feels like I know him. Or maybe it's more accurate to say that I know his *face*; I spent a fair amount of time gawking at it in our art class last year. But the lip ring is new; he must have gotten that done sometime this summer.

He hands me a cup. "You were in my art class last year, weren't you?"

I nod, accepting the drink while my heart starts hammering against my chest. Is there anything more exciting than being recognized by a cute older boy?

Him and his friends slide in around us, but he sits next to me on the log. "I knew it! You're the quiet girl in the back... with the eagle painting."

"Oh, my God, that eagle!" I shriek, remembering the oil painting that I'd worked so hard on, only to have Mrs. Lionel say that she thought it looked like an abstract butterfly.

He smiles. "It definitely looked like an eagle."

"Thanks. I'm surprised you even noticed me, what with all the girls that used to walk you to class." My hand flies to my mouth. "I'm sorry... I... um... can't believe those are the words that just decided to come out of my mouth right now." I can't even blame it on the alcohol because I haven't taken a sip of whatever is inside the cup.

He spits out his beer, laughing loudly, and when he recovers, he says. "What can I say? I have a thing for pretty girls." And as if that isn't charming enough, he reaches over and gently pinches my cheek. *Swoon.*

Tucker stays close to me for the next hour or so, telling me about his guitar and his plans for the future, the road trip he wants to take to L.A. after he graduates. If I could get a word in, I'd tell him that a road trip sounded cool, that I hoped to do one myself one day. "I'm going to grab another drink. Do you want a refill?" He stands, pointing to my abandoned cup.

I shake my head. "I'm good, thanks."

He leans in close to my face, his breath smelling like beer. "When I get back, do you want to get out of here?"

He doesn't wait for an answer, so I'm left alone with my disdain. There is absolutely no way I'm leaving with him, but how do I say that without offending him? Or should I even care about offending him when he's the one who's putting me in this weird situation, anyway?

I look out into the woods, noticing some strange flashing lights in the distance. My first thought is the most obvious - alien invasion, but then someone screams, *cops!* and chaos breaks out around me.

I watch the bodies rush by; *jocks, drama students, members of the debate team,* all the while aware that I'm frozen in place. I'd always imagined myself as the kind of person who would take action in emergency situations like this, but not even the new awareness that I'm *not* that person is enough to encourage my body to follow what my mind is screaming: *run!*

I'm snapped back to reality when I see Adam running toward me. "Bee!" He takes my hand, trying to pull, but I'm pretty sure that even the Jedi Force wouldn't work right now.

He glances over his shoulder where the lights are getting closer now. Turning back to me, he moves the side of his face against mine, so his lips are only inches away from my ear. "Bee, we have to get out of here."

It's like my body says, *there you are!* Apparently, Adam speaking sensually into my ear is the password I'd been waiting for. I let him pull me away.

He doesn't let go of my hand, leading me down another path in the opposite direction from where the shouting is coming from. It's hard to believe that in all of this darkness, he even knows where he's going, but he never breaks his stride, moving quickly around bushes and trees like he's one of those woodsy outdoorsmen on those shows Dad is always watching.

He pauses finally so we can catch our breath. "You okay?" he asks.

"Yeah," I pant. "Do you know where we are?"

"Yeah... the golf course is right up there. Ready?"

I move to take a step in his direction, but my foot catches

and I trip, tumbling forward so hard, I fall directly onto his back, taking him all the way down to the ground.

Thump.

Admittedly, I'm in no pain at all, but Adam, for all I know, could be dead. "Are you all right?" I whisper.

He shifts slightly, groaning. "What happened?"

"I think the cops shot a missile at us."

Thankfully, he laughs, and then I realize how nice it feels to be on top of him. It's sturdy up here, like I'm so light, he can't even feel me. I could sleep like this. I wonder if he could do a push-up.

"As much as I'd love to lie like this all night, we should probably get going."

I shoot straight up, blushing from every part of my body. "Sorry about that."

After another minute of walking, we come up on the clearing of the golf course, speeding up again when we see a small group waiting by the edge of the woods.

A flashlight is pointed at us, and I hear Kyle let out a sigh. "See... this is why you shouldn't have come."

"I got away, didn't I?"

"Barely," Adam says under his breath.

"Are you drunk?" Kyle asks.

"No, she's not," Adam tells him.

Before I can contemplate that exchange and how I wasn't even a part of it, we're moving again. My adrenaline starts to wear off, and I have this overwhelming urge to laugh, until I realize that Adam and I are still holding hands. What is this life? First, we're sharing truths in the basement, then I'm catching him watching me, then I'm lying on his body, and now, we're just holding hands? What is happening?

He leads the way again, but if I didn't know any better, I'd think he was deliberately lagging behind everyone else, slowing our steps so that we naturally fall behind the rest of the group. When they're finally out of earshot, he stops, dropping my hand as he turns to me. It's too dark to see his face, but I can tell by his posture that I'm not going to like what he's about to say. "By the way... if I were you, I would not get involved with Tucker."

I laugh. "Okay... your Grace."

He stiffens. "What?"

"You sound like a broody Duke from a romance novel. They're always all protective and overbearing trying to hide their feelings for-"

"For what?" If I could see his face, I'd know that his lips are turned upward, that he knows exactly what I was about to say.

"Nothing... what's wrong with Tucker?"

He's quiet for a moment before saying, "He's not someone you want to get involved with."

"Riveting insight, Adam, thanks."

He shifts from one foot to the other, like he wasn't expecting me to challenge him on this. And to be honest, it's not his concern that's irritating me right now; it's the fact that he hasn't even considered that I've already figured Tucker out myself. "He's just... I don't know... a player?"

"Really? I thought he was *so* nice." I'm trying to egg him on but to what end, I don't know.

"Oh, come on. You're not really falling for that whole rocker boy vibe, are you?"

I shrug. "Maybe."

Someone whistles from the stone wall ahead of us, so Adam takes my hand again, pulling me toward it.

When we reach the wall, he takes out his phone, shining the light on the stones. "Put your foot here and here." He points. "I'll give you a boost."

I put my foot in the first spot, reaching up to the top, but the absurdity of the situation hits me, and I start giggling. Tonight... everything... it's been such a bizarre day. But I have to admit, I don't hate it.

I step down, slipping at the bottom. My back goes crashing into his chest, and I try to ignore the fact that it feels like I just hit a cement wall. "Sorry."

I see him nod. "You ready to try again, Giggles?"

I climb back up, but this time, he moves behind me like a barrier. I can feel the heat of him, and I know that if I let go again, I'd fall right into his arms. I'm tempted to try.

"I'm going to push you up, okay?" he says, and I nod because words might be lost to me forever. If I turned around, I'm pretty sure that I'd find his face only inches away from my butt, but before I can think too much about it, his hands are *on* my butt, pushing me up enough so I can climb over.

I wait on the other side, trying to slow my breathing.

He hops over easily. I can see him better now from the street lights, and there's a curious smile playing at his lips. He holds his hands up in defense. "I did not mean to touch your ass, I swear. I was aiming for your legs and my hands slipped."

"Right." I smile to myself.

We're both surprised when my phone goes off with a text from Stacey. It's the yellow scooter emoji, so I send back a toothbrush. We'd created our own emoji emergency distress signals freshman year after Sara French kissed Ross Baker in the movie theater. Apparently, his breath smelled like expired mayo, and Sara was looking for a way to escape, but none of us knew what she was saying, so we created a system. A secret, undercover language, using emojis that only made sense to us. *Statue of Liberty - time to go. Rocket ship - create a diversion. Honeypot - I need help. Purple umbrella with rain - I'm in love. Yellow scooter - I'm okay, you? - Toothbrush- I'm alive.*

I look toward the group, realizing how far behind we are

now. But I don't care, and Adam doesn't seem too, either. I want to ask a million questions; first, what is going on between us? But all that comes out is, "So, did you have fun tonight?"

He shrugs. "It was okay. More fun than it usually is."

"Why?"

He smiles. "Some new faces."

"Whose?" I pry, then, "Ow!" I smack my neck when I feel a sharp pinch. I don't think there's another living soul that gets bitten by mosquitos more than I do. I read once that it was because of my O-Blood type. Kyle called me an idiot, but I'm convinced it's true. "I'm getting eaten alive out here."

He takes my hand, pulling me toward the street. "They're attracted to the coconut smell from your hair."

I pause. "What? How'd you know it was coconut?"

"It's new, right?" And then, "Don't forget what I said about Tucker." He steps away casually, like he didn't just drop a major bomb on me. And before I even get a chance to respond, Kyle's yelling at us to hurry up.

Adam doesn't even drop my hand until we spot a group of Caroline's friends in the parking lot. He breaks away then, but at the last moment, he turns back around. "I had fun tonight."

Something is going on between us. I've seen enough episodes of Law & Order to know that when things seem suspicious, they are.

Dear Journal,

Have I always loved him? No, I distinctly remember a time when it wasn't love. Before there was love, he was just another one of Kyle's friends, a regular boy with cooties. He was definitely my favorite, though, even then. I guess everything changed the summer we had that epic fourth of July block party, the one with the bouncy house and the slip-and-slide. I was ten, and he was twelve. I was minding my own business when I overheard some of the older girls talking about how cute he was. All of the boys had just gone through puberty, and while it was excruciating to witness how awkward they were, I couldn't deny how different Adam seemed. But it still wasn't love, not yet, that was just when I started thinking about him a little more. But that day in my backyard, under the maple tree, that was when things got more serious for me. Kyle and I had just gotten into that epic fight over the computer, and I stormed out of the house, crying and crying. Adam came out to try and cheer me up. The maple pods had fallen, covering the grass, and he picked one up and told me to watch. He opened the center, took out the seeds and stuck the pod onto his nose. I was stunned. I'd never seen anyone do that. Then he picked up another one and did it to me. That's the day he went from being a boy I thought about, to the boy I loved.

2

I'M EATING AN ENGLISH MUFFIN AT THE KITCHEN ISLAND with Mom and Kyle when Dad rushes in, frazzled, like every other weekday morning. "I'm in a rush. I have to get to the job site before the building inspector." He twists the lid on the *Yeti* thermos I got him for Father's Day, but the coffee spills, landing on his pants. This happens at least twice a week.

Mom looks up, sucking in her breath, and Dad whips his head around, already defensive. "I can't change now, Liz, I'm going to be late!"

She stands, walking over to him, the very picture of calm. She's the kind of person you want around during an emergency because nothing ever riles her. When Kyle broke his nose last year during a playoff game, she talked him through it like she was explaining how to use the toaster oven, even with all the blood pouring out of his nose. The crowd clapped for Kyle as they walked off the court, but I always suspected part of the applause was for her, too. "Is there anything that I can do to help you?"

He smiles, surrendering his mood; he can never stay frustrated long when she gives him that smile. "Just a kiss," he says, wrapping his arms around her waist.

Kyle flinches beside me. "Dad, I'm trying to eat here. Aren't you late?"

He shakes his head. "I've got a few minutes." Then pulling back, he smiles, looking at Mom again. "But do you know where my keys are?"

Mom and Dad have a special marriage, and I knew from an early age that I wanted one just like it one day. They say their connection was instantaneous, like lightning striking, and I've heard the story so many times, it feels like it's my story. They met in Boston, while Mom was visiting on a college trip and Dad was still working as a foreman for the construction union.

The actual meeting part was simple; they were introduced at a party, but it was what happened after that made their story interesting. Mom moved across the country from Seattle and married Dad, two months after meeting him. My grandparents had been furious with her. They are fancy people, the kind of people who use words like *alacrity* or *acquiesce,* and the fact that she married a man that would be running a bulldozer for the rest of his life did not sit well with them at all. But in the end, it didn't matter - they never let my grandparents get in the way.

After breakfast, I hop into Kyle's car, unfolding my schedule to look over it again. The sheet is already worn and crinkled from all the times I've gone over it. I know it by heart - we are already into the third week of school - but I'm still scarred from getting lost in the hallways last year. There's only so many times the hall-monitor can hand out a detention slip before you're scarred for life.

I go through the room numbers: *English 105, Advanced Spanish 210, Science 302.* But all that really matters to me is *Sewing 101.* It's the first time since the early nineties that

Graves is offering home-economics classes, and I'm the only underclassman who got a spot in the sewing program. I begged my guidance counselor, Mrs. Mooney, for a week straight, and even then, it didn't work until I bribed her with a *Hostess Cupcake*.

Stacey and Rochelle are waiting by the back door when we pull into the student parking lot. Call it *Friendtuition,* but I can tell by the look on Stacey's face that she has something to tell me, and I'd bet a hundred dollars that it has to do with Tucker Williams. He's sought me out a few times since that night at the woods party; only in the hallways and sometimes at lunch, but the girls have it in their heads that he will be my boyfriend by homecoming.

Stacey whispers. "Guess who I just saw?"

"Taylor Swift?"

She rolls her eyes, looping her arm with mine and Rochelle's. "Tucker" she whispers again, as if we were discussing nuclear codes. She waits for a reaction, frowning when I don't give her one. "Do you think he'll ask you to hang out soon?"

The warning bell rings, and we pick up our pace, trying to make it to class before Ms. Moreno. She hates tardiness, and if you're late to class, you have to stand in front of the class and recite Robert Frost's *The Road Not Taken.* In *Spanish.*

We make it just before the last bell. "So, do you?"

"I doubt it. I'm sorry to disappoint you, but I don't like him like that." I take out my book, trying to ignore the look they're giving each other. They're acting personally offended that I'm not falling for Tucker's charms, but I could never be into someone who only ever talks about himself. I'm still surprised he even remembers my name, what with all the *I's* and *me's* he's choking out all the time.

Stacey scoffs. "You're no fun!"

I smile. "Soy tan divertida!"

Later, before the last period of the day, I stop at my locker before study hall to grab all of my school supplies, planning to organize everything during my free period. I rush up three flights of stairs, scurrying through the hallway, making it to the doorway just in time for the bell to go off. I pause, catching my breath, but I lose it again when I see who's sitting in the front row of my classroom. Adam.

"Oh, my God," I scream as everything I'm holding falls to the floor. The class erupts in laughter, but I can barely hear it over the pounding in my chest. My eyes stay locked on him as I try to make sense of why he's here, in *my* class. It must be a mistake; our schedules are set for the quarter, but he looks positively at home at the desk.

He walks over to kneel down beside me. "Hey," he whispers, handing me a folder.

I force a smile, mortified because this is easily the most embarrassing thirty seconds of my life. If I'd known that I was going to be sharing a class with Adam Stanson, I would have hired a make-up team or something, but instead, I make an entrance like this?

I swallow before whispering back, "Hi", and when I can't think of anything witty to say, I focus on trying to collect all of my stuff. Binders, notebooks, gel pens, a butterfly eraser, *why do I have a butterfly eraser?*

When his hand brushes against mine, I jerk upright, dropping another binder.

Mrs. Quinton clears her throat, annoyed. "Ms. McGrath, will you be joining us today, or do you plan on dancing around up there for the rest of the period?"

I stand with a shaking smile on my face. "Sorry." Then I rush to the back of the room, to the safety of my desk.

"And next time, I'll kindly ask you to leave God out of it," she remarks.

More laughs.

"Oh... yeah... sure...no problem...sorry," I say, blushing again.

When the proper amount of time has gone by, seventeen seconds to be exact, I steal a glance at him. To my surprise, he's still standing, looking strangely like he's at war with himself. Finally, he picks up his backpack and walks over, taking the desk next to mine. "Too cool to sit with me?"

"What? *No.* I just didn't want to be weird." I busy myself with a notebook, trying to play it cool. If I stop moving, he'll see that my hands are shaking, and why would my hands be shaking unless he was making me nervous? And why would I be nervous?

I haven't spoken to him since the woods party, not even once, and it feels like deja vu from last year, like he'd forgotten I even existed.

"Are you coordinating your classes by color?" he teases.

I take a deep breath, coaching myself up. *You can do this, you can sit next to him and be normal. You've known him all your life. So what if he watched you the night of the party. So what if he held your hand for longer than he needed to. So what if he knew that your hair smelled like coconuts.* I pull out a label, carefully writing *History.* "Of course I am."

He smiles. "You're a dork."

Ignoring his comment, I ask, "So, did you just switch in?"

"Yeah, I had to move a few classes around in order to make room for away games." He's the star of our basketball team, what adults call *a natural athlete,* and he's always getting little privileges from his status.

I nod, reaching down to pull up a blue binder. "Cool."

He smiles. "How has your first couple weeks been?"

I write *Science* on a label in my neatest handwriting, slipping it into the flap. "Good, good. You know, same old, but I like my teachers so that's nice, and I'm taking a sewing class so that's pretty exciting. Did you hear about that? It was in the student newsletter, do you read the student newsletter? Anyway, there was a whole write-up about Mrs. Holmes, that's our teacher. She just moved here from New York City. She's very cool, super stylish, and she was on a season of *Project Runway*. Do you ever read the newsletter?" I look up at him, faltering. "Sorry, you're bored... I'll stop."

He shakes his head. "You're not boring me. I think it's cool."

"Then why are you smiling? Wait... don't tell me... because you think I'm a dork?"

He nods. "You're definitely a dork, but not because you're excited about your sewing class. I've always thought it's really cool that you like to sew. Remember those kitchen towels that you gave your Mom for Easter? Those were pretty sweet."

I laugh, relaxing into my seat, surprised that he even remembers. It was one of my first sewing projects, one of my first successful ones, anyway. I'd just epically failed at making a mini-skirt out of a lime green stretch knit that I found in the discount section at the fabric store. After that, Mom suggested I start small, so I tried my hand at the kitchen towels, and they had come out just as they were supposed to. We didn't have them for long, though, because Kyle spilled orange soda all over them. Still, it's touching that Adam remembers, especially when I haven't thought about them in years. "You have a good memory, huh?"

He holds my gaze. "About some things."

I cough, trying not to notice that he's still turned toward me and hasn't taken anything out of his backpack. Sara made me watch a TED talk once on body language, and Adam is showcasing what they would have called an open posture, like he's prepared to spend this entire period talking to me.

"So... have you talked to Tucker?" he asks when there's a lull in our conversation for all of three seconds.

I look up, studying his face, trying to figure out what it is that he wants to know. If I like Tucker? If we text? If I'm going to get a tattoo of his name on my butt?

"You know I have," I challenge because I caught him looking at us earlier when Tucker came to sit at my lunch table for a few minutes.

He waits for me to say more, and when I don't, he sighs. "It's not a good idea, Bee."

I roll my eyes. "So you keep saying, but do you even know him? I've never seen you guys speak, not even once."

"I don't need to know him to know the type."

I grab my purple Sharpie, tightening my grip as I write *Geometry*. "I never pegged you as being the judgmental type. Plus, he's been really sweet to me." Even as I say it, I'm wondering why I do, what reason do I have to lie to Adam about what's going on with Tucker?

"He doesn't even seem like your type. Why would you want to date someone who wears the same kind of jeans as you?"

I laugh. "I don't have a type, and we don't wear the same kind of jeans."

"Did you know that he has a tattoo of an actual heart on his forearm that says, *I will never break your heart*? I mean come on, Bee, that's so corny!"

"Maybe he's a romantic."

He scoffs, as if Tucker being a romantic was the most ridiculous thing he's ever heard. "He's not worth it. Trust me. I'm saving you a lot of trouble."

"I doubt that."

"Look... all I'm saying is that high school relationships can be complicated, and maybe you're better off waiting until you're older, like in college or something."

I drop the Sharpie, waving my hand around to shake out a cramp. "Says the guy whose been in a relationship for all of high school."

He ignores the comment. "Here," he says, gesturing for me to give him my hand. "I know a trick from when my hands get stiff in basketball."

I hesitate, but he waves me on as if he's talking about something as neutral as *Athlete's Foot,* so I put my hand in his.

He presses his thumbs into my palm, massaging in small, purposeful motions. If I could breathe, I'd be suspicious of these fingers because there is no way he learned this in *basketball.*

"How's that feel?" he asks, his eyes rising to meet mine.

God, don't ask me that!

I can't find my words, can't even look him in the eyes, so I just nod once, shifting my gaze down so I can focus on the fact that our skin is touching. Like, actually touching. In all the years we've known each other, he's never felt me like this before.

"He's just not the kind of guy you want to get involved with." He throws it out there casually, but I notice his eyes shift back to mine, hoping for some kind of confirmation that I'd heard him. But I'm hardly listening now - my concentration has left me as easily as my senses. Somewhere, probably in the rational side of my brain, I'm being urged to pull away, but the other side is stronger, telling me not to move a muscle. *Abort. Abort. No, stay!*

"What kind of guy should I be getting involved with, then?" *There, a challenge. What do you say to that, Adam Stanson?*

Shannon Myers turns around, reminding me that Adam

and I are not the last two people on the planet. Her eyes fall to our hands, and I try to pull away, but he just tightens his grip, not noticing or caring about Shannon Myer shooting laser beams in our direction.

His fingers move up to my wrist, pressing deeper into my skin. Up and down, up and down.

"I don't know," he says, suddenly looking desperate. "Not someone that's going to hurt you."

He might as well have just poured a bucket of ice water on my head. The fact that he has no idea that *he's* the only person who has that kind of power over my heart is infuriating. I pull my hand away, turning to face the front of the room. "You don't have to worry about me getting hurt."

I know I've made things awkward, so I turn back, saying, "We're just talking a little... it's nothing."

He tries to play it off like it's all good, but a heavy silence settles between us. It feels like I've let him down, and I consider apologizing until it occurs to me that I have nothing to be sorry for. I accepted my fate a long time ago, I've done a good job of living my life without him, watching from a distance, and *he's* the one coming around and making things more difficult all of a sudden.

When the bell rings, he pulls on his backpack, turning to me, the tension wiped clean from his face. "Alright Baby Bee, hand over your stuff, I'll walk you to your locker."

Relieved, I hand over my binders.

In the hallway, we walk in silence, but our bodies occasionally brush up against each other and I know, *I just know*, that he keeps stepping toward me on purpose. He has better coordination than anyone alive; the way his body moves on the court borders on dancing, and there's no way he's suddenly become clumsy.

By the time we step onto the second-floor landing, I'm

buzzing again. How many times have I daydreamed about this exact scenario?

But then Caroline sees us, her face twisting in a scowl as she looks from him to me.

I pause for half a second, unsure if I should stay or book it out of here, but I don't have enough time to decide as she barrels toward us.

"Slumming it with sophomores now?" she asks him.

I step back, blushing. She has this remarkable ability to make me feel small without saying much at all. Maybe it's just from the fact that she's constantly going out of her way to make fun of me. Like that time I stitched peace signs onto my new jean overalls, only to have her announce to everyone that I looked like a *sad little farmer*. No one even laughed, but it was enough to make me tear them off the second I was alone.

"We have class together," I say.

She holds my gaze, looking angry enough that steam might shoot out from her ears. "Was I talking to you?"

"Oh... um..."

Adam steps in. "Hey easy... Bee's cool. I'm just helping her carry some stuff to her locker." Then looking at me, he says, "I'll meet you there. You're on the first floor by the English rooms, right?"

I swallow, surprised. I haven't even figured out where his is yet. I leave them standing there awkwardly in the middle of the landing, almost out of earshot when I hear him say, "It's just Kyle's little sister, she needed some help." *Just*.

I step away, disappointed with myself. *Here you go again, Bee, imagining things that aren't happening.*

"Hey, Bee, wait up," he says a full minute later as I'm pulling open my locker door. He hands me back the binders, inspecting the photo I have hanging up of me and the Cove Girls from the beach this summer.

"Thanks for helping me. I'll see you later," I say, slamming the door shut.

He frowns, letting out a breath. "I'm sorry about Caroline. I know she gets a little carried away sometimes... but-"

I cut in, uninterested in hearing his excuses for her. There is nothing he could say that would convince me she's a nice person. "Don't worry about it. I'll see you later."

3

THE NEXT DAY, I'M SITTING IN *SEWING 101*, ADMIRING THE room we get to work in all year. Mrs. Holmes calls it *The Fashion Lab,* and it makes me feel like we're on the set of *Project Runway.* I've even gotten into the habit of pretending like we're surrounded by a film crew, recording a reality show about the beginning of our careers as fashion designers. Morgan Freeman would definitely narrate, *the greatest minds in fashion started right here in room 213.*

I started sewing after visiting a craft fair with Mom when I was ten. A woman was selling doll clothes at one of the booths, explaining that she made everything herself. The idea that she could make something from a scrap of fabric was mind-altering to me. I just sort of started from there, looking up YouTube videos of simple stitches, then moving on to lessons with one of my Mom's friends, Peggy, who taught me how to use the sewing machine. She showed me how to lay out a pattern, how to protect my fingers from getting nicked by a needle. She explained all the zipper types and fabric counts. And over time, I learned I had a knack for it, an *eye,* as she would say. I can look at a piece of cotton and envision what it *could* be. There is nothing about sewing that I'm not hungry to learn, and this class is going to take my skills to the next level. I know it.

I'm practically bouncing out of my seat after a few minutes because Mrs. Holmes would be announcing our project in class. As it turns out, everyone enrolled has a fair amount of experience with sewing, so she threw away the syllabus and decided we'll been doing a collaborative project instead.

"Maybe we'll go old school and make *Hilfiger* windbreakers," Amber says while we're waiting for Mrs. Holmes to show up. She's always at least five minutes late, but it just adds to her allure; she has a vibe, and I'm mentally taking notes, trying to figure out how to be just like her.

"Or maybe we'll go more classic, like *Diane Von Furstenberg* wrap dresses," Ricky suggests. Everyone seems to think we would be spending the year perfecting one thing, but I think it will bigger than that; Mrs. Holmes doesn't seem like the kind of person to play it safe. I'm about to say so when the girl with the red lipstick, Scarlett, walks in and sits down next to me. I've been waiting three weeks for a chance to introduce myself.

She's new to Graves, that much is clear; she stands out in her chic clothes and cool make-up, and she looks older somehow, carrying herself differently than the rest of us. I half expect her to have a French accent, but when I hear her speak for the first time, she sounds like me.

She glances over and I smile, holding out my hand. "Hi, I'm Brooke."

She takes my hand, relieved, I think. "I'm Scarlett."

I slide over, moving closer, hoping it doesn't freak her out. "Are you new here?"

She laughs. "Obvious, huh?"

"Where are you from?"

"New York. My parents just split-up, and my mom got a job in Boston, so here I am, starting a new school, senior year."

"Perfect timing," I joke

"What about you? Have you lived in Padstow your whole life?"

I'm about to respond but Bobby, whose sitting behind us, distracts me by leaning over his table to look at Scarlett. When their eyes meet, he clears his throat, cutting in, "I don't mean to be a weird stalker, but are you *Scarlett Red* from Instagram?"

Scarlett blushes, shifting uncomfortably in her seat as everyone in the class stops their side conversations to turn to us. "Yeah, that's me."

Bobby squeaks and, seeing my confusion, takes out his phone, shoving it at me while he goes on gawking at her like she's a celebrity. It's Scarlett's page, *Scarlett Red,* and as I scroll through her beautifully curated feed, I notice that she has a casual hundred thousand followers.

The Cove Girls and I linger around the twelve hundred follower count, adding and subtracting a few every once in a while. Only Sara actively works on growing her following, studying hashtags and reels relentlessly, but she hasn't been able to break two thousand five-hundred and fourteen for months.

"Oh wow... this is so cool... I had no idea... I'm sorry," I say.

"Oh please, I'm relieved, to be honest. I was kind of hoping that no one would recognize me here. People start acting funny once they know." Her eyes shift back in the direction of Bobby.

Bobby, unaware, gushes, "I just knew it. That first day when you walked in, I was like, *I totally know her from somewhere!*"

Ricky interrupts, "*Girl,* I'm so jealous! What's it like to get all that free stuff? Do you make money? Can you teach me?

You must be living the dream! But like, what on earth are you doing here in Padstow!?"

She smiles uneasily. "My mom's after a quieter life."

They start rattling off questions until Mrs. Holmes walks in, wearing the coolest black pants suit that I've ever seen. She must be a sensation in the teacher's room, putting their neutral-colored cardigans to shame.

Their attentions shift off Scarlett and focus on the clipboard that Mrs. Holmes is holding. "Good afternoon, fashionistas. I know you've all been waiting for today, so I'll get right to it. I'm so excited to announce that our entire year will be dedicated to a fashion show that we'll host this spring!"

There's a collective gasp.

"What kind of fashion show?" Amber asks.

Mrs. Holmes takes a sip from her Starbucks cup. It's probably filled with something strong like an Americano. "That's up to you. Over the next couple weeks, we'll brainstorm together to come up with a theme, and once that's settled, we'll start."

"Start what?" Ricky asks, practically leaping out of his seat.

"We'll start making our clothes for the fashion show," Mrs. Holmes says like it's obvious.

Bobby actually stands, waving his hands around his face like he's going to faint. "If you're just playing around, Mrs. Holmes, tell me now because my nerves can't take this!"

She laughs. "I'm completely serious. It sounds fun and believe me, it's going to be amazing, but it's also going to be a lot of hard work. You may not be beginners, but you're still at the beginning, so it won't be easy by any means. I'll be here to guide you and teach you new techniques and hopefully, you'll start to figure out what aspects of this industry you like the most. But the most important thing is that we work together. I want this to be a collaborative experience for us all."

When she's done speaking, the room goes silent, all of us

still processing something this major. I'm excited for this class, grateful for the opportunity to learn more from her, but a fashion show of our own is more than I could have ever hoped for.

I look at Scarlett, and she gives me a knowing smile, feeling it, too.

Mrs. Holmes walks around her desk, making eye contact with each one of us, and I imagine this is the moment the cameras click on. "Let's get started."

I'm sprawled out on Sara's bedroom floor after school, trying to memorize the seven steps of the scientific method for my first test on Friday. "Do you know who *Scarlett Red* is?" I ask. I'm chewing on an already mangled pen cap, a habit that I've never been able to break. Stacey says that I have an oral fixation, something that she learned from when she was still in her Freudian phase. She's always going through phases of research; currently she is studying the suppression of Mary Magdalene.

"Ummm, yes, duh. Everyone does."

I silently applaud myself for knowing something before her. She's usually the first to find out about stuff like that. She practically lives on *Little Lucy,* our school's gossip blog. "I met her today, she's in my sewing class."

She pauses the make-up tutorial she's watching and turns around. "What? Are you serious? She goes to Graves?"

"She sat with me and Rochelle at lunch... I think we might already be friends."

"How nice." She pivots back around, trying to appear unbothered, but I notice her hand drop down to her anklet, fingering one of the seashells there. We each have one, a friend-ship anklet made with seashells that we collected over the years. We spent so much time scouring the sand, we eventually pooled it all together in an old glass milk jar that Mom bought at a flea market. We finally made them this past summer, after watching hours of DIY videos on YouTube.

"Oh, come on... you'll like her."

She picks up her contour sponge, sticking out her lips in a duck face. Out of the four of us, Sara is the least interested in making new friends. She feels like it's unnecessary because our personalities are different enough that she gets everything she needs with us. Stacey is the smartest and most sensitive, Rochelle the sportiest and the most fearless, Sara is practical and the most loyal, and then there is me, the silliest and a bit of a free-spirit. We are all best friends, but because Sara is on the next street over, we tend to hang out the most.

"Oh, my God," she says a moment later, dropping the sponge. "I can't believe I forgot to tell you this, but Caroline was here yesterday, and she was talking about Adam."

I sit up, spitting out the pen cap with more urgency than I intended. I've spent the last twenty-four hours practically consumed with thoughts of Adam, but I'm still no closer to understanding what is going on between us.

She smiles in an irritating way; the Cove Girls love to tease me about Adam, and because her sister, Nina, is friends with Caroline, we always have the insider details about their relationship. "You ready for this? They've been fighting...big time," she says, more serious now, as if, all joking aside, there is something important we need to discuss. "They haven't been getting along for *months,* and I guess they broke up for like, two days this summer."

"What!" I say, surprised. "What happened?"

"He broke up with her when he got back from vacation. He said that he wasn't happy anymore, but she convinced him that he was making a mistake, so they got back together."

"Whoa," I say, feeling mixed up inside, wondering if there's even a tiny bit of a connection between this and the way he's been acting toward me. Probably not. Most definitely not. It *has* to be a coincidence.

"I know, *shocking,* and I guess things were going all right again until the woods party. Now she thinks he's going to break up with her... for real this time."

Without thinking, I jump up and start pacing the room. "Since the woods party?" I ask, a little breathless. *The woods party when he was saving me from the cops and telling me not to talk to Tucker?*

She eyes me suspiciously. "Yeah... why? Do you know something?"

I look away, my mind spinning in so many directions. I should tell her about Adam, about how it feels like something is happening between us, but she would shut down the idea immediately. No, I can't tell her now, not until I have it figured out. Not until I know I can laugh about my cluelessness later.

"Bee?"

"What?" I ask, looking over at her.

"Do you know something?"

I clear my throat, trying to pull it together. I'm acting weird, and she can tell, but I still can't say what I'm thinking. *Does this have to do with me?*

"No," I say, taking a breath. "I mean, Kyle never said anything, but you know him; he hates to gossip." I check my blackheads in her mirror, trying to play it cool. "Anyway, what do you want to do this weekend?"

"Wait, Bee... are you serious? I'm shocked. I thought you'd be pumped to hear news like this. Wouldn't you be happy if they broke up?"

"I am! I mean... you know... I'm just surprised. I guess I

never imagined them actually breaking up. They've been together forever."

"Nothing lasts forever." She presses play on the tutorial, clearly disappointed by my lack of enthusiasm. "Maybe he's not your lover boy anymore. Want to stay for dinner? My mom's making tacos."

"Yeah, thanks," I say, grateful for the change in subject. I lie back down, glancing through my notes again, but after a few minutes of looking at the same line, I stop. There's no way I can study now.

Dear Journal,

As if things weren't confusing enough with Adam, he's been over at my house ALL weekend. I know this is going to sound crazy because he's always over, but I SWEAR it was for me this time. There's only so much will-power a person has, you know, before they cave and start a private Pinterest board on destination weddings. I keep trying to remind myself that there is just no possible way that he likes me but really, when was the last time that he stayed a whole weekend? A WHOLE WEEKEND? And he's acting suspicious, too, like on Saturday morning when he said he couldn't shoot hoops with Kyle because his shoulder hurt but then hung around me for like, AN HOUR, while I was sewing. Or later, when Kyle said he wanted to get burgers from Patty's and Adam INVITED ME TO COME. And then when we got there, he just talked and talked to ME, even Kyle was looking at him like, WTF? And then later, while we were all watching Inception, Kyle fell asleep and Adam totally fake dropped his phone and scooted closer to me. Then he touched my leg "acciden-

tally." And here's the kicker... this morning, I was hanging out with the Cove Girls in the living room and he invited us to go to Coloniel Park to watch them play basketball. He's never, ever, ever done that, not ever. I was all like... no, let's just hang here but Sara thought that Sawyer would be there and basically forced us to go. And guess who was looking at me the whole time????? Yup, Adam Stanson. He'd shoot and look, dribble the ball and look, take a sip of water and look, take off his shirt and look. He didn't even care that they lost the game, he just walked up, all sweaty and sexy and irre-sistible and passed me the ball saying, "You wanna play a little one-on-one?" And then I died, for approximately five seconds, only to come back and say... "Um, yeah, sure, whatever, that's cool" but then Cruella de Ville aka Caroline showed up with her friends and he looked at me like I was the actual plague. It's all so weird and confusing and frustrating. Am I losing my mind? What's going on? And what happened to his shoulder injury?!?

4

On Monday morning, I'm in the locker rooms changing for PE when I realize I packed mismatched socks in my rush to get out of the house. It was Kyle's fault, really; he was honking the horn so incessantly, I stuffed whatever I could find into my gym bag. "Is there anything worse than when your socks don't match?" I ask Rochelle as she ties the laces on her new red New Balance sneakers.

"Um... systemic racism? The wage gap? Society's unrealistic expectation of the female body?"

"Yeah, obviously, but it's still one of my pet-peeves. I'm going to be self-conscious about it for the whole period."

"No one will be looking at your feet. Trust me." She pushes open the locker room door and steps out into the hallway.

The smell of baked bread fills my nostrils, making my stomach growl. The locker rooms are located right next to the kitchen, and it smells like pizza day. I silently curse Kyle, again. Another thing I didn't get to do earlier was eat breakfast.

"So, are you and Charlie officially boyfriend and girl-friend?" Her new love interest is a boy she worked with at summer camp. She talked about him nonstop - it was all *Charlie this* and *Charlie that* - and by the end of the summer, they shared not one but *two* make-out sessions up against the back of the camp office building.

"Yup, I'm going to post a photo of us together on Instagram later... making it totally official," she says, giddy. "I'm exhausted. We were up until like... two last night talking about it. He was all like... *so I really like you and was wondering if you'd wanna be my girlfriend, and I was like, ohmygod Charlie, obviously!* I just can't wait for you guys to get to know him."

"Me, too!" I pull at the hem of my pants, trying to cover my socks. "I really don't want to go to gym right now. My bruises are still healing from dodgeball last week."

"Ugh, I know."

Connor Daly, the person who gave me those bruises from an intense dodgeball game last week walks up then, holding out a bag of Swedish Fish. We've been friends with Connor since first grade, and I was even married to him for an entire recess before he divorced me to get engaged to Jessica McNeil. "I know they're your favorite, Brookey Bee."

I look away, still pretending to be mad at him. "Oh, Connor, hey. We were just talking about you... I was telling Rochelle that my bruises have hardly healed since last time."

He frowns, wrapping his free arm around my shoulder. "Bee, how many times do I have to apologize? *I'm sorry!* Sometimes, I get a little competitive. Here, please, just take the whole bag and accept my apology, or I'll be miserable for the rest of the day."

I snatch the bag. "I accept."

We walk into the gym, standing behind a group of kids who are blocking Coach Brian while he lectures us on the importance of neatly putting away the gym supplies at the end of the period.

I turn to Rochelle. "I bet you a bag of Sun Chips that he's wearing navy-blue with mustard stripes."

"You're on," she says, chuckling. It has become somewhat of a game for us - trying to guess what color tracksuit Coach Brian would be wearing - but I have the one up this time because I know he likes to start his week with mustard yellow.

Through the spaces of the feet in front of us, I see that the floor is sectioned off in squares with bright green painter's tape. I let out a sigh; the only gym game I like to play is kickball, and we hardly ever play. "Four squares," I whisper to Connor. "At least there's a pretty good chance you won't attack me this time."

He rolls his eyes, laughing.

"Get your body moving out there, okay?" Coach Brian shouts. "I want everyone sweating within the next fifteen minutes. And that means you, Louis!" He claps his hands together and the group scatters, leaving him standing there with Adam and Jonathan.

"You've got to be kidding me!" I say, exasperated, not even trying to hide my frustration. After Adam brushed me off at Colonial Park yesterday, I'm determined to avoid him at all costs. It doesn't matter whether he's into me or not because nothing would ever come of it. It's pointless. There is no way I would let his tight-fitted gym clothes distract me. No way.

His eyes focus in on Connor's arm, still draped over my shoulder.

I roll my eyes.

Rochelle chuckles. "I owe you a bag of chips."

Jonathan howls, "Man, this is too good to be true! A whole period to tool on our Baby Bee. You and your posse can roll with us, we'll show you fools how to play four-square."

I begrudgingly follow him over to the empty square in the

middle of the gym, conscious of Adam just a step behind me. "We already know how to play, we're not idiots!"

"Whoa, Whoa, Whoa! Bee! No need to get all feisty with me. Why don't you come here and give me some sugar?" He points to his cheek.

I push him away. "Why are you guys here right now?" *Why can't I get away from you?*

"Extra credit," Adam mumbles, breaking his silence.

Rochelle steps into the square labeled *four* and picks up the ball. "Must be nice to skip class and hang out in the gym whenever you want."

Jonathan makes an injured face. "I'm here to help the lower classes with their athletic stamina. You, boy," he points to Connor, "wait over there. It won't be long before I knock one of these two out." He nods to me and Rochelle.

I step up across from Adam, giving myself three seconds before I look at him. I would

have loved this last year, but since that day in my basement four weeks ago, it feels like I have more to lose now when I find out I've been dreaming this whole thing up.

Finally, we lock eyes, and I notice a smile playing at his lips. "You sure you're ready for this?" he asks.

I'm about to flip him off when Connor comes up behind me and starts rubbing my shoulders. "You've got this, Bee, you show 'em why we called you the *Fantastic Four* in fifth grade."

I laugh out loud, remembering the nickname vividly - I was the standing champ for two weeks. Leave it to Connor to remember something like that. Instead of walking back to his spot on the side, he stays, coaching me up like he's my own personal cheerleader. He means it to be funny, but the whole thing comes off as strangely personal, and I can't help but notice when Adam's face falls. Suddenly, I find myself very intrigued by the idea of making him jealous.

"I won't let you down." I turn around and pinch his cheek.

Connor's eyes me curiously – he's a flirt, probably the biggest one in our grade, but I don't typically return his affections. But the way he's looking at me now says that he knows what I'm doing, and he's down to play along. "You never do, my Sweet Bee."

I take my place again, facing Adam, but this time with more confidence.

His expression has turned downright sour, and I turn my face, hiding my smile. This is going to be too easy.

"Your socks aren't matching," he says, going right for the jugular.

I flinch, looking down. "I'm aware, thanks."

"I *like* your socks, Bee!" Connor shouts. And just like that, I'm smiling again, with the upper-hand.

Coach Brian blows the whistle. "Go!" and then "Louis! You come down off those bleachers right now!"

Rochelle serves, bouncing the ball to Adam, and the game begins.

Jonathan wastes no time with the trash-talk, trying to psych us out, but we hold steady, bouncing the ball back and forth, unfazed by his taunting. He's easily the most obnoxious out of all of Kyle's friends, but he's also the funniest. "How did you get your nickname, Bee? Was it because you love the sound they make when they fly by your face? Buzz, buzz, buzz," he says, trying to freak me out.

"You'll have to do better than that," I retort, spiking the ball at him.

He jumps, startled, almost missing the ball.

Adam's eyes dart up to meet mine. His expression is soft now; he seems surprised, maybe even a little impressed.

Rochelle smiles, comfortable enough with the pace now that she can join in on the conversation. She's competitive, and

I know if she doesn't win, she'll be talking about it for the rest of the day. "She got the nickname the day she beat Danny Ouellette in the Cork-Screw-Dipsy-Doo. By twelve seconds."

"The Cork-Screw-Dipsy what?" Jonathan asks. "How have I never heard this story before?"

"It was an obstacle course that Danny made up at the Colonial Park playground. You had to climb the ladder backwards, jump twice, go across the monkey bars, cross the bridge while hopping on one foot, spin twice, go down the slide frontwards, climb back up, and go back down again. Danny had the fastest time at forty-five seconds, and she beat him!"

Jonathan looks surprised. "Wow Bee, respect. But what's that got to do with bees?"

Adam clears his throat then. "Kyle had her convinced that she'd turn into a bee if she ever got stung." He looks at me again, his expression thoughtful, as if acknowledging that he'd been there that day, that he's always been there. We share a lot of the same memories, though we definitely have different versions of them.

Jonathan laughs. "Classic Kyle."

Rochelle adds, "And on the way down the slide, the second time, she sat on a bee and got stung."

"So you actually thought you were turning into a bee? How old were you?" Jonathan asks, teasing.

"She was six," Adam says, his eyes focused on the ball.

I remember that morning well; I can almost feel the adrenaline that pulsed through me as I flew through the course. I knew I was making good time because Danny looked worried, but before I could get excited about it, I felt a sharp blast of pain, followed by a dull ache. Everyone was shouting my name until they realized that something was wrong. The Cove Girls ran to get Kyle, and he came back with Adam knowing I was upset about turning into a bee. Kyle told me the truth. He said, *you won't turn into a bee but I think I'll call you Baby Bee, anyway.* And then they carried me home like a queen, lifted up high on their shoulders. I was too young to have feelings for Adam then, but he'd made me feel special by promising to buy me a candy necklace from the corner store.

I look at Jonathan, waiting until I have his attention. "And to answer your question, *yes*, I did think I was turning into a bee." I spike the ball at him again but this time, he misses. "You're out!" I shout, jumping up and down.

Jonathan lets out a grunt and shakes his head. "I think you were working together on that one. Good story though," he says as Connor jumps into the game.

Connor serves, not missing a beat. "Bee, can I take you to the game on Friday?"

Adam winces, trying his hardest to appear unfazed, but when I notice the vein in his neck pop out, I smile. It always happens when he's upset about something. He doesn't say a word, refusing to look in my direction, but when he finally gets the ball, he whips it at Connor. If Connor notices, he plays it off like he doesn't.

"I could pick you up, we could get something to eat first."

Rochelle snorts. "Since when do you have your license?"

"Whoa! Way to bring a guy down, Rochelle," he says good-naturedly. "Okay, so I can't physically pick you up in a car, but I could call an Uber. Uber Deluxe, if you're lucky."

I laugh. "Maybe... let me think about it."

Adam cuts in, barely hiding his annoyance now. "You have to be eighteen to take one on your own. Maybe your mom could come along to chaperone."

Connor shrugs. "I'll bring Mom along if that's what it takes for you to come on a date with me. Plus, you love her, don't you?"

I nod. "I *do* love Kim, she's the best."

When Adam stiffens, I cough into my shoulder. It's the only way to hide my laugh. *Victory!*

Later, after putting the balls away, I'm sitting alone on the bleachers when Adam walks over, holding out his hand.

I take it cautiously, aware that the last time I let him touch my hand, I hadn't been able to think straight for days. I wish I had the nerve to ask him outright, *has something happened between us?* But I don't know if I could recover from the letdown I'd feel when he'd inevitably respond, *nothing.*

"Good game." He sits down next to me, so close that our knees are almost touching.

I smile. "You, too."

"Rochelle takes no prisoners, she deserves that win."

"Yeah... she's the sportiest of us."

He's quiet then, focused on his shoes. I watch the side of his face as he struggles to get out what he's about to say. "Are you going to go to the game with that kid on Friday?"

"You know his name is Connor," I remark, also knowing I never had any intention of going with him. I've had plans to go with the Cove Girls since yesterday when I asked Dad to drive us.

"He's just another tool," Adam frowns, looking across the gym at Jonathan who's flirting with two Freshman girls.

I shrug. "It seems like you'll find something wrong with any boy I'm interested in."

He whips his head up. "So... you *are* interested in him?"

I *almost* laugh until I realize how close our faces are. "No, that's not what I'm saying."

"What are you saying?" he asks, looking down at my lips. My heart starts beating at that rapid pace again. I'm starting to realize that it only picks up like this when he's around. I shouldn't be surprised by it, but I am. I can't believe anyone could move me this way.

I giggle nervously. "I don't know what I'm saying. What are *you* saying?"

He breaks into a smile, meeting my eyes now. "I don't know what I'm saying, either." Then as if by reflex, he lifts his hand and moves it toward my face, pausing before touching me.

"You have something in your hair" he says, waiting for my permission to go on.

I nod, speechless.

He reaches over then, his fingers pushing through a mass of hair. I hold my breath, closing my eyes. How long does it last? Three seconds? Three minutes? Three hours? I couldn't say because I'm so caught up by him, so caught up by the feel of his fingers gliding through my strands, it sends chills to my spine. I want to lean into him, make the distance between us less and less.

He pulls away too soon, and to center myself, I clear my throat, but it ends up sounding like a bark. "What was it?" I ask as he sits back into the bleachers.

His eyebrows push together, confused. "What was what?"

I laugh. "What was in my hair?"

He lets out a nervous laugh and then the impossible happens right before my eyes -Adam Stanson blushes.

"You know what I want to know," he says a beat later as the pink slowly clears from his cheeks.

"What?"

"What's the rest of your list?" When I look confused, he clarifies, "Your travel list. You never finished telling me."

"Oh, Spain. Spain is my number one, I want to study abroad there one day."

He nods, mulling it over. "I can see you in Spain, sitting at an outdoor cafe, drinking a sangria... knitting."

I bust out laughing, and then he's laughing too.

When I envision myself there, I'm sitting on the steps of a

busy plaza, wearing a long white flowy dress from fabric I bought at an ancient shop that only the locals know about. I see it so clearly sometimes, like it's not my imagination but a memory I'm looking back on.

"There's more," I continue, trying to read his thoughts and wondering what he really thinks about my dreams of seeing the world. Too often, it's met with doubt, people thinking it's unrealistic, that I'm a small-town girl that will live here forever.

He waves me on. "Go on... let's hear it."

"Okay, I want to road trip through the south of France, eat a sausage at the Christmas markets in Germany, buy something at the Grand Bazaar in Istanbul, sip high tea in the English countryside, and take a run on the Great Wall of China."

He laughs. "You don't even like to run!"

"No... but I'd definitely do it there."

"That's a good list, Bee."

"Really? You don't think it's too cliché?"

His face drops. "No way, it sounds amazing. I hope I can see it with you."

My eyebrows raise in surprise and then he looks embarrassed, like he hadn't meant to say it out loud. "Ah sorry, that sounded weird. What I meant was, maybe you can start a blog or something and I can follow along."

I look down at my fingernails, wishing they were painted. "Yeah, maybe I will." I can't look up at him just now because if I do, he'll see right through me, see the giddiness that I'm feeling for no good reason. "What about you?"

"All of the places you said... plus New Zealand so I can pay homage to the *Lord of the Rings*."

I smile, looking at the students lined up by the door, waiting for the dismissal bell. "I would rather spend one lifetime with you, than face all the ages of this world alone."

He looks up, stunned. "Oh, my god, Bee, did you just quote

the *Lord of The Rings?"*

I shrug, feeling myself blush. "Well, you guys have watched it enough times that I probably know every line by heart. But that one is definitely my favorite."

A half smile breaks out on his face. "You're so different than the girls I know," he says, almost disappointed by it.

I know that he means Caroline because she always complains about the movies the boys want to watch, calling them weird. There have been so many times I've wanted to shout back, *there is nothing weird about Captain America!*

"Can I tell you something... a secret?" he asks.

I nod, holding my breath. *Tell me you love me. Tell me you love me.*

"Earlier today, Mr. Twomey called me into his office and told me about an internship I could apply for in Ecuador for Marine Biology next year."

"Oh," I say, surprised. "Sounds incredible, but Marine Biology? I didn't realize you were into that."

He nods, perking up a bit. "I am, I'm *really* into it, but nobody knows."

"Why not?"

He shrugs. "My Dad would laugh... he'd say something like, *why would you study coral when you could be making millions on the stock market.*"

"What would Caroline say?" I can't help asking.

He looks up, meeting my eyes as he considers it. "She'd probably say something similar. They're a lot of alike - I think that's why he likes her so much."

It gives me a sick satisfaction knowing she's shallow enough to dissuade him from pursuing his dreams, but at the same time, I hate that his dad likes her. In my head, his family hates her and can't wait for the relationship to end so that he can be with me. I wish I had the guts to tell him that I'd support his dreams, that I'd encourage him to do the things that make him happy. "Tell me about the internship."

"Mr. Twomey has it all figured out. Apparently, someone who graduated a few years ago did it. I could take a gap year, go down there and do the internship, learn Spanish, *really* learn it, you know? Not just like... sitting in Ms. Moreno's class reciting words."

I sit up, practically bouncing. While the thought of Adam moving so far away from here is devastating, it's also exciting imagining him live that kind of life. "You have to do it Adam! It sounds amazing!"

"Imagine? He said that part of the internship is spent off of the Galapagos islands studying Grapsus grapsus."

"What's that?"

He laughs. "A red crab."

"It seriously sounds so cool. I'm really happy for you."

He studies my face, equally excited for a moment before shaking his head. "I probably won't do it."

"Why not?"

"My dad wants me to play college ball and study finance. He has a five-year plan for us, and by the time I graduate, he'll be ready to open his own office. He wants me to work up to be partner with him. I can't let him down, he'd never forgive me."

"Are you interested in studying finance?"

He shakes his head, looking away. "Not even a little."

"You can't pass up an opportunity like this!"

He frowns, his eyebrows pushing together. "We can't always get what we want."

I wonder if we're playing the innuendo game again and if he's actually talking about more than the internship now. "Sure, you can, you can get everything you want," I urge. Maybe if I say it enough times, I'll start to believe it myself.

The bell rings and he jumps up, offering me his hand again

to pull me to stand. We are getting more comfortable with each other, and I can't help but be excited about it. He's trusting me, telling me things regularly now, things he doesn't share with anyone else. It has to mean something.

Dear Journal,

OHMYGOD. Let me just get this down on paper now so that I have it in writing. On October 3rd at approximately 10:43am Adam Stanson said to me, "You're so different than the girls I know." He had to have meant Caroline. The girl he's supposed to be able to trust with everything, doesn't know that his dream is to be a marine biologist! BUT HE TOLD ME. HE TRUSTED ME. The pieces to the puzzle of Adam are totally starting to make sense now. I had no idea he was such a tortured soul!! Which, if I'm being totally honest, completely adds to the allure of him. IMO, anyway. Real talk though, that completely sucks that he feels so much pressure from his dad. It's a very medieval situation - like Adam's a prince and needs to follow in his king-father's footsteps or else the entire kingdom crumbles. But like, it's modern day and people are supposed to have freedom and all that. I can't imagine living under that much pressure from my parents. I also just can't believe that he trusts me with one of his big life secrets! He must LIKE ME LIKE ME. When did this happen? How did this happen? Where do we go from here? I feel like I should start getting regular manicures. Maybe I could convince Mom to take me shopping for new clothes. He's probably a really good kisser. Oh god... I'm probably a really BAD kisser. I wonder if YouTube has tutorials on how to kiss?

5

AFTER A SYNCHRONIZED DANCE ROUTINE, TWO PRANK phone calls, a cheese pizza, six grape sodas, and a few outfit changes, we're on our way to the football game. Katy Perry's voice fills the car, "*I kissed a girl and I likeddd itttt,*" we sing while Dad slouches in the driver's seat like he's hoping he might disappear. When we finally pull up outside the stadium, he lets out an obvious sigh of relief and smiles. "You sure you don't need a ride home?" he asks, queuing up a Pearl Jam song.

"We'll find a ride," I say, batting my eyelashes at him, hoping to plead my case one last time for a later curfew. "Eleven o'clock? *Please?*"

He shakes his head. "Ten, Bee, final."

I contemplate complaining again, but it's not worth it. They've never budged on curfews, so I lean over and plant a kiss on his cheek.

"Call if you need a ride. I don't mind coming back," he says.

"Bye Dad!"

The stands are already full by the time we walk in, and

after a quick scan of the sections, we see some year tens all the way at the top.

We squeeze in with Connor and Johnny. "Well, well," Connor says, looking at me, "look who it is."

"Hey, guys" I say, trying to be casual, like I didn't ignore the text message he sent after school asking about the game. In my defense, I hadn't realized he was being totally serious when he asked if I wanted to go with him. I thought we were just playing a game together, that he was playing around. Then when I realized he wasn't kidding, I felt bad for using him to make Adam jealous. "Sorry about earlier. I had plans with the girls."

He pulls me in for a side hug. "It's cool, Bee... I didn't really think you'd come with me, anyway. Plus, Adam practically had a heart attack when I asked. What's up with you two?"

I flinch. "What's up with who two?" I glance at the girls to see if they've heard the question, and when I see they haven't, I look back at Connor with an uncomfortable feeling in my stomach.

"You and Adam."

It feels like Connor has reached into my soul and pulled out my deepest, darkest secret. On the one hand, I feel solidified, like if Connor noticed that something is going on between us, then maybe I'm not losing my mind. But it still makes me feel uneasy - as much as I want Adam to like me, I know how bad it would look from the outside. No one cares about what the boys do, but if a girl is caught going after someone else's boyfriend, she'd be ostracized. Harlow Frank got heckled so bad last year for something similar, she switched schools.

"Nothing at all, why? What do you mean?"

He's not convinced, giving me a look like, *come on.* "It didn't seem like it was nothing... you had this weird, heavy vibe going on between you. Wasn't that why we were flirting? To make him jealous?"

"We always flirt," I say, but we both know it's a lie. Why is he grilling me right now?

Thankfully, Sara interrupts. "Connor, come take a selfie with me."

He reluctantly stands and sits next to her. "Make a funny face," she says.

At halftime, Stacey and I go to the concession stand to bring back hot chocolates for our group. It's when she leaves me in line to go to the bathroom that I feel someone brush up against my shoulder.

"Hey," Adam says, surprising me.

"Oh... hi."

He's bundled, wearing the fur-lined bomber hat that his aunt sent from Colorado last year. He'd worn it so often, the edges are rough and sticking together in some places. Depending on the stitch, I might be able to replace the fur.

After a few quiet moments, he tries again. "Mind if I wait in line with you?"

"Sure." I wasn't purposely trying to be quiet, but I have a lot on my mind, mainly the conversation I just had with Connor. Until now, I'd assumed no one knew that anything is going on between Adam and I - especially because I don't know for sure that something is. But I have to figure it out soon or risk people getting the wrong idea about me.

Adam looks like he's about to say something until we hear a quiet sob from behind us. We both turn, surprised when we realize the girl behind us is crying. I recognize her from school. She's a grade under me.

He glances at me quickly before turning back to her. "Are you all right?"

She looks up, eyes widening when she sees him. "Oh... I'm okay... I just got in a fight with my best friend."

He nods in such an understanding way, it makes my heart tighten. It's how he looks at his sisters, Jenny and Jo, how gentle and sweet he can be toward them, even when they're crying about something as silly as dolls. "What's your name again?"

She practically swoons. "Isabelle." And I want to laugh because it's such a charming thing to say to her right now, especially because I'm pretty sure he's never seen her before.

His eyes light up. "That's a pretty name. This is Bee."

"Hi," I smile. "Nice to meet you."

She smiles back, and her mood seems to have completely reversed itself. Before Adam has a chance to charm her some more, her friend comes over, wiping her own tears and apologizing.

We turn back around, our shoulders brushing again. "I'm pretty sure you just made her whole life," I tell Adam.

He ignores my comment, scanning over the menu. "Let me guess... hot chocolates with extra whipped cream?"

"Yup."

He laughs. "How were you planning to bring them back?"

"I was going to balance a few on my shoulders," I say before ordering. I reach into my wallet, but before I can hand over my card, he gives the concession mom cash, asking her to add two more hot chocolates to the order.

"Oh... I only have my card. I can ask Kyle to pay you back?"

He shakes his head. "I want to buy them for you."

My cheeks immediately blush, feeling embarrassed and pleased by the gesture. "Thank you, that's really nice." But part of me can't help wondering if the other two are for him and Caroline. Despite telling myself not to look for him in the stands earlier, I did, finding his arm wrapped around Caroline's shoulder.

The mom hands over the hot chocolates one by one, smiling at Adam. *Is there anyone who doesn't fall in love with him?*

He grabs two trays, helping me adjust the cups, then he takes the last two hot chocolates and hands them to Isabel and her friend. And my heart tightens again.

He follows me to a picnic table. "So... you ended up coming with that Connor kid, after all?"

I push my eyebrows together, shaking my head. "No?"

"You're sitting with him."

I almost laugh. "No... I came with the *Cove Girls*, Dad dropped us off. He's just sitting with us."

His relief is obvious, but I find myself even more confused. He's worried about Connor, but he still has a girlfriend - it doesn't make any sense.

Stacey walks up. "Look who I found," she says, moving aside for Tucker.

"Oh, hey Tucker."

"I haven't seen you all week," he says, debating on whether or not to come in for a hug and ultimately deciding not to.

"Yeah, I know. How have you been?"

Adam stands there, stiff, listening to our conversation until Caroline storms over, glaring at him. "I was just helping Bee carry these drinks back to the bleachers."

She rolls her eyes. "You're always helping Bee with something," she snaps, looking at me like I'm the one to blame.

I remind myself that this is why I have to be careful. Now that I think about it, her dirty looks linger a little longer these days, like she suspects that something is going on. She's mean enough as it is - I don't need to give her a reason to go after me.

Tucker steps in. "I'll walk back with you, *Bee*," he says, smiling because he's never called me by my nickname before.

"Ok, cool," I say, eager to get away from Caroline. Turning to Adam, I say, "Thanks again."

Tucker walks close, getting right into a story about his new graffiti tag, and I listen quietly, all the while waiting until we're far enough away that it's safe to look back at Adam again. And when I do, he looks how I feel: disappointed by the interruption.

My parents are already asleep when I walk into the house right at ten. Kyle won't be home until later; his curfew got pushed to eleven-thirty in September, and I overheard his friends talking about Brittany Gordon's party after the game. Since no one thought to invite us this time, we went to George's sub shop with the rest of the underclassman and split an order of chicken fingers.

I don't feel like going right to sleep, so I change into sweats and rummage through Mom's junk food spots. She doesn't leave the good stuff out in the open, but if you know where to look, there's always something. I find Twizzlers and turn on the TV.

I'm about twenty-five minutes into *The Notebook* when I hear a noise from the back room. I pause the movie and wait, thinking that now is a really inconvenient time to remember all of the *Dateline* episodes I've seen. I can hear Lester Holt's voice clearly: *Murder during The Notebook.*

There's a bang, followed by a *nooo,* and I finally let out a breath. It's just Kyle.

I find him in the den, sitting on the floor with Mom's favorite painting lying face down beside him.

He looks up and half smiles. "Bee, the room is spinning," he slurs, the smell of alcohol filling the room. He burps, moans, and after a moment of what looks like confusion, lies his head back and falls asleep.

"Kyle, wake up." I kick him lightly, but he just grunts and rolls onto his side. I lean down with every intention of pulling him up, but after two tries, I give up - he's dead weight and in no condition to help.

I hate this. It makes me nervous that he's this drunk, plus it's such a bad look. Why would you want to drink so much that you can't stand up?

Suddenly, Dad calls down in a groggy voice, "Kids, is that you?"

I leave Kyle and run to the bottom of the stairs. "Yeah, Dad, just us. We're going to watch a movie," I say. He's barely awake, looking at me with one eye open, but if he remembers that Mom's oatmeal cookies are on the kitchen counter, he'll come down.

"Ok, Sweetheart. How was the game?" he asks.

"It was really fun. We won."

"That's great. I'll see you in the morning," he says, turning away. When the door clicks shut, I rush back over to Kyle, hoping that he's somehow roused himself enough to go downstairs, but he looks even more settled into the floor.

I'm still weighing my options when the back door opens and Adam steps in. The last time I'd seen his pupils this small was at Mrs. Walters' Christmas party, two years ago, when they stole a bottle of whiskey. "Hey, you," he says, closing the door. "You're just the person I wanted to see."

"How did you guys get home?" I think of the drunk driving demonstration that the school put on last year. Neither of them are big drinkers, but this is the drunkest I've ever seen Kyle, and the thought of him driving around like that is enough to make me go snitch him out to my parents.

Adam shakes his head, like he knows what I'm thinking.

"Andrew was the DD tonight."

It's only then that I can consider what he said a moment ago: *just the person I wanted to see.*

"Can you bring him downstairs?"

"Sure, I can, my little Beehive." He bends down, picking Kyle up as if he weighs no more than a feather.

I follow him out of the room, chuckling when he starts humming Whitney Houston's *I Wanna Dance With Somebody.*

"Whitney? How did that get stuck in your head?"

"I *love* Whitney," he says, dancing around, knocking Kyle's head into a wall. "Whoops, sorry bro," he laughs, patting his back. "*I wanna dance with somebody,*" he sings. "Will you dance with me, Bee?"

I roll my eyes, smiling. Maybe drunk Adam would be kind of... *fun.* "I'm going to get Kyle a water... I'll meet you down there."

"Suit yourself... you couldn't handle these moves, anyway," he says, flashing another smile.

A minute later, I find Kyle lying face down on the couch. I set two water bottles on the coffee table, watching Adam struggle to pull off his hoodie. My smile fades though when his shirt lifts, exposing the patch of hair underneath his bellybutton. I've seen his stomach before, the boys rarely wear shirts in the summer, but in this setting, it makes me blush.

I look away. "Goodnight." I pause with one foot on the stairs, willing him to ask me to stay. My resolve to be careful around him apparently goes away when the option to be alone with him is presented.

He looks up, kicking off his shoes. "You going to bed?"

"No, I'm watching a movie."

"All right, I'll be right up."

Yes!

In the kitchen, he moves in and out of the cabinets, looking for snacks, knowing the secret spots as well as I do.

"I have Twizzlers in the living room."

He finds a box of chocolate raisins, tossing one up in the air and catching it in his mouth.

"Bee, you know I'm more of a chocolate guy." He does it again, but it bounces off his cheek and lands of the floor.

Okay. Drunk Adam is definitely fun.

"Good one," I say, walking into the den.

He trails behind me, and when I lean down to pick up the painting, he reaches over and takes it, placing it back on the hook. It's an abstract sunset that I've never particularly liked but right now, with him standing so close, I find it comforting. I feel unsteady, nervous, because we're alone, *really alone*, for the first time since this whole weird thing began between us.

When his gaze shifts from the painting to me, I panic. "I want popcorn!"

He doesn't miss a beat, following me back into the kitchen. "So, did you have a good chat with Tuck-*her?*"

"Yeah, I did actually."

He scoffs. "His tag name is Eclipse? Come on." He plops down onto the couch, still rambling.

"It's *E-Clips* not, Eclipse," I say, pouring the popcorn into bowls.

"Even worse! What does that even mean?"

"Why don't you like him?" I ask, handing him a bowl.

He shrugs, as if surrendering. "I don't know... he's really not that bad, I guess. He actually *just* started to annoy me... what's this?" he asks, pointing to Ryan Gosling's frozen face on the TV screen.

"The Notebook."

He smiles and lays his head back. "I've never seen it."

"You're kidding me. I've watched it with the *Cove Girls* at least twenty-five times."

"Nope, never," he says, shaking his head. "Can I watch it with you?"

I swallow, managing a quick nod. I've been anticipating him going back downstairs since the moment he followed me up. I wanted this, hoped for it, but I can hardly keep my thoughts in check now that it's happening.

"You don't mind hanging out with me, Cookie?" he asks with puppy dog eyes.

I laugh. "Cookie?"

"Yeah," he smiles, "you're my little cookie."

I restart the movie, hiding my blush. He could have called me his little hippopotamus just now, and I still would have found it endearing.

We're only a few minutes in when he starts talking again. "I already know what's going to happen. They meet, they fall in love. Her parents put the kibosh on it, but they come back together in the end."

I roll my eyes. "That's not how it happens."

He reads my face and laughs. "That's exactly how it happens!"

I throw my popcorn at him. "It's about how true love conquers everything, okay? Just watch!"

He turns to me again, more serious this time. "Have you ever been in love?"

I stuff a handful of the popcorn into my mouth, saying the first thing that comes to mind. "That's a loaded question."

Oh God, oh God, oh God.

"Why is it loaded?" he asks, his eyes fixed on me now.

I look away, knowing that I can't explain it without sounding like I've been obsessing over him for years. "Have you?" I ask, trying to take the heat off me. "I guess that's already obvious."

"What's obvious?"

"That you're in love. You've been in a relationship for years, which by default means you are."

He looks down at his hands. "Not necessarily."

"What's the point, then?"

"I don't know," he says. "I don't know what the point is."

We're quiet for a long moment, the movie still playing in the background. He focuses on his hands again, starting to pick at his fingernails. "It's like, I'm stuck. I've been with Caroline for a while now, and it's fine, you know, it's completely fine, but there's something missing. I don't know..."

I clear my throat, ignoring the pounding in my heart. "Why are you with her, then?"

"I don't know how to explain this without sounding like a douche, but sometimes I think we're together because of what we represent as a couple. Like, at some point, we were just like, *okay, this works fine, people seem to think this is a really good idea,* and it was just easier to play those roles. But, I don't even think she knows me."

"By people... do you mean your dad?" I ask, trying to piece together all the little bits of information he's given me over the last few weeks.

"Yeah, sure, my dad, but also everyone else in this town who expects me to be the best athlete and student and friend and son. It's exhausting. And Caroline's a part of that, too. There's so much pressure on me to be perfect, and sometimes it's easier to just... do what everyone else wants."

"I'm sorry," I say, pausing. "That's... *a lot.*"

He laughs. "Thanks for saying that... it actually makes me feel a little better because it *is* a lot. And I'm not trying to take for granted my privilege in all of this but man, sometimes it stresses me out."

"For what it's worth, I know what you mean. There was a

boy, once, and I wasn't myself around him, either."

"Tyler?" he asks.

I nod, taken aback. Tyler and I weren't together long enough for him to get to know my family or by extension, Adam, so it's surprising that he knew right away who I was referring to. "I was never myself around him."

"I get it," he says. Then he turns to face me, making himself more comfortable on the couch. I mirror his position on the other side, the two of us now quite literally *lounging* together.

"Do you know Tyler?" I ask.

He shakes his head. "No, not really. I noticed when you started hanging out with him, though. He walked you to a lot of your classes and one time, I saw you together at George's. You had him cracking up, and I wanted to get closer, to hear what you were saying, but I didn't. You never saw me."

I *had* seen him. My back was facing the door, but I'd heard his voice and turned just in time to see him leave. Tyler had taken me to the movies afterward, but all I could think about was Adam, wondering what it would be like to go to the movies with him. Would he share a coke with me, instead of buying me my own? Would he kiss me in the back row?

"You should have said hi," I say with a shy smile, aware that with each passing moment, the walls feel like they're closing in on us.

"I was jealous." His eyes meet mine.

I twitch, not trusting my ears. "Jealous? Why would you be jealous?" Instead of looking away, I hold his gaze, not about to let this moment pass. These last few weeks have been building up to this conversation, and if I wanted answers, I'd have to press him.

He looks up at the ceiling, his eyebrows touching, like he's thinking about what to say next. "Something changed..." he pauses, hesitating. "It was the summer before you started at

Graves. We saw each other a lot that summer, do you remember?"

"Yeah," I whisper.

"You were different; just, like, not a little kid anymore. Like in my mind... you were always Bee, Kyle's goofy little sister, but then one day... you weren't... and it took me by surprise. You were sewing all the time, and I thought that was cool, I was impressed." He stops again, and I want to scream, *don't stop now, not when things are getting this good.* But then his eyes meet mine, and there's a dark sexiness to them now. "And you were always in that red bikini... driving me *crazy* with that damn bathing suit."

Oh.My.God.

"I guess my feelings for you had been changing all summer, but I was so confused by it. Then we were at the Willow Glen that day, on your birthday and I," he looks down, hesitating, "I read your journal."

"Ohmygod! I knew it!" I'd spent weeks wondering about it.

"I'm sorry! I'm not proud of it. But knowing you saw me like that made me realize that I felt the same way. It freaked me out, though." He moves closer. "I spent the whole next year trying to avoid you, trying to deny the way I felt about you. I couldn't even look at you without those feelings coming back. I still can't."

"Feelings?"

His eyes focus in on mine, and then he's finding his way closer, moving so our faces are almost touching. "What are you thinking right now?" he asks.

"I don't know what to think," I say honestly.

What does one think when it feels like their dreams are coming true?

"I think about you constantly," he says.

I want to say something important, something meaningful,

but all that comes out is, "I think about you, too."

He lets out a breath and smiles. "Good."

"Good" I repeat, my throat dry, knowing somehow that he's going to kiss me now.

There's a ringing. In my body, in my ears, but before I can make sense of it, Adam's pulling away.

Oh... there's actually a ringing.

His phone. He shoots across the room where it lies on one of the chairs, clicking it off, then he's walking back over to me.

It goes off again.

He stops to check it but this time, his face falls. "Caroline's here. I'm really sorry... I'll go talk to her for a minute, but I'll come right back. Don't move," he says, rushing out of the room before I can say anything.

After five minutes, I look out the window, desperate for a sign; anything that might tell me whether I should stay or go. And then I get one, when she leans over and kisses him.

I run upstairs, falling into bed, hoping -despite everything- that he'll come knock on my bedroom door. But he never does and eventually, I fall asleep.

The smell of bacon rouses me from a disorienting dream. I know something bad has happened, but I can't recall any of the details... not yet. I open my eyes and my stomach tightens as a hollowness creeps over my whole body. Adam. Me and Adam. Adam and Caroline.

I go downstairs, listening to the normal sounds of a weekend morning: the rustling of pans, the teapot whistling, Mom's favorite jazz station. My parents smile when I walk in, busy preparing a full breakfast. "Morning, Babe. How'd you sleep?" she asks as Dad looks over and winks.

"Good," I say, sitting at one of the stools. I could tell them the truth, that it might have been the best night of my life until it all fell apart on me, but I don't want them to be mad at Adam. I don't want to be the one responsible for breaking up our family dynamic; they love him and treat him like a second son. "The game was really fun. We won, and I went to George's after with the girls. How was your night?"

"It was good, Sweetie. We have exciting news... we've figured out what to do for Christmas vacation." She stops short when she hears Kyle stomping up the stairs. "Oh, I'll just wait for him."

He pushes open the door, groggy, looking at me first. He doesn't say a word, but I know him well enough to know he's thanking me for last night. Mom hands him an orange juice and he sits, running his hand through his hair.

Then, to my absolute horror, I hear a second pair of footsteps coming up from the basement. There's no way Adam would have stayed here last night, not after everything that happened, but then he's there, right in front of me, avoiding eye contact.

"Oh, good! We can tell all of you now," Mom says, handing Adam a glass. He takes a seat beside me but focuses his gaze on Dad, who is whisking the pancake mix.

"So," Mom says, looking excited, "we've booked a house in Vermont for winter break! The Cove Family ski weekend is on! Your family is coming too, Adam!"

Kyle chirps right up. "Yes! Shred sesh," he says, turning to Adam, holding out his hand for a fist bump.

When I don't react, Dad looks over." That sound good to you, Bee?"

"Yeah," I say, "should be great." *If you like torture.*

Adam just sits there, avoiding my gaze. It's like last night never happened.

6

I spend the rest of the weekend in a somber mood, trying to distract myself by knitting Stacey a scarf for her birthday next month. It's a navy-blue wool/cashmere blend; a score from an Etsy shop during their mid-summer sale. The fabric is soft but thick enough that she can wear it all winter.

I bailed on a movie night with the Cove Girls. I knew I wouldn't be able to hide what I was feeling from them, and I just couldn't say the words out loud - *Adam left me hanging*. There also might have been a small, tiny part of me that stuck around in case he showed up and apologized, but he never did, and that's when I decided that no one would ever find out about what happened or *almost happened* between us. By Sunday night, Mom knows something is going on, and she invites me to go for a walk with her after dinner.

I've always enjoyed our walks because it's how I've gotten to know her over the years. It was on a walk when she told me she was going back to work after almost fifteen years as a stay-at-home mom. I was surprised, not because she wanted to work but because she was so nervous to tell me. There was a part of her that believed she was letting us down by wanting more. But the opposite was true; I was glad she had something for herself after so many years of giving herself to us. She started part-time at our local museum, and within a year, she was the chief curator for the art department.

It's almost dark when we set out, bundled for the first time since the season change a few weeks ago. I take a deep breath, letting the cool air fill my lungs, and it shakes me almost immediately out of my funk. Mom says being out in nature can cure a bad mood, but I tend to forget about that when I'm actually *in* a bad mood. It's easier to lock myself in my bedroom and wallow in my misery by scrolling through Instagram, looking at other people's perfect lives.

We stop first at the Henry's elaborate Halloween display, taking in every horrifying detail. It use to terrify me, especially after the year they did the *Stranger Things* theme, but not so much anymore. Now I can appreciate how much time it takes to put it together; how generous it is that they keep it going even though their kids are full-grown and live in other towns. "Look at the witches' circle," Mom says. "I love that."

We move on, walking at a slow pace. The leaves are everywhere, a reminder that summer is well and truly over. *Step, crunch, step, crunch* - the sound is so familiar, it takes me right back to when we were kids and Dad used to rake up big piles for us to jump into. It was my favorite part of autumn, that and the apple cider donuts that we buy every October at McConnor's farm.

"Oh!" Mom bends down, picking up a bright red leaf and giving it as much attention as she would one of her paintings. She's always finding beauty in the simple things: a seashell, a piece of bark, a shiny rock. She brings them to her office to use as inspiration for later and sometimes, those little treasures inspire an entire collection at the museum.

"So, what's up, Bee?" she asks, blocking me with her arm as we leave our neighborhood and head downtown. Kyle calls it the Mom-arm, and she's been doing it to me for as long as I can remember. It used to annoy me; I felt like I was perfectly capable of crossing the street without getting hit by a car. But now, I kind of like it. It makes me feel safe, like no matter how old I am, she'll always be there to support me if I need it.

I look up at the sky as if I'll find the answer there. My life just feels like a big, complicated mess right now, and how could I possibly explain that the last five weeks have been both exciting *and* horrible? Thrilling *and* draining. "I don't know, nothing much," I lie.

"Well, how's the sewing class going?"

Relieved to move on, I say, "Great... I really love it - I'm super excited about the fashion show. Our theme is *the working woman,* and we each have to decide on an occupation and create a whole look for it."

"Wow. I can't wait to see what you come up with."

We turn downtown, about to pass *The Dream Cream,* when we see June, Adam's mom, and his sisters coming out.

"June!" Mom beams, rushing over.

The girls run into me with so much force, I step back a few paces from the impact. Nina is twelve, and Jo just turned seven. Being their favorite is a proud accomplishment of mine - all it took was braiding their hair during basketball games and occasionally sneaking them Skittles. Only the red and yellow one's though - the rest, they always say I can keep for myself.

"Brooke," June gasps, "look at you! You're *so* beautiful. Adam was not exaggerating!"

Say what now?

Maybe she's just trying to be nice. Maybe she's making conversation. Or maybe Adam is telling his Mom that I'm beautiful.

Jo interrupts. "Will you come over soon and play Barbie's with me? Please?"

I nod. "I'd love to!"

The door to *The Dream Cream* opens, and Adam steps out carrying one of their hot pink paper bags. When he sees me, he stops short, his mouth practically falling to the ground. We live in the smallest town, it's not that surprising when you run into anyone, but he literally looks like he's just seen a ghost.

June waves him over. "Adam, look who we just ran into!" Then turning to us, she adds, "We were just getting some peppermint ice cream."

I almost laugh; the Stansons are the only people alive who actually like peppermint ice cream, and I was teasing him about it last week in study hall.

He walks over, smiling politely at Mom. "Hey, Mrs. McGrath."

June directs the attention back on to me. "So, Brooke, Adam tells me that you have a class together this quarter?"

Okay, so they've definitely been talking about me.

Mom turns her head, surprised, and that's when I *know* that she *knows* Adam has something to do with why I've been moody all weekend. I don't know what her secret is but she's always figuring these things out with almost no information.

I fidget, trying to deflect her gaze burning into the side of my face. Maybe she really can read minds; it's something I've long since suspected of her. But then my talk with Connor pops into my head, and it seems more likely that my feelings for Adam are just too obvious now. It's my very own Scarlett letter.

"Yeah, it's just a study hall," I say.

"And your sewing class! How exciting! It will be such a great opportunity for you. You're so talented!"

Gotcha!

I look at Adam, but his eyes are locked onto his feet like he's just discovered that they're made of gold. I want to scream *coward! What about everything you said? What about the red bikini? What about the almost kiss?* The least he could do now is look at me and acknowledge the fact that he's been talking about me with his mom. *His mom!*

"Thanks... and yeah...I feel really lucky. I know I'll learn a lot from our teacher, Mrs. Holmes."

"Did you know my mother was a seamstress, too? She made all of our clothes growing up."

I smile, surprised. "No, I didn't know that. That's really cool."

She nods, looking back and forth between Adam and me until Mom cuts in, asking her a question about Vermont. The girls run to a nearby bench, leaving me and Adam standing there alone.

"How was your day?" I ask after a few long and uncomfortable seconds of silence.

He looks up, watching the girls. "It was fine."

A pit forms in my stomach, already disappointed in the way he's acting. He's cold, closed-off, and clearly trying to avoid talking to me. I expected this to happen, but a teeny-tiny part of me had hoped that he'd seek me out and explain himself without the armor of night-time and drinking to cover up what almost happened.

I told myself I'd never bring it up, but something tells me that this might be my only chance to learn the truth. What's a little more humiliation, anyway? "About the other night... we didn't get to finish our conversation."

He looks right at me then, his face going through a slideshow of emotions. *Surprise, recognition, understanding, frustration.* He lowers his voice, stepping away from our Moms before he whispers, "Yeah... I just... what do you want me to say, Bee?"

I want you to say that we should be together.

I clear my throat instead, embarrassed that he's asking me to spell this out for him. He said he liked me, he admitted that he thinks about me constantly, and I'm ninety-nine percent sure we were about to kiss... *while he still has a girlfriend.* I'm pretty sure if you're willing to cheat on your girlfriend, your feelings must be serious. Unless you're a jerk. And he may be a lot of things, but a jerk isn't one of them. I almost wish he was, it would make this so much easier. "I guess I was hoping to have a follow up?" I chuckle lightly, looking away. This is mortifying. Why do I have to be the one leading this? He's older, the one with real relationship experience. "You know... I thought we were having a moment, and it sort of stopped..."

"I know," he runs his hand through his hair, "but I can't do anything about it, so just forget about what I said, okay? Nothing can change, you should know that better than anyone after all the stuff I've told you about my dad. I drank too much and I let myself say more than I wanted to. It's my fault."

I take a step back, startled by how quickly it feels like I could cry.

"Look... if it makes you feel any better, I can't remember everything" he says, trying to throw me some kind of consolation. But then his eyebrow twitches and that's when I know for sure that he's lying. It's his tell - you don't obsess over a boy for years and not pick up a few things about them along the way. But the worst part is that it doesn't matter if he's lying or not because he's trying to erase what happened.

At least I have enough dignity to drop it. "Yeah...totally... it wasn't important...never mind."

He flinches, and I know he feels awful and helpless and probably a million other things, but before he can say anything else, Mom asks if I'm ready to go.

June pulls me in for a hug. "I'm so glad that I got to see you,

Brooke. It's been too long. And please, stop by any time... we'd love to have you."

I can feel Adam's gaze on us, and I wonder if he's surprised by my act right now – or maybe I really am just putting on a brave face. Maybe he has no idea that it feels like my heart has been split in two. "Thanks. It was nice to see you, too."

Jo takes my hands. "Please, come! I'll even let you use my *Moana* doll."

I muster a smile, then we turn away, walking through the rest of Main Street.

"So, you have a class with Adam?" Mom asks.

There's no point in trying to cover it up now. "Yeah, just study. We sit together, though. We've been talking more."

I catch a glimpse of myself in the bakery window, mesmerized for a moment by my own reflection. I don't even recognize the girl staring back at me. Since when am I desperate enough to go after a boy who already has a girlfriend? Why was I willing to kiss him without even a second thought about Caroline's feelings? And despite all of that, why am I still so disappointed that he doesn't want me?

"How's that been?" she asks.

"Fine, mostly fine," I say, teetering. I know that if I say it out loud, it all becomes real, and I won't be able to pretend like none of it matters anymore. "It's hard to explain," I say, my throat tightening.

She looks at me thoughtfully. "Try me."

I tell her everything, and once I start, I realize how good it feels to get it out. My instinct whenever anything goes wrong is to go inward because it seems easier than dealing with the truth. Why would I want to *feel* sad? But now that I've said it out loud, I realize it's not as bad as it was inside my head. When I'm finished, she doesn't seem surprised, confirming my suspicion that she'd already figured it out.

"Thanks for sharing all this with me, Babe. It does seem really confusing."

We keep walking, talking it through, and it's only when she stops to pull me in for a hug that I burst into tears. I nuzzle into her neck, overcome with the familiarity of her smell: lavender and clean linen soap and just *her*. I'd spent years entangled in that smell, and it reminds me how far away I am from those earlier days when she could take all my troubles away by lifting me into her arms. I wish she could do that now; take it all away. "What should I do, Mom?" I sob. I feel helpless and sad and ridiculous. It's embarrassing that I can cry this much over someone who isn't even my boyfriend.

She holds me until the tears stop falling. "What do you want to do?"

The million-dollar question. *What do I want?* "I know what I want to do, but I *feel* like I should be doing something else. I *want* to be with him; I want to call him out for lying, for being too scared to admit that he likes me. But I *feel* like there's no point. He's made it clear that he's not willing to change anything, so I'd basically just be pining after a boy who has a girlfriend, and I don't want to be that person. I just feel like such an idiot."

"First of all, you're not an idiot. You need to give yourself a break. It's a really complicated situation. You've known Adam for a long time... so it's not like he's just some boy to you - he's very involved in our lives. It seems to me that you've been trying to talk yourself out of what's happening, and my advice would be to honor your feelings. You like him, and that's okay! If it's meant to be, it will be. For now, just let yourself feel whatever it is you feel. Angry? Sad? Disappointed? Feel it... don't shut it down. One of the hardest things you'll learn in life is that you can't control other people. So, if Adam is going through something right now, it's not your job to step in and figure it out for him. For now, just focus on yourself." She looks over my face. "You okay?"

I take a deep breath, knowing what I have to do. "I will be."

Dear Journal,

I've been sitting in my room for two hours, mulling over the situation I've gotten myself into. Mom's advice was good, and I intend to do exactly what she says - I'll feel my feelings in private but I also have a new plan - I am going to get Adam Stanson OUT of my life. Sure, he's beautiful, funny, sensitive and smart, but I WILL SQUASH THAT CHARM WITH A POKE OF MY PINKY FINGER. He thinks he can play these games with me? Flirt, not flirt, confide in me, then take it back. ***I think about you constantly... Oh, Bee, Bee, your red bikini... I don't know another girl like you...don't date until you get to college... he's not the guy for you.*** *LIES, LIES, LIES.* ~~You know what rhymes with lies? Pies, thighs, colonize. Never mind.~~ *Here's what I'm going to do...first thing tomorrow, I'm going into the guidance office to volunteer to help Mrs. Mooney put together those packets on safe sex that I saw scattered all over her desk last week. Then, I'll offer to come by for the rest of the week to help organize her office, and she'll be so grateful for the help that when I ask her to switch out of study hall on Friday, she'll say yes, even though the period to switch classes ended weeks ago. If I can do that, I'm well on my way to winning because my strategy is this - out of sight, out of mind! I will ignore Adam if it's the last thing I do.*

7

THE NEXT DAY, I'M SITTING AT LUNCH WITH THE GIRLS, silently congratulating myself on having successfully avoided Adam all morning. It was easier than I imagined it to be; all I had to do was skip study hall and find new routes to my second and third period classes where I usually see him in the hallway. I felt a renewed sense of purpose; I could do this.

Sara looks at us with a sly smile. "Jeremy pulled me into the janitor's closet earlier and kissed me!"

Stacey drops her sandwich. "Shut up! What happened?"

"I don't even know. We were flirting a lot in class and then later, when we were walking the halls together, one thing led to another."

Rochelle lowers her voice, leaning in. "What do you mean, *one thing led to another*? Did you do more than kiss him?" Sara had been talking about him since the first week of school when she first realized they had French class together. But we were all skeptical - he has a reputation for being a player.

"What's borderline made-out mean?" The teenage jargon for hooking-up is constantly changing; between *tindering* and *shipping* and *smashing*, you can never be sure of what something means.

Sara rolls her eyes, frustrated by our lack of enthusiasm. "Ok, fine, we didn't make-out, but there was definitely tongue."

Rochelle's eyebrows push together. "I don't know, isn't he kind of a slime ball? I heard that he took a video of Amber while they were hooking up last year and then showed the entire swim team."

Sara looks offended. "No way, those rumors are not true. Girls, come on... be happy for me! He mentioned Homecoming!"

"Ok, you have my support," I say - after all, who am I to judge her bad-boy when the good-boys can break your heart, too?

"See? Thank you, Bee." She starts giving us the play-by-play of their janitor closet kiss but somewhere between mop head and disinfectant spray, I notice that Adam's walked into the lunch room.

I silently curse myself; I must have miscalculated his schedule because I thought he had first lunch today. As he nears our table, I feel my resolve faltering - it's so much easier to declare war on the boy you like when you don't have to see him face-to-face. In all my preparation for today, I hadn't considered how he would act toward *me*. Or how cute he would look in that navy-blue polo.

I force my eyes onto Rochelle, holding my breath while I wait for him to pass our table. But instead of graciously passing by like a normal person, he stops, gaping at me with his mouth open. After too many seconds without any reasonable explanation for his behavior, Stacey clears her throat. "You okay, Adam?"

He snaps out of his daze. "Oh... yeah...um... yeah... I'm good. Have a good lunch."

They turn to me, confused. "What was that all about?" Rochelle asks. "Why was he looking at you like that?"

I shrug. "Who knows," I say, catching my breath. "Is there something on my face?" For a second there, I thought he was going to blow up my entire plan by proclaiming his love for me, right here in the cafeteria. But since he's not, I realize his reaction to me sitting here can only mean one thing - he knows I skipped class to avoid him. If I could do a cart-wheel without Mr. Bryant writing me up, I would.

When I'm finished eating my salad, I walk up to the snack shop to buy a pack of cookies. I'm deciding between *Oreos* and *Chips Ahoy* when he appears at my side. "Hey," he says, "why weren't you in class earlier?"

I step forward, trying to be nonchalant, having just spent the last five minutes coaching myself up for this exact scenario. I had a feeling it was coming, but what I hadn't anticipated was him doing it here, in front of the entire lunch room. But as I take another deep breath, I remind myself not to cave; I don't owe him any answers, just like yesterday, when he felt like he didn't owe me any.

A tit for your tat.

I ignore him, stepping up to the counter. "Can I have a pack of Oreos, please?" I ask our lunch lady, Ms. Janet. I can still feel him behind me, all tension and angst, and I have to admit, as awkward as this is, it feels good to finally have the upper hand. For Adam to be standing behind *me*, waiting for an answer to a question he shouldn't even be asking. *Because he has a girlfriend.*

"What can I get you, Adam?" she asks, passing me the cookies.

"Nothing, Ms. Janet, thanks."

He follows me out of line, waiting for an answer. There's something in his expression now - it's not desperation exactly but a kind of regret, like he knows how bad he messed up yesterday. But it's not my problem anymore. He's not playing fair, so I won't, either.

I take out an Oreo, eating the frosting first. "I'll be helping Mrs. Mooney in the guidance office for the next couple of weeks." It's not an out-right lie; I *was* in her office earlier and while we haven't talked about me coming back, I do plan on being somewhere other than study-hall for the next couple of weeks.

"What!" he shouts, then adds, quieter, "Why?"

I finish the Oreo, glancing behind him. He seems unfazed by the attention we're attracting, but it's enough to make my heart start to pound. The lunch room is definitely not an ideal location to have this conversation - what will Caroline do when she finds out about it?

"Extra credit," I lie.

It sounds like a bark comes from his mouth.

I raise my eyebrows, waiting, but he's stuck, and we both know it. He can't explain why he's upset unless he tells the truth about his feelings for me. Which we both know isn't going to happen. A part of me feels bad, but I'm looking out for my own heart now.

Connor comes up, saving the day. "Hey Guys," he says. "I'm not interrupting, am I?"

I shake my head just as Adam says, "Kind of."

I take a step back, not acknowledging it. "No, you're not interrupting. What's up?" I offer him an Oreo. "You want a cookie, *my little Cookie?*"

Adam coughs, his cheeks turning the perfect shade of pink.

All is fair in love and war.

Maybe it's below the belt, but now I have my confirmation that he was lying yesterday. He remembers calling me *Cookie*, just as clearly as he remembers telling me about the red bikini.

Connor takes an Oreo. "Can I borrow your history notes?"

"Sure, I have them right over here," I say, stepping neatly away.

"What do I have to do for a study date?" Connor asks, following me.

I dig through my bag, handing over the notes, chancing a glance at Adam, who is still standing over there like a dog with his tail between his legs.

One point for Bee.

8

Every Halloween, Graves hosts a costume contest, and most students take it more seriously than studying for the SATs. The winner gets added into Mrs. Mooney's *Halloween Hall-O-Fame*, which should be ridiculous since all she does is add your photo to the glass case that she keeps outside her office - but it's competitive. There hasn't been a new photo since Molly Caldwell's *Mother Nature* look from three years ago, so Mr. Cummings upped the ante this year by adding a week's worth of home-work passes to the first place winner. And that's when Kyle - who has never once cared before - decided he had to win. So naturally, I enlisted Scarlett's help.

"Ok, one more layer of brown, and I can start gluing on the hair," she says, dabbing the side of his face with make-up paint. I've been sitting with them since she got dropped off at five-thirty this morning, amazed by the process; he actually looks like a werewolf.

Kyle has been oddly quiet during the transformation, happy, it seems, to listen to us talk about sewing and *Sanditon*. "So, who are you, anyway?" he finally asks.

Her eyes widen. "Oh, he speaks! I'm Wednesday Adams."

He makes a confused face and she stops, glaring down at him. "From the Adam's Family? Please don't tell me that you've never seen it. It's a classic."

He shrugs. "I've seen it... I just think it's weird... why would you want to dress up as someone so depressing?"

She rolls her eyes. "She is *not* depressing, she's ironic. But let me guess, you'd prefer to see girls dressed like a sexy nurse or something."

He chuckles. "What's wrong with that?"

"For starters, I'm not dressing for you, I'm dressing for *me*. And the very idea that a nurse would dress in a skimpy outfit like that is ridiculous. Do you know what they do for a living?"

"I do," he says simply. I brace myself for a snarky response; Mom nicknamed him *The Great Debater* because he'd argue anything just for the fun of it, but instead of challenging her, he just smiles, his new false teeth pointed to perfection.

"I can't get this wig on right" I say, trying to change the subject just in case his smile turns into something more sinister.

He shakes his head. "Another weird costume. No one our age even knows who Bob Ross is."

I give him a dirty look. "Whatever... it's easy, and I already had all the stuff for it."

"Bob Ross is a legend," Scarlett says, winking at me. "I'll help you in two minutes."

"Are you almost done?" he asks, looking down at his phone. "Adam is going to be here soon to get us."

I whip around, knocking the box of bobby pins on to the floor. "What?"

He doesn't even look up. "Adam's driving us in today."

I throw myself onto the floor, furiously picking up the pins. There are times when I'm aware of myself overreacting, but this is not one of them. "Why?!" I practically cry. I can think of nothing worse than getting into Adam's jeep dressed as Bob Ross. "No I can't...I won't be ready in time... and I still have some homework to finish, and I'm actually not feeling so well. You two can go, and I'll have Mom drive me in later."

Scarlett leans down beside me, helping with the pins. "I'll go with you." Then she stands and swats Kyle's hand away from his face.

"It's itchy!" he whines.

"I just spent the last two hours turning you into this creature, and you will not mess it up before we even get to school," she warns. Then with a few more strokes, she steps back. "Okay, I'm done!"

He stands, looking in the mirror for the first time. "Whoa... I'm seriously impressed." He looks back at her with a new appreciation. "On second thought... I think I will drive us in."

When Kyle goes upstairs to finish getting ready, Scarlett looks at me thoughtfully. "So, whose Adam?"

Great. Just another person who knows. I pause a moment, stalling, wondering what I said to give myself away. "Kyle's best friend."

"Yeah but who is he to *you?*"

I raise a finger to my cheek, feeling the heat rising up to the surface. "To me?"

She smiles knowingly. "You can tell me, you know... whatever it is that you're trying so hard not to say."

I hesitate. "I like him." And with a deep breath and not much thought, I tell her everything. When I'm finished, it feels like I've peeled back another layer of the onion, letting go of all that I've been holding onto for these past weeks. Telling Scarlett now feels safe; maybe because she's new to our school or maybe it's just because she seems like the kind of person who can keep a secret. Either way, I feel good about telling her. "I know I sound pathetic."

She grabs my hands, squeezing tight. "You do not sound pathetic!"

"Thanks, but I'm such a cliché... I honestly thought that something was about to happen. I've always liked him, but then I got to *know him know him,* and he sort of just flipped my world upside down. There's more to him than this image that he puts out into the world, and I don't think he shows that side of himself to anyone."

She smiles. "But he showed *you.*"

I nod. "He showed me."

"That has to mean something."

I shrug. "I think it does mean something, but I don't know if it means enough."

"Maybe he's still trying to figure it out."

I think of what Mom said before, about how Adam might be going through something. Maybe I can't see the whole picture because my feelings are too invested. "But it feels like he's trying to figure out a way to *stop* having them."

"But so are you! He sounds just as confused as you are." Not until this very moment had it occurred to me that we are both doing the same thing. Sure, he denied our most monumental conversation after the football game, but haven't I been trying to disregard my own feelings for him this whole time? Maybe we both understand that being together would be messy, on many levels.

I look up. "So, in addition to being an influencer and make-up artist and seamstress... you're also a therapist, too?"

She laughs. "I'll send you my bill."

Once Kyle is parked, he throws Scarlett a cheesy smile. "Thanks again, Scar."

The *Cove Girls* are waiting for us in front of the school, dressed as rock, paper, scissors. Sara's sulking, probably still mad that no one agreed to be the *Kardashians* with her.

Scarlett laughs. "You girls look great."

"Thanks," Stacey beams, clearly pleased with the compliment. They still treat Scarlett like a celebrity, even after she met us for fries at *George's* last week. I can tell that Stacey and Rochelle like her a lot, but Sara still needs some convincing.

"Kyle looks amazing, by the way... how did you even do that?" Rochelle asks.

A group of junior girls rush by us, dressed as M&M's. "My friend Nathaniel is a make-up artist in New York, and he sent me a video breaking it down for me. It's easier than it looks."

I step forward, holding open the door for us. "She's being modest! She literally came over at five-thirty this morning."

"Wow, that's so cool!" Stacey says.

Principal Cummings is in the lobby dressed as Professor Dumbledore from *Harry Potter,* trying his hardest to use an English accent. "Welcome, fine students of Graves, and happy Hallows eve, mu-ha-ha-ha."

"That's not even something that Dumbledore would say," Stacey complains. "If you're going to go for it... *at least go for it.*"

His gray cloak is long enough to cover his feet, and I find myself wondering whether it was something that he owned already. I can picture it, hanging up in his closet right next to his *Star Wars* shrine. "Please gather round, if you dare."

We shuffle forward, listening as he recites Edgar Allen Poe's *Spirits of the Dead.*

> *"Thy soul shall find itself alone*
> *'Mid dark thoughts of the gray tombstone—*
> *Not one, of all the crowd, to pry*
> *Into thine hour of secrecy"*

Sara loses patience first, pushing her way through the crowd of costumes. "I literally have no idea what he's saying."

As we walk further on down the hallway, it's like we're lost in a sea of costumes. It seems like everyone's dressed up as something until I see Marcus from my gym class, looking completely unaware of the fact that it's Halloween.

"Kyle has a good chance, but did you see those freshmen back there, dressed as the whole cast of the *Guardians of the Galaxy*?" Stacey asks.

"Or Annie Libby's Khaleesi? I think she's wearing contacts," Sara adds.

After Scarlett says bye, Rochelle turns to me, giving me the same look that she had four summers ago when she begged me to go tubing with her on Lake Winnipesaukee. I ended up with a bloody nose, and I swore I'd never give into that look ever again. "Bee, guess what we're doing tonight."

I stop at my locker. "I thought I was coming over? I got the last pack of orange frosted Oreos." Stacey and Sara exchange a look, trying not to laugh. They aren't around tonight, so Rochelle and I are going to make a Halloween inspired snack board and watch *Hocus Pocus*.

"Nope! Tuck those cookies away for another time my friend... I've got something even better for you! We're going to Musters!"

I laugh out loud until I realize she's not joking. "Wait, what? Musters the old insane asylum?"

She gives me a half-hearted smile as Stacey and Sara bust out laughing. "We'll leave you two to it, then. Good luck, Rochelle." Sara laughs again before walking off.

"Good luck?" I call after them. "Why does she need luck?"

Rochelle leans back against the locker next to mine, pleading her case. "Okay... before you say no, just hear me out. Charlie goes up there a lot, I guess." She leans over, lowering her voice. *"For ghost hunting,* and a bunch of upperclassmen are going to break in... tonight. He's leading one of the groups."

When I shake my head no, it loosens my wig. "There's no way I'm going ghost-hunting! Just no way!" Out of all of us, I'm the least likely to ever do something like this. I still can't watch a scary movie without hiding under the blanket for most of it.

"Okay, but I haven't even told you the best part! It would be a double date - with Erik Roth!"

"Erik Roth, the kid that got caught making out with the German exchange student in the athletic director's office last year?"

"One and the same." She nods as if that fact alone should convince me.

I slam my locker door shut. *"Hard no,* Rochelle. No way!"

She follows me down the hall, practically begging. "Please? I don't want to go alone."

"Then don't go!"

She jumps in front of me, blocking the entrance to my class. "Come on, Bee, he really wants me to go, and it will be fun. I don't know Erik that well, but he's cute, you might like him."

"Nothing about being at an old insane asylum on Halloween night sounds fun, Rochelle." I look away just in time to see Adam and Caroline turn down the hallway, dressed as peanut butter and jelly.

"Very original," I mumble. It's been two long weeks since I waged my war on Adam, and I'm beginning to wonder what counted as winning and losing. I haven't spoken to him since that day in the cafeteria, and as much as it's what I want, I'm disappointed that he hasn't pushed back at all. If anything, he seems relieved that his *Bee Problem* has been dealt with.

"What?"

"Nothing, nothing."

"So, what do you say? Pretty please, with orange frosted Oreos on top?"

Adam walks by, doing a one over on my costume, a smile playing at the corner of his lips. The thought of him seeing me like this earlier had embarrassed me, but I should have known that he would find it just as funny as me. We always laugh at the same things.

Maybe breaking the law with Erik Roth would be a good thing. If nothing else, it might take my mind off Adam. "Fine," I say, turning back to her. "But I'm going to be pissed if I see a ghost!"

9

AFTER DINNER, I'M HELPING DAD DRY THE DISHES WHEN I get a text from Rochelle saying they'll be out front in five minutes. "I remember how excited you kids used to get about trick-or-treating," he says, reminiscing. "Those were the days."

I smile at him as I dry the last bowl. He always gets sentimental at times like this, like the holidays are a reminder that we've grown up. "Oh Dad, we're growing up too fast."

He chuckles, elbowing me in the ribs. "Then slow down a bit, will ya?"

Kyle's sitting at the kitchen island, scrolling through his phone, still annoyed with me from earlier when I told him I was going to Muster's. Even winning the costume contest hadn't set him right. *Why do you pick the riskiest things to come to?* he asked, frustrated. *If we get caught, we could seriously get arrested this time.*

I didn't respond because I didn't actually know why I'd agreed to go; one minute, I was saying no and the next, Adam was there in his stupid couple's costume and I thought, why not?

But the fact still remained; she convinced me to do something I didn't want to. It was reminiscent of the assembly Mr. Cummings hosted last year on peer pressure, when he wore his baseball cap backwards with other faculty members and chanted, *no, man, I'll pass on the grass - nah, mizz, that ain't your bizz!* His hope was to encourage us to follow our instincts and not let others influence our decisions. However, it got lost in translation due to his ridiculousness. The hashtag, #MrCummingsisoncrack circulated for weeks.

Charlie honks, and Kyle follows me out.

"Be safe and call for anything!" Mom shouts after us. It makes me feel another wave of guilt. For the first time ever, I'm going to do something illegal, something that they would definitely be disappointed in me for. I wonder if every criminal feels this conflicted before their crime, or if I'm just not cut out for the hard life.

Rochelle's hanging out the window of Charlie's car, waving me on. "Ready for something scarryyyy?"

Kyle comes up and hip checks me. "Oh Brookey Bee, you didn't tell me it was a date!"

I roll my eyes. "Shut up, Kyle. It's not a date!"

He looks through the window, then turns back to me. "Ooof... Erik Roth? Good luck with that!"

He pinches my arm before running over to his car.

"Ow!" I wail, pulling open the back door to Charlie's car. I climb in, smiling uneasily at Erik.

Rochelle turns around in her seat. "Brooke, this is Erik, Erik, Brooke," she says, looking very pleased with herself. And why wouldn't she be? This all worked out exactly as she'd planned.

Erik smiles. "Hey, Brooke, I've been looking forward to meeting you."

Despite myself, I blush, tucking my hair behind my ears. *Maybe this won't be so bad, after all.*

Charlie pulls off down the road. "So, Brooke... are you nervous?"

Rochelle reaches her arm out toward Charlie, resting her hand on his shoulder. The comfortableness of it makes me pause. While I've been obsessing over a boy who's already taken, she's been securing her status as a *real* girlfriend. It makes me feel twisted up inside. I'm happy for her, but I'm envious of what she has. I wonder if they've gotten close enough yet to have pet names like *Babe* or *Lovebug*.

"A little," I say, honestly.

Erik reaches over, squeezing my knee. "Don't worry, we'll take good care of you."

Ugh. I've experienced boys like this before, the ones who feel entitled to reach out and touch me without asking, and it always gives me the creeps. So I turn away, looking out the window, watching the last of the trick-or-treaters run up and down the streets. It makes me long for that time in my life, when things were simpler, when all you worried about were bed times and cooties.

A while later, after stopping so Erik could get a *Red Bull,* Charlie's pulling into a small industrial park right off the highway.

I look around, partly amazed; I've driven by these buildings all of my life, without ever really noticing what is in them. There's a tech company and a pharmaceutical sales building and a sign out front of another one that says *we buy houses,* but all of the parking lots are empty, except for the one that we're driving to in the back.

He parks and starts filling his backpack with flashlights. "We have to park here, but we'll walk up through the woods to get to the hospital."

When the boys get out, Rochelle whips around to face me. "I can't believe we're about to do this. I'm actually really nervous."

"Me, too. It's okay. We'll be fine," I assure her, but in the next breath, I find myself frantically searching the crowd of people outside until I find Kyle. He can be a real pain sometimes, but I feel safer knowing he's around - he'd never, *ever*, let anything bad happen to me.

I look back at Rochelle. "*Cove Girls* for life."

Over the next few minutes, my nerves feel like they're all over the place, like *I'm* the ball in the pinball machine. One second, I'm panicked, and the next, I'm excited. Besides the obvious risk I'm taking, it's most likely something that will be talked about at school on Monday. There might be a *Little Lucy* post about it and as far as I can tell, we're the only underclassman here. So, I guess that's pretty cool.

Bobby Miller whistles, and a circle forms around him. Charlie pulls Rochelle in, but I'm happy to hang back by the car, absorbed in people watching. He starts explaining the plan, something about basements and flashlights and rotted flooring, but I stop paying attention when Caroline's car pulls in.

She jumps out with Dina, the both of them dressed in matching camo outfits. Adam steps out next, stretching his arms above his head as he lazily scans the crowd.

I know I only have about three seconds until he realizes I'm here, but I can't pull my eyes away. Thankfully, just as he's about to notice me, Andy Linberg runs up and chest bumps him.

Bobby makes a whooping sound and claps his hands together. "Let's do it!"

I walk beside Rochelle and Charlie as we climb a steep, muddy hill, annoyed that I put on my new white Ked tennis shoes. A few muffled conversations are happening around us, but for the most part, it's just darkness and silence.

Erik brushes up against me. "Awe, Brooke, you look nervous. Don't worry... I'll protect you." I push on, ignoring him. There is no way he can see my face right now to know I'm nervous, anyway.

We stop at the top of the hill, and thanks to the creepy full moon, I get my first look at the asylum. It's just as frightening as I'd imagined it to be. It's ancient and uncared for with the outside covered in brick and graffiti. Most of the windows are missing, and there are chipped statues of mystical fairy children scattered throughout the top of the building. Maybe it's supposed to be comforting, but it would have been nice if they considered us, *the kids who would be breaking in a hundred years later*, and how terrifying those statues would look with missing limbs. If there is a place to shoot a scary movie, this is it.

Someone behind us yells, "Oh, hell no," and runs back down the hill, and for a split second, I think of following him. I could be sitting on Rochelle's couch, stuffing my face with Oreos, *watching* a scary movie not *participating* in one.

Because I apparently do things that make me uncomfortable, I follow the group as they jog across the road.

Bobby rushes up the stairs, pushing open the intricate wooden door and one by one, we step into the building. There must be thirty of us; way too many people for this kind of thing.

Charlie looks at me as if he can read my mind. "By law, the guards aren't allowed to come in here...so, at least there's that."

Inside, it's dark and cold and musty, every sound echoing through what seems like the entire building. I knew it was a big place, you can see it from the highway, but I never realized just how massive it actually is - the kind of place you could get lost in.

I'm well and truly terrified by the time Bobby shuts the

door behind him. "Let's separate in two groups," he says, and then there's shuffling and shifting until I'm standing on the opposite side of the room from Kyle. Before I can freak-out about it, Rochelle's pulling me down a long, empty corridor.

"He's really smart, isn't he? Like, showing everyone around like this?"

I let out a breath. For some strange reason, she seems more relaxed now that we're inside. "Definitely."

"You like him, right?"

"Yeah, *he's* great, but I don't know about his friend." But it's not the time to explain how I really feel. We'll talk about it later, when I'm sleeping at her house.

"He told Charlie that you are hot."

"Cool," I say, walking on my tip toes.

Charlie pauses to pull open a wooden door with elaborate carvings all over it. "This is the chapel," he says, stepping aside so we can walk through. The room is still in decent condition compared to what we've seen so far, and I find myself hoping it brought the patients joy in an otherwise doomful existence here. Musters had a reputation for being especially brutal to its patients and officially closed down in the seventies due to malpractice. "Chapels are hubs for supernatural activity," Charlie says as we gather around him. He has a direct, easy way of talking, and I find myself genuinely interested. He points to the piano. "It's been said that people still hear this piano being played, but as you can see, the keys are missing."

I step away, only half listening now, taking a seat at one of the pews. I point my flashlight up at the ceiling, reading the graffiti; *Love not hate, War is hell, Free Britney, E-Clips was here.* I smile to myself, wishing, despite everything, that I was touring this creepy hospital with Adam. He would find a way to make this all funny.

Our next stop is the kitchen, where Charlie has promised

us a story about stolen knives and a chef held hostage, but just as we're about to go in, group two comes walking past us. Kyle stops when he sees me. "You alright?"

"Yeah. I'm okay."

"You can come with us if you want," he suggests. "It won't matter."

Out of the corner of my eye, I see Adam stop, turning around to walk back to us.

"No. I'm good, I'll see you after."

I meet back up with my group in the cafeteria. "Let's hang here for a minute," Erik suggests. "I'm bored with this place already."

He follows me around until he walks right up behind me, so close, I think he's going to touch me again. "Are you in a relationship?"

I flinch, feeling chills run up my spine, and not the good kind, either.

"No," I whisper.

"How come a pretty girl like you is single?"

I fidget a little, wishing the group would come back. "I guess I just haven't found the right person yet."

He walks around to face me, and his expression gives me pause. He seems genuine. Maybe I've been judging him unnecessarily. Sure, he was too handsy earlier, but maybe I've been too closed off. It's not lost on me that I compare every boy to Adam, but in the end, who could live up to that kind of adoration?

I've just about decided to be more open when a loud bang stops us both in our tracks. He jumps back, pushing me toward the sound, and I squeeze my eyes shut, anticipating the inevitable death that's coming my way. *This is it, they've come to get me*, I think, not sure who they are or where we're going.

It bangs again, sounding the same. I slowly open my eyes, stepping forward to look out the window. *Bang. Bang. Bang.*

"What is it?!" Erik whines in such a pitiful voice, it almost makes me forget about my own fear because I'm so distracted by his.

Bang.

I let out a breath, realizing it's just a shutter slamming against the window. "Just the shutters," I say, stepping back. I check on Erik; he's still squatting on the floor with his arms covering his head. I want to laugh and say *thanks for the protection,* but he's probably embarrassed enough.

The group comes back in, and Charlie announces that we've been wandering around the building for close to two hours and it's time to head out.

The walk back is more relaxed, all of us a little more at ease now that the hard part is finally over. We can say that we successfully toured Muster's without dying. I'm even looking forward to hearing the stories that come out about it on Monday. Maybe there were some hookups or ghost sightings, after all.

When we step into the room we started in, the lights from a security truck are rounding the building, moving slowly with their flashlights pointing outside their windows.

"Shit," Charlie says, "turn off your flashlights. We're going to have to wait until they pass the building. Don't move and be as quiet as you can." He takes Rochelle's hand. "No need to worry. Like I said before, they do this all night."

Then, as if things weren't tense enough, there's a scream from somewhere in the building. The sound carries, echoing through walls and staircases; it's so loud and deafening, I'm convinced the guards can hear it, too.

It's silent in the following moments, all of us waiting for something, *anything* to happen. Then... there's a pounding. I can feel it more than I can hear it; the room shakes under the pressure, like the floor is going to cave in. It's a teenage stampede, and it's headed our way.

Charlie holds up his hand, urging us not to move, but the steps are getting closer, and it feels like we're waiting to be trampled on. It's the not knowing that's the worst - they could be running from anything: a giant spider, a man with a chainsaw or a snake with three heads.

I look at Rochelle, watching her face turn from confusion to sheer panic. She whips her head away from the hallway, looking outside at the security truck.

"Steady," I tell her, reading her mind. She wants out; as far as I can tell, she's waiting for the zombie apocalypse, and I doubt I could say anything to convince her otherwise. "We're fine," I try again, but then the other group comes bombing into the room, and it's over; she takes off, running right through the doors with the truck directly in front of us.

"Wait!" Charlie yells, but there's no use; everyone scatters fast.

I dash out, moving, stopping, moving, stopping, until I find a tractor to hide behind. I hadn't noticed when we first walked up, but the building is under construction; I've been around enough job sites to recognize the signs. I crouch behind one of the tires, listening to the chaos. I'm panicked, but somewhere in the back of my mind, I'm pumped that I'm not frozen in place this time.

The guards scream *stop!*

I inch closer to the front of the tractor, trying to come up with a plan. The guards are blocking the entrance to the path where we came from, so it's clear I need to go in the other direction. I take a deep breath, looking back once, then I dart out, not stopping until the shouting becomes faint.

I know I'm on the road. It's logical to assume it goes all the way around the building, but it's what waits for me on the other side that makes me nervous.

I hear footsteps and move closer against the building, too nervous to show myself in case it's a guard. They stop, quiet for a moment before calling out, "Hey! Who is that?"

Adam.

Relief floods through my body. "It's Brooke," I say, running over and throwing myself into his arms. "I'm so glad to see you."

I feel him relax against me. "Yeah?"

I step back, breathing deeply.

"I followed you," he says.

I pause, letting the words hang in the air between us, not sure what I'm supposed to say to that. "We should keep moving. Charlie said there's a security booth up here, so there must be another road out."

He clears his throat. "Yeah, there's a path through the woods that opens up to Chris McGuire's old neighborhood."

We walk slowly, not speaking until we see the security booth. I should be terrified right now; I could get arrested, or there might be a murderer walking about, but I'm excited, *electrified,* like my night can finally start now that we're alone together. Maybe it's the adrenaline, but I know now that the distance over the last two weeks was for nothing because I just can't let him go.

"I'll go see if anyone's in there, and if it's clear, I'll wave you on," he whispers, leaving to get closer to the booth. When he gives me the signal, I rush over, leaning my back against the tree that he's on.

"I think we're good." I go to step out, but a police cruiser pulls in. Adam grabs me, pulling me to him, my back against his front.

Oh God.

"They're driving around back," he says, breathing deeply.

Neither of us makes a move to change this position we're in, but he does reach into his pocket to pull out his phone. "I'm going to text Kyle to let him know we're together. I'll have him pick us up outside the path."

A moment later, his phone lights up. "He'll pick us up in front of Chris's old house." He raises his hands to rest on my shoulders. "On three, we run to that opening right over there."

I take a deep breath. "One... two... three."

We dart out, running as fast as we can, stopping when we reach the path. My throat is on fire now, the same feeling I get when Coach Brian makes us do sprints. "We're good," he says, trying to catch his breath. He looks at the hospital, then back to me, and all at once, we bust out laughing. "That was nuts," he says. "No pun intended."

I catch my breath, looking into the woods. "And just when you think the scary parts are over."

He laughs, taking out his phone again to use as a light. "If anyone can walk through the woods on Halloween night, it's you." He leads us in. "What happened with Erik? I thought he was going to protect you."

I hadn't realized he was close enough to hear that. "Yeah, not exactly. How was your tour?"

He walks slowly, the path too dark to see anything beyond what's in front of us. "We went down into the basement... in these sketchy underground tunnels. I couldn't wait to get out of there."

I bite back a laugh, appreciating his honesty. "But no ghosts?"

"No ghosts."

When he stops short, I step on his heel. "Sorry... so... what were you all running from?"

He scoffs. "Dina walked into a spider's web and freaked out

and then... I don't know... someone ran, and then the whole group started following. It was a disaster."

"Figures."

He turns to me, holding the light in a way so we can see each other's faces. "I was surprised to see you tonight."

I shrug. "I didn't think you saw me."

"I saw you right away."

He starts walking again, but it feels different, the silence more magnified. We ghosted each other for two weeks, but it doesn't feel that way now. It feels like no time has passed at all.

I look past him, to the glimmer of light peeking out from behind the trees; we'll be out of the woods so soon. I wish I could pause this moment, make it last all night.

"So... are you coming back to class next week?"

Without thinking, I blurt out. "I think I'm switching out." When I spoke to Mrs. Mooney earlier today, she agreed to a class change, but she said we'd talk more about it on Monday.

He stops, turning so suddenly that I jump back. He doesn't raise the light this time, but I can still see the outline of his face. "I... I don't want that."

I step closer to him. "What do you want?"

He takes a deep breath, and we both know that what happens next will determine everything. "I want you... I want to be with you," he says without hesitation, fear or regret.

Heat and relief practically burst through my body. *Finally. The words.*

He closes the distance between us, his chest lining up with my head. I stand on my toes, unsteady and unsure, my mind feeling disconnected from my body. I'm reaching up to kiss him, or rather, to put my lips against his, feeling everything happening at once: adrenaline, excitement, fear.

Time stops or slows down or maybe it doesn't even exist at all... but *Caroline.*

I pull away just as quickly as I pushed in. "Oh, my god... Adam, I'm sorry. I don't know why I just did that."

But he closes the distance again, his phone dropping to our feet in the process.

His hands cup my face, and then he's kissing me - properly, expertly, beautifully. Whatever I imagined, it wasn't this. He tastes fruity, like he's been eating *Skittles*, and I want to devour him.

His phone goes off, and that's when we both come up for air.

I'm breathing heavy, barely aware when he reaches down to pick up his phone, telling Kyle we're coming out.

He cups my face again. "Are you okay?" he asks, concerned, but I can see the outline of his smile, and I know he's just as dazed and excited as I am right now.

I nod. "I'm okay."

There are so many things we could say to each other, but all that comes out is delirious laughter, from both of us. It's not until we reach the street opening, when he turns and smiles at me, that I realize I'm seeing him clearly for the first time all night. And maybe ever.

10

THERE'S A GAME THE COVE GIRLS AND I CREATED CALLED *No Go Phone* for the times when we're waiting for an unlikely text to come in. The rules are simple: you put your phone in an out of reach spot, like above the refrigerator, and assign tasks to yourself before you can touch it again. But if you touch it before you've finished the task, you tell yourself that something really, really bad will happen.

I woke up on Saturday morning in full on *No Go Phone* mode, knowing that I'd be glued to my screen, with the hopes of Adam getting in touch. I started small - *if you check your phone before you've showered, you'll wake up in a bed full of spiders,* and then later, *finish your English homework or you'll get stuck on an elevator that smells like pee.*

But by night, my scenarios had escalated in an unprecedented way - *if you check your phone one more time, you'll never see your parents again.* So, I locked my phone in Dad's safe.

I'm almost asleep when my laptop pings with an e-mail from Sara. She must be really desperate if she's e-mailing me.

It's a link to a Little Lucy post - *When Romeo dumped Juliet*. I sit up, my heart pounding against my chest, knowing what this post has to be about.

When Romeo dumped Juliet

Roses are red, violets are blue, Adam Stanson dumped Caroline and she said F you. It's true, Graves Nation... your favorite power couple is no longer [insert sobs here] or [applause here]. We're guessing this split will leave our readers with mixed emotions; sad, cause it's the end of an era or happy because um, Adam Stanson is SINGLE! For all of you romantics out there, don't count on a reconciliation. Rumor has it that they've been headed towards Dumpsville for months, having already taken a break this summer when Adam went on vacation. You'll remember, *my loyal subjects*, that's when Caroline partook in some questionable "flirting" at Joshua Nelson's backyard rager. Anywho, multiple sources saw them on Saturday night arguing in the parking lot of George's and then again Sunday morning at the Bagel Stop where Caroline looked like she'd officially accepted her defeat. BUT she is the debate team captain, so we suspect the fight has just begun.

I throw myself back down onto my bed, putting a pillow

over my face. I want to scream - *Yes!* or *No!* Did I just break-up Graves' favorite *It Couple?*

I get up out of bed, pacing my room. Sleep, unfortunately, is now out of the question. *What should I do? What should I do?* I need to talk to someone! But who - because I'm a genius and didn't tell a living soul what was going on between Adam and me, I literally have no one I can call. The Cove Girls would require too much backstory and apologies for not mentioning it earlier, and Kyle, well... who knows how he's going to react to the news that Adam and I kissed the other night.

No... don't freak out, I tell myself.

There's a strange tapping sound on my window. At first, my reaction is to hide under the blankets, but when it persists, I crawl over, peeking through one of the blinds. For a moment, all I see is darkness until Adam steps out from under the maple tree. *Ohmygod, my very own eighties rom-com moment!* He points to the front door and I nod, even though all he can see are my eyes.

"What's going on? Why are you dressed like a navy seal?" I whisper a minute later, after changing out of my flannel pajamas with the pigs on it. He, on the other hand, is wearing all black, his hood tightly pulled over his head.

He smiles. "I'm on a mission. I needed to blend into the night."

"You walked here?" I ask, aghast, even though he lives a few streets over.

"Yeah... grab your eskimo Ugg boots and come out here with me. We should... talk."

"Do you want to just come in?"

He shakes his head. "No way... can't risk anyone seeing us right now."

He's right. We are in a very temperamental place and can't

risk being caught hanging out alone at midnight. "I'll be right back."

I find him under the maple tree, hugging one of his knees to his chest while the other leg is sprawled out in front of him.

"Hey," I say, sitting beside him.

He shifts, turning to face me. "Hey."

The air is cold, but I'm sweating in my North Face bubble coat. Mom had just taken out all of our winter stuff earlier this week preparing for what the weather-woman said would be *a very chilly November*.

"So..." he says.

"So."

He shifts again, seeming just as nervous as me. I've been waiting for him to call all day, but now that he's here, I don't know what to do with myself. "Um... did you hear? About me and Caroline?"

"Yeah."

"And?"

I cross my arms over my chest. *Say something!* But what do I say? "And... are you okay?"

He sigh-laughs, looking out into the street. Like in the woods, I can't see his face clearly, but I can read his body language - his frustration, confusion. And it's no wonder - he broke up with his girlfriend for his best friend's little sister. I think.

I pick up a maple pod from the ground, flicking at the dried edges. "Do you remember when we were younger and Kyle and I got in that huge fight over the computer?"

He laughs. "You were so butt-hurt that he ended your game. What was it? Barbie Dreamhouse?"

I push him. "It was an outfit design program, thank you very much!" I loved that game. I'd spent hours "cutting" out clothes and mixing colors and patterns to customize all of my outfits.

"What about it?"

"You followed me out here... to check on me, and you stuck one of these pods onto my nose." I pull open the one I'm holding, picking the seed out from the middle and bending back the sides.

"I remember."

I reach out, feeling my way through the air until I'm touching his face. I take the maple pod, sticking it onto the bridge of his nose. "I think that's the day things changed for me," I say, exhaling. "My feelings, I mean. For *you*."

He swallows, shifting slightly so he's facing me. "So, you *do* want this."

"Of course I do. I always have."

"Yeah. I'm sorry I've been such an idiot these last few weeks. I've been confused. Not about you but just, I don't know, what to do about how I *feel* about you. I've never felt this way before, and it's exciting, but it's kind of freaking me out, too. You make me feel like I can be myself, and it scares me a little, especially since I've just been going through the motions all these years. And there was Caroline, obviously - it's not like I set out wanting to hurt her. I was dreading it, and it probably wasn't fair to put it off this long but — I don't know. Does any of this make sense?"

Trying to lighten the mood a bit, I nod. "You're saying you like me."

He lets out a good-natured sigh, running his hand through his hair. "I like you, Bee. I'm in like with you."

I laugh out loud. "I'm in like with you, too. So, no more games?"

He groans. "Ugh - I've been a real ass, haven't I?"

"*Such* an ass! But I dished it out in the end."

He reaches over, wrapping an arm around me to pull me closer. It feels so natural, *so right*, to be cuddling against him like this. Maybe it's because we already know each other so well, that the physical stuff would be a natural next step. "I can't believe you called Connor your little Cookie! That was below the belt, Bee."

"All is fair in love and —"

"War, I know, but now that we've truced, we need to figure out what we're going to do next. I have to tell Kyle ASAP."

My stomach tightens, thinking of Kyle and Caroline and the entire school freaking out when they find out that he broke up with *her* for *me*. I spent so much time dreaming about being Adam's girlfriend, never considering the messy stuff. That the world might hate us. That Caroline might actually kill me.

"I could tell him tomorrow —" he says as I start picturing all the ways Caroline could end my life. I wouldn't put murder past her - not with something like this. She'd probably do something sneaky like put poison in my PSL.

"What if we don't?" I interrupt as he's considering whether he should tell Kyle over burgers or a roast-beef three-way. "What if we just... wait?"

"Wait. What?"

"Not wait to be together but wait to tell everyone. Only for a little while... maybe just until things cool down and your break-up with Caroline isn't so... fresh? I mean, how do you think people will react when they learn that we kissed before you were even broken up?"

He's quiet, thinking it over. "I guess that's true, but how would I see you?"

"We could... sneak around a little?"

"Are you sure? I mean, after everything, do you really want to do that?"

I picture Caroline coming at me with the heel of one of her

stilettos. "Yeah... I think it's the best thing we could do... for now."

"Okay... so we'll be together but in secret... just until things die down a bit?"

"Yup."

I rest my head against his shoulder, savoring the feeling of having him this close. I've wanted this for too long to make any mistakes now. I have to find a way to figure out how to keep him.

"But just so we're clear," he says, looking down at me, "we're doing this... we're together now."

I nod, trying hard not to giggle. "Yup. Does this mean you're going to start calling me Babe?"

11

EVERYONE IS TALKING ABOUT THEIR BREAK-UP IN SCHOOL the next day. I'd convinced myself that it wouldn't be a big deal, that despite the Little Lucy post, no one would even care. But I was wrong. In the hallways, in the bathrooms - students, teachers, they all have something to say. I heard Shannon Finkle calling it the most devastating split since Gigi and Zhan. And the rumors are getting more far-fetched as the day goes on. Last I heard, Caroline broke up with Adam to date the water polo captain from Boston College.

Between my third and fourth period, Kyle walks up to me in the hallway. "Have you heard about Adam and Caroline?" I didn't see him this morning, having sent Scarlett an SOS-text last night asking her to pick me up early. She said yes without hesitation, not even asking any questions.

"Um, yeah. Who hasn't?" I look into the classrooms as we pass by, acting like I'm looking for something while inwardly freaking out. *Why is he asking me this?*

My brain tells me to *relax, be casual. Whatever you do, don't look him in the eye.* Kyle is constantly surprising me, and to write him off as clueless would be a mistake. He might have already started to suspect something is going on. But that doesn't mean I have to throw in the towel already.

I feel his eyes on the side of my face, silently urging me to turn his way. And then, because I just can't help it, I do turn his way, but in an instant, I regret it. It only takes seconds, but it's like he's downloading all the information he needs without me saying a word, like the answer to whatever he's asking is written on my face. I don't have a poker-face, and he's been known to use it against me.

I knew this would happen, I think to myself. Isn't that why I asked Scarlett for a ride in the first place? Because I didn't want to give myself away somehow.

"What?" I ask, defensive now as I stop outside my class. Maybe I'm exaggerating - maybe he doesn't know anything. So far, I haven't heard anyone say anything about Adam kissing an underclassman.

He seems to be thinking really hard about something before taking a breath. "Nothing. I was just wondering."

Phew.

"Well, I better get inside." I hold my breath, not letting it out again until I'm sitting behind the safety of my desk. It was a coincidence; for the first time in his entire life, Kyle just wanted to gossip.

I'm mostly quiet during lunch - happy to listen to the outrageous stories that are going around about Adam and Caroline. I can't deny that all of it is kind of thrilling. No one knows about us - we share this secret together. *Me! I, Brooke McGrath, broke up Adam and Caroline.* It makes me feel empowered, invincible, special.

Sara is telling Stacey and Rochelle what she's already told me weeks ago about them breaking up over the summer, adding that Caroline had gone to their house on Saturday and spent the day alternating between crying and eating Ben & Jerry's ice cream. That part gives me pause - despite everything, I don't want to be the reason she is upset.

Needing a moment to be alone, I get up to go to the bathroom. I haven't spent much time thinking about Caroline or the fact that Adam and I kissed while he was still with her. She'd become almost like a faceless part of all of this. She was there, *always there*, but she never mattered enough to change my feelings. Maybe if she had been a nicer person, if she hadn't spent the last two years going out of her way to be mean to me, maybe then I would have abided to the ethics of girl-code.

As if materializing from my thoughts, the door opens, and she walks in, storming over to me. "Oh... Hi, Caroline."

"Don't Hi Caroline me." She grabs my shoulder, shoving me back against the wall. It takes a second for me to realize that we're the only ones in here. My heart starts beating against my chest as the hot feeling of dread starts to flow through my body like a slow-moving current. Everything is a contradiction. My mouth is dry, my hands are sweaty. I want to run, but I can't move.

"What's going on?" I manage to get out, though my voice sounds small even to my own ears. I'm terrified, and she knows it. Even through her rage, I see the satisfaction on her face.

"I know that you have something to do with this!" she barks, stepping forward again so our faces are mere inches apart. Her lip gloss smells like cherries.

Did Adam tell her?

"To do with what?"

Her face twists together. "To do with what," she mimics.

"Don't be stupid. I know that you've been pining after him for years."

"I don't... I don't," I stutter, hating myself for being this scared. Why can't I be strong enough to face her? To stand up for myself? "I don't know what you're talking about."

Ignoring me, she goes on. "I don't know how you did it... *not yet,* but when I figure it out, I'm going to make your life suck. I promise you that. Adam will regret the day he ever left me for a sad, desperate girl like you."

And then she's gone, leaving me standing there alone. It was so brief that it feels like it couldn't have been real, that I just conjured up a scene from my nightmares.

I storm into one of the stalls, locking it behind me, taking a few deep breaths before I burst into tears. I just... *stood there,* letting her tear into me. I don't want to be that girl, the one with no backbone, but I was really scared, especially because I saw that she was telling the truth. She's going to ruin my life.

Dear Journal,

I love life. November, it turns out, is my favorite month. It's chilly enough to wear my new parka, Thanksgiving is a few weeks away and I just so happen to be in a secret relationship with ADAM STANSON. Okay, to be fair - he's never said the word, "relationship" and we haven't hung out at all BUT we're inseparable through text message. AND we've talked on the phone before bed for the last four nights! I had to change his name to **Claire from Science** *because he blows up my phone so much, I was worried someone would see his name and ask questions. It's not a fairy-tale beginning but I'm practical and clearly well-schooled in LOVE (another word we haven't said yet). I imagine him lying in bed,*

*shirtless, still a bit damp from a shower, thinking about
how cool I'm being about this. How *low-maintenance*
and *different* than all the other girls he knows. The
secret part is just how our story begins. It's only temporary, until his break-up isn't so fresh and we can figure
out how to tell Kyle. That's the part that really gets
Adam all kinds of stressed out. Twice now, he's freaked
out saying we can't keep this from him. But I very gently
remind him that it's not a big deal. That we've got this.
I'm the very picture of ease these days... but how could I
be stressed about anything when Adam, I repeat,
ADAM STANSON, calls me at 9:30 pm and says, "I've
been thinking about you all day."*

12

Two weeks before the boys' basketball season starts, the booster club sponsors a student/faculty basketball game to raise money for the team. The whole community packs into the school gym to watch the young face the old, and if the students win, Mr. Cummings has to sit in a dunk tank this spring for *Spirit Week,* but if they lose, they have to organize the gym equipment on a Saturday morning. Kyle would never admit it, but he's nervous this year because it's rumored that the new computer science teacher, Mr. Sampson, played in college.

During one of my late-night calls with Adam, he asked me to go. *I always go,* I had said, trying to downplay my excitement that he was asking me to be there for *him. Yeah but it's different now.*

And it is - in only a few weeks, we've managed to get to know each other in a whole new way. I held on to every word, wanting, *needing* to hear more about this boy who is baring his soul to me, trusting *me,* of all people, with things he said he hasn't told anyone. It's surprising, given how close our families are, that we can learn anything new, but every night, he calls again and we talk until my eyes practically close on their own.

On our way to the game in Charlie's car, I'm dancing and singing with the Cove Girls to Ed Sheeran's *Shape of You* with an excitement reserved only for weekend nights. Between the four of us girls, we're wearing at least half of a bottle of *Victoria's Secret Love Spell* and enough padding in our bras to fill a Build-a-Bear, but we're young and alive and on our way to a high school basketball game.

When the music switches from Ed to Rhianna, Sara pauses, looking at me like I have food stuck in my teeth. "Bee... you curled the left side of your hair wrong again. It's going the opposite way it's supposed to." Sara is always up-to-date on the latest make-up and hair trends, something that hasn't particularly interested me until now.

I panic, pulling out my iPhone's camera to use as a mirror. I've been trying a little harder to look nice - nothing too extreme, just face masks and painted nails and more bronzer but apparently, hair is still not my thing. I'll probably never get it to look as perfect as Caroline's.

"What am I supposed to do now? Does it look bad?"

"You can't even tell!" Stacey sings, *"We found love in a hopeless placeee!"*

Understatement of the year.

Rochelle turns around, teasing. "Since when do you care this much about your hair, Bee? Do you have a secret lover that we don't know about?"

I laugh a little too loud, but no one notices.

Pulling into the parking lot, my nerves suddenly take over as questions pop into my mind. *Is my hair really bad? Does he have strong enough eye-sight to see this pimple on my chin? What if he doesn't look at me? How often should I look at him?*

What if I'm already looking at him every time he looks at me, does that make me look desperate?

As we walk up the steps to the gym, the sound of basketballs hitting the floor mirror the pounding in my heart. The sights are all the same - booster Moms working the concession stand, younger siblings hanging in the hallway, Mr. Cummings handing out raffle tickets by the door. But none of it eases my anticipation.

I find him right away, warming up with the rest of the team. I want to scream *I'm here! I'm here!* I want everyone to know about us. I want the world to know I'm his girl. Maybe it's just that if I say it out loud, it will be easier for me to believe it. His feelings still surprised me; how does a boy like that, with his easy charm and tight butt, like me? *Me.*

We find a spot on the bleachers with Charlie's friends.

I let my eyes wander over to Adam again. He hasn't seen me yet, still too busy warming up, but I'm pretty sure I won't be able to breathe again until we make eye contact.

"Did you ever try out for any sports?" I hear Stacey ask Charlie.

He shakes his head, looking uneasily at Rochelle like he's nervous that what he's about to say will make her think less of him. "I tried soccer my freshman year, but I'm just not very athletic."

"Me, neither," Rochelle lies.

The referee blows her whistle, and as the team huddles up, Adam finally looks out into the crowd. I watch his eyes scan the sections, searching, pausing to wave at his family, and just when I think I'll die from anticipation, he sees me.

He smiles, a secret smile that says nothing and everything at the same time.

We're only a few minutes into the first quarter when Caroline and her friends walk into the gym, sitting right in front of us. They're all dressed in blue and white, but it's Caroline's face that makes my stomach flip because in bold glittered make-up, is the number eight. *His number.*

It feels like I've been punched in the stomach. *Why would she wear his number on her face?* Adam and I haven't talked much about her in the last few weeks. I take this as a good sign - like with every passing day, she's becoming less of a thing to us. But wearing his number takes guts - it makes a statement. It says, *things aren't over between us.*

For most of the first and second quarter, I find myself glued to the back of Caroline's head, following her movements as she follows his. When he finally sits on the bench for a break and looks up in our direction, it's hard to know whether he's looking at her or me. She catches his eye, waving enthusiastically, and he nods back.

"So, what's the deal, Caroline?" Britt Murphy asks. "Are you getting back together?"

Caroline nods, her eyes still fixed on him. "Definitely... he's just confused right now. It's not even a break-up, *per se,* but more of a break."

I'm leaning so far over my seat now, I'm surprised I don't fall forward.

"So, you still talk?" she asks.

"Oh yeah... all the time."

"Will he go to UCLA with you?"

She shrugs. "We've talked about it. He really wants to study finance, and he can do that anywhere."

It should put me at ease to hear her say something that is so clearly incorrect, but I find that it does nothing to lessen the anxiety I feel over the fact that she still thinks that they're getting back together. *Would she lie to her friends?*

I'm in a sour mood by the time Scarlett texts at half-time asking me to meet her outside. I walk over to the door with my head hanging low, unable to shake the things Caroline was saying. *It's just a break. UCLA in the fall.*

I slam right into a solid chest. When I look up, I realize it's Adam, coming back in from the locker rooms. I should be embarrassed - I look like a total stalker, waiting for him to come out, but I'm just relieved he's smiling at me.

He pulls me to the side.

"I'm just going to meet Scarlett," I explain, hoping I sound casual.

He steps closer, bending like he's going to whisper in my ear. "You sure you aren't waiting for me?" He adds, "Do you want an autograph?"

I push him away, smiling. "You wish."

"A guy can dream, can't he?" he flirts. "What are you up to after this?"

Coach Brian calls over, "Stanson! Huddle up."

"I'm not sure," I say quickly, watching as Coach Brian starts to walk over.

"Want to hang out?"

"Um...okay... How?"

"I'll call you after the game."

Outside, I meet Scarlett in a daze. "You okay? You look like you've seen a ghost."

"Yeah, sorry. I'm ok," I say, leading her into the gym while I still try to process the fact that I just agreed to hang out with Adam later. I knew this was coming; we can't carry on over the phone forever, but the thought of being alone with him feels very intimidating all of a sudden. *What if I freeze up? What if I act so weird that he changes his mind about me?*

"So, besides Adam, do I know anyone else on the team?"

"Kyle," I say, pointing to him.

She turns eagerly, and they lock eyes at the same time. For some reason, Kyle looks surprised, maybe even a little embarrassed, but he recovers quickly, giving her a nod before dropping his gaze back into the huddle.

As we walk back over to the stands, I realize that Caroline and her friends are watching us with an intimidating curiosity. The Cove Girls and I call it a Code Red - anytime a group of upperclassman girls are looking at you at the same time, you should dive for cover because something bad is about to happen.

The closer we get, the clearer I see Caroline's rage. They must have seen me talking to Adam, and I curse myself for flirting with him in front of a gym full of people. *Have I lost all sense? Is Caroline memorizing my face so she can put the finishing touches on my voodoo doll later?*

Just when I'm almost out of the red zone, Britt puts her leg out, making me trip. I'm seconds from falling flat onto my face until Scarlett grabs my arm and pulls me back up. She turns to Britt. "Why would you do that?" It's a bold move, but her Instagram celebrity holds some weight with these girls.

"Whoops!" Britt mumbles, clearly surprised by being called out.

As soon as we sit, Caroline starts talking, a little louder than she had before. "Do you know who I saw the other day, working at the pretzel stand at the mall?"

"Who?" Britt asks.

"Harlow Frank... remember her? She's that sketchy girl who went after Matthew Kent when he was still with Miranda."

"Oh ya... I totally forgot about her."

My stomach tightens, dreading whatever comes next.

"I know, me too. But there she was... selling pretzels and looking *horrible.* Her face is covered in acne now, probably from the anxiety of being cast out by everyone."

"I heard she dropped out of school."

"I wouldn't be surprised. I mean, you don't just recover

from something like that. It basically destroyed her life, and you know what the saddest part is?"

"Besides the acne?"

Caroline chuckles. "Matthew ended up getting back with Miranda in the end." She turns, looking right at me with a smile on her face. It's a warning. Another threat. It's almost enough to make me want to lock myself in my bedroom and never come out.

Almost.

The rest of the game goes by quickly with Scarlett telling us stories about what it's like to live in the city, including the time the New York Knicks invited her to an influencer event where she got to sit in a VIP box with Meghan Trainor.

"You guys coming over?" Sara asks when the game's over and we're walking out. Turns out, Kyle had nothing to worry about - the students won by twelve points.

Rochelle shakes her head. "I'm going back to Charlie's after we drop you off."

"Ohhhhhh," Sara teases. "Boom chicka wah wah."

"You should come," I say to Scarlett while trying to calculate roughly how long it might take Adam until he calls me. *He'll need time to meet with the team, get cleaned up, eat. But should I even go? Maybe I should stop this now. Would I turn out like Harlow?*

Sara turns her head away, pretending like she didn't hear, and Scarlett shrugs. "I'm tired. I think I'll just call it a night."

I frown, about to protest, but my attention is drawn to the side of the gym where Caroline is walking toward Adam with an unnerving speed. She reaches her arm out, touching his back. He turns, but Sara grabs my hand, pulling me out before I can see what happens next.

"It's a law, somewhere, that you can't watch any holiday movies before December first," Sara says, snatching the remote from Stacey. "It makes the actual season less special."

Stacey dives, grabbing it back, and falls onto Sara's bed. "*Love Actually* barely counts as a holiday movie, it's just a background characteristic. You can watch it any time of the year without even noticing it's in December."

Sara steps in front of the TV, blocking her view. "House rules."

Stacey submits, tossing her the remote. "Fine, but I'm not watching *To All the Boys I've Loved Before* again."

I'm gripping my phone, trying to play it cool, but it's been exactly fifty-seven minutes since the game ended, and I still haven't heard from Adam. *What if he changed his mind? What if Caroline changed his mind?* I reach up and place my phone on the top of Sara's bookshelf.

She looks at me and mouths, "No go phone?"

I shrug, hopeless, picking up her nail polish box to distract myself.

"So, what's Scarlett's deal?" Sara asks, flipping through the movies.

Stacey sits up. "Can you imagine growing up in New York City? That must have been so cool."

"I know," I say, picking up a yellow polish called *Barbuda Banana*. "She's the best. I've never met anyone our age who likes to sew as much as me, plus she's super worldly and just like... chill."

"But she's not *our* age, she's a senior. When do older girls ever want to hang out with younger ones? It's weird," Sara snaps.

Stacey ignores her. "Did you see her latest post? The one with that red crop-top? She's the only person who can make a crop-top look chic."

I nod in agreement. "I took that photo!" We spent all of Saturday morning driving around, scouting locations -as she called it- for Instagram.

Sara rolls her eyes and presses play on *Bridesmaids*. "She's not chic. Meghan Markle is chic. Scarlett is something else."

"What flavor hater-aid have you been drinking?" I ask. "What's your problem with her? You're always so rude."

She sits on the bed, ripping open a bag of *M&Ms* and pouring them into her mouth. "I'm not hating, and I don't have a problem with her, I just don't see the draw. Sure, she has a bazillion followers on Instagram, but so what?"

Stacey holds out her hand. "Can I have some blue ones?"

I put the nail polish away and walk over to the mirror, scouring my nose for blackheads. *Not the time to pop them,* I remind myself. "People like her because she's cool... not because of how many followers she has. You'd see that for yourself if your nose wasn't so high up in the air."

Stacey agrees. "Yeah, she seems *so* cool!"

My phone goes off then with a call from *Claire from Science* so I grab it and scramble out of her bedroom. "I need to pee."

"Hi," I answer, whispering, even though no one is around now.

"Hey, how's it going?" he asks. "Why are you whispering?"

I clear my throat. "I'm at Sara's."

"Can I come pick you up?"

"Yeah... totally... Cool... That works."

He laughs. "Meet me at the end of her street in ten minutes, okay? I think Caroline might already be there."

"Ok... bye." I hang up, trying not to look too much into the fact that he knows where Caroline might be. I wonder what they talked about after the game, if they still talk all the time like she said.

I clutch my stomach as I step back into Sara's room. "Ugh... I gotta go home... my stomach is killing me."

Stacey looks concerned. "You okay?"

"Yeah. I just need to sleep. I think." It's getting harder and harder to keep this from them. I almost caved twice and told them everything, but Caroline's threat stopped me in my tracks. I can't risk her finding out, even if it means I have to lie to the Cove Girls for a little while longer. "I'll text you tomorrow."

I quietly pad through the house, relieved to find Caroline's not here. With a deep breath, I step outside into the cold night air, trying to push away my nervousness. *He's just a regular boy,* I remind myself.

And then I see him, leaned against his passenger door, waiting for me. *Waiting for me!*

"Hey, you," he says as I approach. He has that after-a-game look, sleepy but glowing, and if I were brave, if I weren't scared out of my wits right now, I'd lean in and kiss him.

When I respond with a shy smile, he turns and opens the door for me.

I get in.

Once my seat belt is on, he pulls out onto the road. "What time's your curfew?" he asks.

I look out the window, embarrassed. "Ten," I say, wondering if Caroline has one. Probably not.

He glances at the clock. *Eight-thirty-nine.* I've been in his jeep for less than sixty seconds, and it's already going by too fast. Despite my nerves, I wish I could pause this moment and savor how it feels. "Sorry," I say, "I know, it's lame."

He takes a sip from a water bottle, shaking his head. "It's not lame. I have to be home by eleven tonight. "Do you want to drive around a while?"

I nod, looking out the window. A drive would be nice, low-pressure, but it would still give us a chance to talk. "Congrats on your first win of the season. How did it feel to be playing in front of a crowd again?"

He chuckles, switching his hold on the steering wheel from his left to right hand. It's funny seeing him from this vantage point; I've driven with him a thousand times, but I'm usually stuffed into the back seat with backpacks.

"It was cool. I liked seeing you out there," he says, turning to look at me. "Although, you weren't watching me as much as I would have liked."

I smile. "You weren't watching me!"

"I was watching you the whole time," he says.

I turn to look at him, blushing. I guess I wouldn't really know who he was looking at because I was so obsessed with what Caroline was doing. I didn't plan on mentioning her - in fact, I told myself not to bring her up at all, but I want to know the truth more than I want him to think I'm cool. "Caroline had your number on her face."

He sighs, pulling down another road. "I know... I'm sorry, this must be so weird for you. To be honest, I'm not sure what to do about it. She still fully thinks we're getting back together."

"Are you?" I ask, hoping that I don't sound desperate. "Going to get back together... eventually?"

He stops at a red light, turning to meet my eyes. "No, I don't want to be with her anymore, I haven't for a long time." The light turns green, and he looks back at the road, turning onto the causeway as we head out toward the public beach.

"Do you still hang out?" I ask.

He shakes his head. "No, I haven't hung out with her alone since the weekend we broke up but like... I still talk to her, you know, if she calls... I always answer. I feel bad."

I stay quiet, looking out at the choppy water. It reminds me of the day Sara and I stole Jonathan's kayak. The water was too rough to go out, so the boys decided to throw around a football but when they weren't looking, we stole the kayak and slipped into the water. We only got up to our knees before they came running over to stop us.

He turns into the parking lot, driving right up to the sand. "This okay?" he asks, cracking the windows.

I nod, then kick my sneakers off and hug my knees to my chest.

"It's not ideal, I know but it won't be like this forever. I just feel like I broke up with her and now she's all sad and I don't know... I don't want to bail on her completely."

I look out the window, at a cluster of fancy houses that sit on top of a cliff nearby. I know he's asking for my blessing; he wants me to say that it's okay for him to talk to his ex-girlfriend while he's starting something new with me. And as much as I hate the idea of them talking, I have to admit that I admire his consideration for her feelings.

"Bee," he says, "I'm not getting back together with her. I promise you."

I smile, knowing that I'd agree to hop into quick sand with him right now if he asked me to.

"What are you thinking?"

"Nothing, just... at the game, Britt Murphy asked Caroline what is going on between you guys, and I wanted to see if your stories matched up."

He chuckles. "Oh, so... this was a test? Did I pass?" He reaches over and gently pinches my arm. It's meant to be funny, but my stomach flutters from his touch. Then I realize how nervous I am about potentially kissing again. We only had that one kiss... in the middle of the woods.

I smile. "Yes, you did."

His phone buzzes, and he picks it up, typing something quickly before putting it down again. "Sorry. Just my Dad, sending me videos from the game tonight. I can't even play in a stupid student/faculty game without getting a full rundown of what I did wrong."

"What did you do wrong?" I ask, surprised. He always looks so beautiful when he plays. Anyone with eyes can see that he stands out from the rest of the players. It's hard to believe anyone, let alone his own dad, could find anything wrong with him.

"The usual...I looked tired... my footwork was lazy... Mr. Sampson was running circles around me." He sighs. "It was a fundraiser, no one cares. It's not like it was a real game."

"Is he always like that?"

He starts cracking his knuckles, something he does when he's frustrated. "Yeah... he's always like that *now*. It sucks... we used to just play ball together for fun, but he's obsessed with my future and all the little steps I have to make to get to the end goal. Like... I know he just wants what's best for me, but I hope I can live up to his expectations."

"What's best for you?"

He thinks about it for a few moments. "I guess if you asked him it would be playing college ball and starting the firm with him."

"What if I was asking you?"

He smiles. "I honestly don't know."

"What about Ecuador?"

"I mean... yeah sure... it would be amazing, but I wasn't

really serious. It's not realistic... he's counting on me too much, and I can't let him down."

"Why do you care so much? I mean... about what he thinks?"

He looks out at the water, quiet for so long that I start to think I've upset him. "This is going to sound weird... but he's just so different than he used to be. When I was a kid, he was the *man*. He took me everywhere with him. I remember I'd go out of my way trying to come up with ways to make him laugh. It was the best feeling. He'd give me a noogie and be like, *Adam you're hilarious,* and that made *me* feel like the man. But then he got a promotion, and things have been different ever since. I think part of me wants to do what he wants so that I can get him back."

"Oh wow. I'm sorry."

He shrugs. "Don't be, I'm used to it now."

His phone buzzes. "I'm going to shut this off." He picks it up again. "Oh, it's Kyle." He sighs, sinking down into his seat.

"What?"

"I hate that I'm lying to him. You sure we can't just tell him?"

I shake my head, recalling the story Caroline told about Harlow Frank earlier. She wouldn't stop until she made sure my life was ruined. "Not yet. Plus... isn't this kind of... *fun?*"

"Kind of." He smiles, turning to face me. "I just can't believe it's finally happening."

"Since the red bikini..." I taunt.

He looks up, his eyes narrowing in on mine. "That image of you is like, imprinted into my memory... I think I pretty much associate the color red with you now. " He laughs. "Like every time I see a stop sign or a strawberry, it's like, *boom, Bee, bikini.*"

I laugh, blushing. "I like that. I want you to think of me in that way."

When he looks surprised, I look away, embarrassed. I want to be honest about everything, but I'm so new to this romance thing, I could have easily missed the memo that you're not supposed to tell your crush that you *want* him to think of you in a red bikini, that you want him to think of you *without* a red bikini, too. "Sorry, that was weird of me to say."

He reaches out for my hand. "Don't apologize. I'm just not used to someone being so open about how they feel. Like sometimes, when we're on the phone, you say these things that are so honest about yourself, and I think, *she is so cool* and I want that. I just think it's going to take me a minute to get used to it." He's quiet for a beat before he says, "I think about that summer a lot still, *the summer of the red bikini.*"

I laugh out loud, my heart picking up a beat, excited to hear his version of another memory we sort of share together. "What about it?"

"Just you and how different you were even then. That was the summer I was working as a life guard, and you were always here." He points to the water. "I'd watch you... more than I should have been, considering I was on duty." He laughs. "Every other girl on the beach was there to work on their tans, but you'd be like bouncing around, begging someone to bury you in the sand." He looks down at our hands and starts tracing a circle in my palm. "I obsessed over you all summer... telling myself that I was being protective, like an older brother, but at the reservoir, it's like it all clicked. I knew I liked you... more than I should have, and you and the girls were asking about Graves and what high school was going to be like, and I was sour because I knew some kid was going to scoop you up and it wouldn't be me."

I look up into his eyes. "But you never said anything."

He sighs. "I know. I wish I had." There's relief in his admission, but there's also regret, and I can't ask why when I don't feel prepared to hear his answer. Maybe it's simple - he regrets waiting so long. Or maybe, I'm the problem. Maybe he's been hesitant because he knew being with me would complicate his life in a lot of ways.

"Well, it doesn't matter now." I clear my throat. "Look how far we've come."

His eyes soften, and I get the feeling that he's started to think about something else entirely. "I really want to kiss you."

I swallow. "Okay." My voice is barely more than a whisper.

In a movement that seems both fast and slow, he leans over the console, parting his lips just before they reach mine. One quick kiss, then another before his lips start moving with intention. When our tongues finally touch, my body feels like it's been ignited in flames, and my thoughts are all over the place, *ohmygod this is happening, ohmygod this feels so good, ohmygod do I suck?*

He reaches over, cupping the side of my face, and a surprised gasp escapes my throat. It's not hard for me to gather that Adam knows how to kiss. Not just kiss but *kiss*. It's both thrilling and nerve-wracking, especially because I don't want to do anything that could mess up the perfectness of this moment.

When he pulls away, our lips make a smacking sound. "You have no idea how much I've been thinking about this."

I manage a smile, but all I can think about is the sliver of space between us now that he's pulled away. "Um...I think I can imagine." I lean in for another kiss.

He kisses me, holding my face between his hands, pulling back again just as I feel myself getting lost. "This might sound weird, but when I'm with you, I feel like I can just be myself."

I clear my throat, trying to ignore the humming in my ears. The irony is not lost on me; I've spent years dreaming about

Adam saying these things to me, but now I want him to *stop* saying these things so he can kiss me. "That doesn't sound weird at all."

It's like he knows what I'm thinking because at once, he leans back in, and in an instant, his hands are everywhere. My neck, my hair, gripping my shoulders. I'm buzzing, floating, not even embarrassed by the sheen of sweat that materializes out of nowhere.

The kisses deepen, the touches grow more urgent. In contrast to my own movements which are clumsy and stiff, he has a subtle finesse in how he moves around me, like he's known me -in this way- all along. He's confident but curious, firm but gentle. He takes my awkward movements and makes them his own, never rattled, never steered off track. There's a clear difference between us, by his experience and my lack of, and I'm jazzed and flustered at the same time.

I pull back a little, trying to catch my breath.

"You okay?" he asks, sitting back in his seat. "Was that too much?"

"Yeah," I nod, then shake my head. "I mean no... no, it wasn't... I liked it... it's just, I kind of feel like an amateur compared to you right now, and I don't want you to be disappointed."

"What?" he says, confused. "How could I be disappointed?"

"You know, I don't know, I just haven't done any of this before. I don't have a lot of experience with hooking up, I've only ever kissed and I don't want you to be turned off by that."

"Who have you kissed?" he teases, a smile spreading across his face. He reaches back over, taking my shaking hand. "I'm not. I couldn't. Believe me, everything we were just doing *really* turned me on."

My cheeks burn as I take the hair elastic around my wrist and put my hair up in a messy bun.

"Look, I get it... it's overwhelming at first, but there's no rush. Let's take our time." He smiles, and I can see now that despite his ease with the physical stuff, he's nervous, too. He looks out the front window. "This all feels new to me too, you know. Nothing about this relationship feels the same as my last."

I hiccup a laugh. "So... is that what this is? A relationship?"

Maroon 5's *Won't Go Home Without You* plays softly in the background, and I realize I didn't even hear the music playing until this very moment.

His gaze is hopeful. "What do you want this to be?"

I poke my finger against my face like I'm thinking. "I want to be with you. I mean... I want to be in a relationship with you."

"That's what I want, too." He leans back over, planting a quick kiss on my lips. It almost feels more intimate than what we were just doing because there's a familiarity to it now. He brushes his nose against mine, smiling from cheek to cheek, and the saying *love struck teenagers* pops into my head. I couldn't be more smitten if I tried.

"Now what are you thinking?" he asks.

"I think this might be my favorite moment, *ever*."

He leans up, kissing my forehead, trailing his lips down to meet mine again. "It's definitely mine." Somehow, he tears his eyes away from mine long enough to check the clock, and I'm delighted to see another version of him that I've never experienced before. *Panicked Adam*. "Oh man," he spits, suddenly trying to put himself and the car to rights. "I have to get you home!" He doesn't say anything again until we're pulling off the causeway, when it's clear we'll make it back in time.

"Thanks for tonight," I say, getting out of the car.

He smiles quickly, his eyes darting around, still paranoid that Kyle will pull down the street and see us. "I'll text you when I get home!" he says, practically taking off before I can get the door shut.

I laugh, skipping into the house, and by the time I hop into bed, he's already texted. *I had the best time tonight. Are you too tired to talk on the phone?*

13

"How OLD ARE YOU?" RICKY ASKS MRS. HOLMES ONCE she's finished telling us about the five-years she spent as a designer's assistant in Hollywood. I started to daydream somewhere between *accidental nip slip* and *purple wig,* but her age is actually something I've been wondering about myself. She has so many stories about her time in New York or Milan or Los Angeles, but she doesn't look old enough to have that much life experience. "You've lived a lot of life for someone who doesn't seem very old."

"I'm thirty-one," she says, chuckling, "and you're right. I took advantage of every opportunity that came my way. I was basically a nomad for the entirety of my twenties, and I encourage you all to do the same."

"So, how did you end up here in *Padstow?*" Bobby asks with an air of disgust.

She smiles coyly. "A boy. He grew up around here."

"What! You traded in your glamourous life for a boy from the burbs?" He's disappointed.

She presses her hand against her heart, feigning insult. "Isn't that always the case?"

And then, "Kidding. I didn't trade it in, it was fate."

"Preach, sister," he says, and we laugh.

"I think it's romantic," I say, cutting out white cotton for the button-down blouse I'm working on, having finally decided on an occupation as a stay-at-home mom. It received mixed reviews from the class, but Mrs. Holmes said it's *unexpected and surprisingly edgy*, and it highlights the role as a stay-at-home Mom as a *job* rather than something a woman just decides to do.

I already sketched out my look; I'll be making a pair of high-rise jeans, a button-down blouse, and a tote. It seems straightforward enough, but the jeans would be difficult to get right. I tried working with denim last year, and it was harder than I thought.

"I do, too," Scarlett says. "What's better than love?"

Ricky scoffs. "Travel, experience, cultural awareness. Need me to go on?"

More laughs.

Mrs. Holmes stands, walking over to Scarlett as she pins a piece of faux black leather onto one of the mannequins. "It's true. I'm not sure that I'd be the person that I am today without those experiences."

"What if you had met him when you were twenty?" Bobby asks.

She glances down at his sketch, nodding. "That would have been a shame because I'm not sure if it would have worked out then. I knew I wanted *experiences*; I wanted to work and travel and learn. Without that, I wouldn't be the person that I am right now."

"But couldn't you have done that *with* him?" I ask, weary of her answer. "You know, learned and traveled and all that but stayed together?"

"Maybe, but hopefully you're a different person at thirty than you are at twenty, and the growth is difficult to make with someone else. It's not that it can't happen, I'm sure it happens all the time, but there are some murky waters you need to swim through, and that's easier to do when you aren't in love."

"Love makes you blind, I would know," Ricky pouts, referencing his recent break-up from his boyfriend, Carson, a saga we're all invested in now because he's been confiding in us for weeks.

"But," Mrs. Holmes says, swinging around to face him, "you can learn a lot from heartbreak, too, though that's difficult to be excited about now, I know."

She walks over to me, sensing my concern. "It's not the case for everyone, though. I'm only telling you my experience. If you find a big love, it won't matter."

"Big love?" I ask a little quieter.

She looks at me thoughtfully, like we're the only ones in the room. "You know, the kind of love that changes everything, a soul-mate." *Is Adam my soul-mate?*

"How did you meet him, anyway, this knight and shining armor?" Ricky calls, circling back.

She winks at me before walking to her desk. "We met through friends."

Ricky whines, "That's it? Not like, you locked eyes at a rave in Soho?"

She laughs. "Nope, it's not one of my more exciting stories, I'll admit. We just hit it off at a mutual friend's party. He did change my course, though; I was leaving for a new position as a buyer for Sezane in Paris. It was a dream job."

"You didn't go?" Scarlett asks.

"I did, but everything was different after I met him because

I wanted *him* to be my future. We stayed in touch, wrote each other romantic letters, he even visited me a few times, and as much as I loved Paris, I wanted to be where he was. So, I packed up earlier than I'd planned and came home to get my guy."

"Do you regret leaving? How did you know that he'd wait for you?" I ask, needing to hear more. She's become a mentor to me, but more than that, I feel like we are similar. I want to live a life just like hers; I'm inspired by the places she's been and the people she's met. I can imagine having those same experiences, but I don't know how a boyfriend fits into all of that.

"No, I have no regrets because I've already experienced so much before meeting him. And I didn't know for certain that he'd wait, but I think you'll find that when it's the real thing, people hold on tight."

Later, I'm sitting in study, pretending to be mad at Adam for teasing me about my knitted sweater. "I'll have you know it took me three weeks to finish this."

"Oh, come on," he whispers, his body turned toward me. "You're not really mad, are you? " He pats my arm. "I love the sweater, seriously - it's so cozy."

As with all new relationships or what Sara calls *the honeymoon stage*, we're still learning about the little things that make us who we are. Like how the word *moist* makes me cringe, or when he eats apples, the inside of his mouth starts to itch. Every day is an opportunity for us to uncover something new about each other, and while he's pretty sure I'm not upset, I can tell by the slight rise of his left eyebrow that he's a tiny bit nervous.

Without looking at him, I take out the note I wrote during

English, inviting him to a picnic dinner, and place it on his desk.

He looks at me curiously, then rips it open. "What's a picnic dinner?"

"Do you accept my invitation?"

A smile spreads across his face. "I accept."

"Meet me outside the gym after your practice for operation '*concession*' *and* don't mention this to anyone. The note will self-destruct in exactly fifteen seconds."

He laughs again, looking around the class to see if anyone's watching, and when it's clear, he reaches over, lightly rubbing his thumb across my bottom lip.

Ohmygod.

"*Easy,* I'm still mad at you," I say unconvincingly.

"Not for long."

Before I have time to consider his suggestive stare, the bell rings for the day, and we walk out, going our separate ways once we're through the threshold. It has been surprisingly simple to carry on a secret relationship; all you have to do is avoid each other in communal areas, limit contact with all your friends, and hang out in obscure places like cars or the finance section of the town library. It's not so much the secrecy that I like, but the privacy that this kind of relationship allows us, where we can easily overlook things like ex-girlfriends and older brothers.

I go straight home to put together the picnic: turkey BLT sandwiches with pesto mayo, UTZ Ripple potato chips, two Pepsis, and the toffee oatmeal cookies that I baked last night. Mom always makes it for ski lunches, and I know it's one of his favorites.

As I'm walking back to school, my phone buzzes; a group text from the *Cove Girls.*

Rochelle: On our way.
Stacey: I'm ready.
Sara: Ready.
Me: Huh?
Sara: the outdoor mall... remember we made plans at lunch?
Me: Oh shoot, sry. Totally forgot... I'm slammed w/ hw. Have fun!!

I bite back the minor surge of disappointment I feel at missing something the Cove Girls are doing. I remind myself that I can always hang out with them, that what I really want right now is Adam. Plain and simple.

Inside the school, it's quiet except for the sounds of sneakers screeching against the gym floor. I don't need to look in to know that Coach Brian is making them do burpees, obvious from the grunting and curses the boys are uttering. It's Kyle's least favorite form of exercise since he puked once during summer doubles.

I walk past the gym doors, down another hallway where I won't be seen, and sit on the floor so I can actually finish my homework. *See, not a total lie.*

At five, the whistle blows. *Soar, score, Eagles, Eagles, Eagles, yeah!* They break, then the door bangs open as they make their way down to the locker rooms.

I pack up, waiting.

Ok 007, where are you? he texts.

I laugh. *In front of the gym.*

My heart beats with anticipation as I hear him mount the stairs, at least two at a time, until he's right there, walking toward me with a smile on his face.

"Hey," he says, leaning down and kissing me quickly. "That

was the longest practice ever. I can't focus when you're around."

I blush, biting the inside of my cheek. "I probably shouldn't go to any of your games, then."

"You take that back!" He pulls me against him. He's taking a risk, being this handsy out in the open, but I like it too much to remind him of that. I nuzzle my head into his chest, smelling his deodorant, probably something that's called *clean breeze* or *simple linen*. "What's for dinner?" he asks.

I take his hand, pulling him to the other side of the concession stand to a door that says DO NOT ENTER.

"Whatever you do, don't make eye contact, okay? It makes them feel uncomfortable." I inhale an exaggerated breath and knock three times.

He pulls me back reflexively.

I laugh. "I'm just kidding," I say, pushing open the door. "It's just a storage closet." The Cove Girls and I had obsessed over what could be inside, things like, Mr. Cummings Beanie Baby collection or Mr. Underwood's stash of fungi or maybe even the entrance to the secret pool, but when we finally got up the nerve to go in, it was just an ordinary storage closet, empty except for a few pep-rally signs and plastic chairs.

"Welcome to my lair," I say. "And by 'my lair', I mean the first time I've ever really been in here."

He picks up a sign that says SHOUT, examining it like it's an ancient artifact. "How'd you get in here?"

I sit, unpacking the bag. "I have my ways."

He smiles, then, seeing all the food, he sighs. If I've learned anything in these last few weeks, it's that he really likes food. "You really do know the way to my heart. I'm starving."

I hand him a sandwich, watching as he takes a bite, waiting for the praise I know is coming.

"I'm going to tell you something, but you can't ever repeat

it," he says, looking serious. "This sandwich might be better than your mom's."

I roll my eyes, laughing. "I thought you were going to drop some major gossip on me."

He smiles, pleased with himself. "It's so cool that you do things like this," he says, waving a hand over the food.

"Like what?" I ask. "Break into storage closets and feed you dinner?"

"No, just like... you baking and cooking and sewing."

I make a face. "How very 1950's of you to say. I should have worn my pearls."

"No, that's not what I mean." He grins. "I just think you're cool, okay?"

"Thanks, I think."

He rinses down the rest of his sandwich with a sip of *Pepsi*, then he reaches over, taking my hand. "I've been wanting to ask you something for the past few days."

I purposely drop my cookie on the plate, making a show of being surprised. "Ohmygod. Are you going to propose?"

He laughs out loud. "Even more important than that, will you go to the homecoming dance with me?"

I sit up a little straighter, actually surprised. "Really?" I've seen the signs hung up all over school, but the Homecoming dance is for upperclassman, and it never occurred to me that he'd want to go. *With me.*

He smiles, seeming nervous, like despite how amazing these last few weeks have been, he's still not sure what I'll say. Which is comforting, I realize, that he's also self-conscious about us still. "Yeah, I don't want this to be a secret anymore, do you?"

I sigh. "No," I say, realizing that all of the lying really has taken its toll on me. It's like I've been living a double life, giving only a portion of myself to my old one while pouring myself into the new one with Adam. I want to combine the two, but once we're out there, we're out there, leaving ourselves open. Celebrity relationships are always tested once the paparazzi knows about them. Not that we're celebrities or anything.

"If you're okay with it, I'll come over this weekend and talk to Kyle."

I take a sip of *Pepsi*, feeling like my appetite is long gone. We've discussed the specifics before, deciding that Adam would take the lead on this one. He'd talk to Kyle because *bro-code,* and he'd talk to Caroline because *murder,* but it still feels really overwhelming for me to sit by and wait. "Caroline is going to flip." My cheeks feel itchy, a tell-tale sign that I'm about to break out in hives. "And what do you think Kyle is going to say?"

He shakes his head. "Leave her to me, and as for Kyle," he sighs, "I think he'll be okay. He's going to think it's lame that we kept it from him, but I think he'll be all right with it. I mean, he can't be totally in the dark. He knows something's up."

"I'm scared. It feels safer to hide."

He reaches over, tucking a piece of loose hair behind my ear. "I know, but it's not right to keep this from him anymore. And I'm happy we're together. I want to shout from the rooftops, *BEE IS MY GIRLFRIEND*. Plus, I'm getting sick of Connor flirting with you during lunch."

Charmer.

"Okay, then," I say, taking a deep breath. How could I say no to him? "Let's go public."

He shakes my hand like we've just struck a deal. "We're going public!"

14

EVERY SECOND SUNDAY OF THE MONTH, THE COVE GIRLS meet for breakfast at *Farine*, a French bakery downtown. It's been our tradition since the spring of eighth grade when we started watching *Sex and the City*. The characters always met for a breakfast or lunch, chatting about everything: love, dating mishaps, work, money, sex and while our conversations tend to be much more PG with topics like science papers and *American Eagle* sales, we like to pretend we live complicated lives while drinking our iced chai lattes.

"Don't forget my almond croissants." Mom pulls up outside of the cafe. I asked her to drop me off twenty minutes before they opened so I could get our favorite table by the window. "If they're out of almond, I'll take chocolate, but tell Juliette they're for me, and she might bring out her secret stash."

"Ok, two plain croissants, got it." I hop out of the car, making a line outside the door.

She puts down the car window, calling over. "Not funny, Bee! There won't be a place for you to come home to without those croissants!"

I'm taking off my coat when Stacey and Rochelle walk in. "You're a *boss*! I'll come early next month," Rochelle says as Emily, our server, walks up. "Hey *Cove Gals,* you want the usual?"

I look up as Stacey says, "You know it!" winking at Emily as she walks away. It takes me a moment to realize she's wearing glasses. *Glasses!*

"Um... Stacey? When did you get glasses?!"

"Oh... I forgot you weren't with us! I got them three days ago."

Rochelle rolls her eyes. "We were at Optical Illusion for two and a half hours helping her pick."

"You were all there?" I ask, disappointed. Have I been that absorbed with Adam that I don't know what my friends are up to anymore? Have they even noticed I haven't been around as much? Do they even care?

"We definitely invited you. I think you said you were working on your sewing project."

A lie, clearly another one of my lies.

I look down at the menu, wondering what else I missed over the last few weeks. "How's Charlie?" I know through *Instagram* posts that he's been coming around more - Stacey even captioned one of her photos *The Cove Girls plus Charlie,* though *The Cove Girls minus Bee, plus Charlie* would have been a more accurate description. I'm happy for Rochelle, albeit a little envious that her boyfriend has joined our group so seamlessly while I've had to hide mine. I hope one day soon, it would be *The Cove Girls plus Charlie and Adam.*

She beams. "He's good... he's been asking about you!"

"I think I'm going to get something different this time. Should I?" Stacey asks, looking at us for approval. We always get the same: sausage, egg and cheese on a biscuit and granola bars to share.

"Nope!" we both say, laughing.

Emily sets down our iced chai lattes. "Where's the fourth member of the band?"

"She'll be here soon. She slept at her Dad's last night," Rochelle says.

After we place our orders, Sara comes bombing into the restaurant, rushing over to us. "You guys have to read this conversation I had with Jeremy last night," she says, taking out her phone.

"Wait, so you guys talk on the phone now?" I shriek.

"Ummm, yeah... that's old news. When you go MIA, you tend to miss things, Bee."

Rude. But at the very least, it answers my earlier question of whether they've even noticed I've been around less.

"Okay... this convo is definitely steamy," Stacey interrupts, scrolling through the text feed while I look on over her shoulder. "But like, what about Harper and Homecoming?"

I blink. "Wait, what? *Please* fill me in, I have no idea what you guys are talking about!"

Sara takes a sip of her latte, looking at me. "Basically, Jeremy and Harper Brown made some like, pact in the ninth grade about going to Homecoming together their senior year, so even though he really, *really* wants to take me, he can't."

"That sounds weird," I say.

Rochelle agrees. "That's what I said! I don't trust him."

"It's fine, I'm not worried about *her*. You've seen her Tik-Toks - they're embarrassing! He doesn't *like her like her,* plus, I know deep down he wants to take me."

"But he could take you... if he liked you as much as he says he does, he'd just tell Harper the truth. Pact or not."

"No offense Bee, but you don't have enough background on the situation."

"What's that supposed to mean?"

"We haven't even seen you for the last month!" She erupts. "You've been spending all your free-time with Scarlett?"

I jerk my head back, stunned. She's right, of course. I haven't been around, but throwing Scarlett into it is unnecessary. I'm allowed to have new friends. "Scarlett doesn't have anything to do with, okay? I have something I need to tell you."

Emily comes back over, carrying the tray with our breakfast. No one says a word until she's gone. Stacey speaks up first. "What's going on, Bee?"

"I've been seeing someone."

Rochelle's mouth falls open. "Ohmygod, seriously? Who is it? Someone from your sewing class?"

I blush. "No... it's... it's—"

"Who, Bee!" Sara practically shouts.

"Adam."

"Adam, who?" Stacey looks up at the ceiling, clearly shuffling through her memory of all of the Adam's she knows.

My stomach tightens. *Adam, Adam... Adam Stanson.*

They say nothing, staring at me in disbelief. I have the sudden urge to bust out laughing, but it's just the nerves. I don't actually think any of this is funny. There is a very real chance they are going to be mad at me for keeping this a secret.

"I wanted to keep it a secret - mostly because I'm pretty sure Caroline knows and is planning my death. She's been threatening me, but I haven't even told Adam that part. I just-"

"Wait, *what*? You're serious?" Stacey laughs uneasily, looking at Rochelle and Sara. "This is real?"

"I'm serious. He asked me to go with him to Homecoming, so you know, it can't exactly be a secret anymore." I'm slightly freaked out by how calmly I'm delivering the news. I can't even imagine what they're thinking right now.

Rochelle starts waving her hands around her face. "Ohmygodohmygodohmygod. Wait, it feels like I'm literally about to faint. Is this even real life right now?"

"I know, I can hardly believe it myself." I laugh, feeling an enormous amount of relief. They aren't mad - shocked, yes, but not mad.

Stacey shakes her head. "Ok, Bee, spill, seriously, details, now."

I tell them everything except for what happened the night of Musters because I don't want our beginning to be associated with cheating. It was cheating, technically, but like Adam said over and over, he was breaking up with her, anyway.

"So, he's telling Kyle today?" Rochelle asks.

"Yup, I'm freaking out."

Sara leans in, her eyebrows touching. "What if he's totally against it?"

I shrug. "I don't know... I think it will be okay."

"Wow, I can't believe it." Rochelle takes a massive bite of her biscuit. "I can't believe you're going to homecoming with Adam Stanson! I can't believe Adam's like, *your* boyfriend. Is he your boyfriend?"

"Yes." I blush, my resolve faltering a bit now that the news is actually out. It's really happening. Everyone would know about us. *Caroline* would know about us. "It's been a whirlwind of a few months."

"It's just so crazy, like, you've loved him since forever, and now you have him!"

"Ah!" Sara looks at her phone, swiftly changing the subject back to herself. "Jeremy just texted again. Look at this."

As we walk out, I fall behind to talk to Sara. While Stacey and Rochelle fired off a million questions about Adam, Sara didn't ask a single thing. She pretended to be uninterested while swiping through Instagram the whole time, even though I'd seen her pause when I told them about how we parked at the beach after the basketball game. "I'm sorry I kept it from you. I just didn't want anyone to know."

"Did you tell Scarlett?"

I take a deep breath, not wanting to lie about anything anymore. "Yes."

She shakes her head. "You've known her for five minutes, Bee, how could you trust her over us with something this major?"

"I don't know. I guess it was because she felt outside of everything - she doesn't know Adam *or* Caroline. I was paranoid that Caroline would find out."

"I would have kept that secret, you know. I would have taken it to my grave."

I nod, feeling terrible. My mind hasn't been in the right place - of course I could trust my friends. "I know. Look, there's one part of the story I left out about the night of Musters. But if I tell you, you actually have to keep it a secret, okay? You can't even tell Rochelle or Stacey for like, ten years."

"I pinky promise."

After *Farine*, I go to Stacey's to re-establish myself within the group and don't get home until after four o'clock. I hear the basketballs in the driveway but I rush by, too scared to face them, and join Dad in the living room instead. We quietly watch football and at some point, I fall asleep.

When I wake up, I'm disoriented, Dad still watching the game beside me.

"How long was I sleeping?" I ask, groggy.

He reaches over, squeezing my foot. "I don't know, about an hour, probably."

When I don't hear the basketballs, I shoot up, rushing over to the window to peek through the blinds. With a sense of dread, I realize they're gone. *What happened? Did they talk? Did they fight?*

"What are you looking for?" Kyle shouts from behind me.

I jump back, embarrassed, and when I turn around, they're both sitting in the kitchen, watching me with amused expressions on their faces. "I thought I heard something," I say defensively though we all know I'm lying.

I join them, my thoughts all over the place, but I'm pretty sure Adam is avoiding eye contact because he's chickened out. I don't blame him; the thought of having that conversation is enough to make me break out in hives, but I thought we agreed that it had to be today. The *Cove Girls* know now, and I didn't tell them to keep it a secret. Half of Padstow might already know about it.

Mom walks in. "Dinner in thirty. I'm making Bolognese. Bee, can you chop some veggies for the salad?"

"Yeah, sure," I say, thankful for something to do.

Minutes tick by, and just when I think I might actually faint from too much pressure on my nervous system, Mom walks out of the kitchen and Kyle gets up to go to the bathroom.

"What's going on?" I ask, frantic.

"He knows," Adam whispers. "I told him everything."

Relief, but also dread, washes over me. "Everything?"

He nods. "*Everything.*"

"And? Is he mad?" I ask, needing to hear word-for-word how the conversation went.

"Not *mad*, no."

Through gritted teeth, I press for more, "*No?* Happy? Sad? Disappointed? Give me something, *Man*, you're freaking me out!"

"He wasn't surprised... I guess... he sort of suspected something was going on."

"So, what now?" I ask, pacing back and forth with a knife still in my hand.

He smiles. "*Now*, we're in the clear, baby. But you should probably put down that knife."

I pause, placing the knife back down on the island as I take a steadying breath. Despite my panic boiling over, I can't help but smile. He's never called me *baby* before.

Kyle walks back in, and I start chopping again. I'm so focused, you'd think I'm performing brain surgery but deep down, the silence is killing me. *I can't look at my own brother! Nothing will ever be the same! I've ruined everything! Finally, the truth and look what it's done.*

Kyle's the one who finally breaks the silence. "This is going to be really weird, isn't it?"

I keep my head down, too ashamed to see the disappointment etched on his face. *The betrayal, the indecency.* I'm the worst sister ever.

"Oh... yeah... super weird," Adam agrees.

I take another deep breath, preparing for the duel that is sure to take place at any moment, but when I look up, they're smiling at each other.

"You can breathe now, Bee," Kyle assures me, just as Mom walks back in and asks them to set the table.

While we're eating, the conversation flows easily, but I can't shake my own feelings of guilt. Sure, Kyle seems okay with it, but I still feel like I've done something wrong. It's just like that time I ate all of the thumb-print cookies that Mom made after Mrs. Carson's hip surgery. She didn't punish me, didn't even yell, but I could tell she was disappointed, and that made it worse. Is Kyle disappointed?

"So, Adam, where did you apply for schools? We don't get

to talk about college too much around here," Dad says, winking at Kyle.

Kyle rolls his eyes. "It's just all anyone ever wants to talk about."

Adam smiles, glancing at me quickly. "I don't mind... I just sent in my applications for Villanova, Duke, and the University of Kansas."

I flinch, feeling like I have something new to be anxious about. He never brought up colleges, and I never asked, mostly because I wanted to avoid the fact that he'd be leaving so soon.

"Oh? You're not applying anywhere around here?" Mom asks.

"No." He looks at me again. "You know my Dad, he has a heavy-hand in deciding where I should apply, and he's already been in touch with some of the coaches from those schools."

"He just wants what's best for you, but we'll sure miss you around here," Dad says.

I'm staring at the garlic bread when I hear Mom calling my name. "Brooke?"

I look up, confused, their eyes all on me. "Yeah?"

"Did you hear me, Babe?" she asks, amused.

"Oh...no... sorry...what?" I mumble, taking a sip of water, hoping to swallow down the sour taste in my mouth. *He'll be gone before we even get started. He'll never want a high school girlfriend while he's away at college.*

"I was wondering if you finished that blouse for the fashion show?"

"I...um...I um...I did," I say, stumbling over my words.

"Great," she says, looking back at the boys. "Have you guys thought about the homecoming dance yet?"

I drop my fork, scrambling to pick it back up. "Sorry, it slipped," I say.

"So, do you have dates yet?" she asks again, turning back to the boys as they exchange an uncomfortable look.

"I'm taking Mandy Nowak," Kyle says.

Mom beams. "I love Mandy! That will be fun!"

"I'm going to homecoming, too!" I shout.

Everyone looks up at me in disbelief; Mom's concerned, Dad's confused, Kyle's trying hard not to laugh, and Adam is horrified. I'm so bad at this kind of thing, but Adam's done so much already with taking responsibility for the talks with both Kyle and Caroline, the least I can do is save him from my parents.

"I'm... I'm... going to the homecoming dance, too," I say, struggling, "because I have a boyfriend now."

Dad puts down his fork, eyes wide. "Boyfriend? When did you get a boyfriend?"

I lock eyes with Mom and bless her, it clicks. She understands what I'm trying to say and somehow, it just makes this easier.

"Come, on, Bee, this is literally the worst announcement ever," Kyle says, trying to lighten the mood.

I take a deep breath. "Adam is my boyfriend... I mean...I'm his girlfriend... we're basically together now... no we're definitely together now...so I'm going to go to Homecoming with him."

Mom smiles, gently squeezing my knee underneath the table.

Dad is still confused. "*Adam* who?"

Mom clears her throat, nodding her head in Adam's direction.

Dad sits up a little straighter, looking right at Adam. "Wow, how did I miss this?"

Kyle shakes his head. "Man, Bee, that was painful."

There's a moment of silence where we're all assessing each other. But then Dad cracks a smile, and we all start laughing.

Later, I'm getting ready for bed when Kyle knocks on my door.

"Hey." He steps in, his eyes focusing on the Rolling Stones t-shirt that I'm wearing. It registers to both of us at once that he asked me if I knew where it was two weeks ago and I told him I had no idea.

"Hey. So... you're really not mad? I mean... you're going to be okay with this?" I ask.

He sits on the bed, letting out a breath. "No... it's going to be weird, but I want you to be happy." His expression is blank as he looks down at the floor, and I wonder, not for the first time, if it does bother him. It has to be weird; the thought of Adam and me together, he *has* to be wondering if this is going to change everything.

"Well, thanks. I am happy. I'm really, really happy." I realize then that no matter how he feels, he *is* happy for me. He could have ended our new relationship with a word and that's not lost on either of us, but he's choosing to be cool.

"Good," he says, reaching over and giving me a noogie. "I'm going to bed. I love you, Kid."

"I love you, too."

Dear Journal,

News travels fast when you're Adam Stanson's new girl-friend. Little Lucy even put up a post about it - they're calling us BRADAM!! It's like I just hit gold status in the high school hierarchy and I gotta say, it feels GREAT. It makes me question why I insisted on the secret in the first place - they love me, they really love me! The only weird thing is Caroline. I may or may not have googled 'what to do in a girl fight' the night he told her, but it was all for nothing because surprisingly, she's gone quiet. Eerily quiet. Maybe she didn't anticipate the public love for Bradam. Or maybe she realized that Adam and I just belong together. I wouldn't want to stand in the way of true love, either. Sometimes when we're walking the halls together, I imagine Blinding Lights by the Weeknd playing in the background while everyone turns to watch us - Adam and Bee, Bradam, the IT couple. "They're just so perfect together" they'll whisper, tossing flowers at us. "A photo for the year book, please!" someone will shout. Adam will bend down, picking up a single red rose, placing it gently under my nose while quoting Shakespeare or something. I can see it now.

15

"Frappuccino's first?" Mom asks, pulling into a parking spot at the mall. We're here to find a homecoming dress but Mocha Frappuccino's with extra whipped cream is always first priority.

With our drinks in hand, we walk slowly, taking in the holiday decorations, always commenting on how they're out too early but how much we like it anyway. When I was younger, we'd come just to see the displays: the oversized ornaments, the colorful wreaths, the North Pole made of Legos. It all seemed so big and exciting, I can still remember the thrill.

"Any idea what color you want?" she asks as I follow her into the dress section of Nordstrom, my stomach flipping with excitement. It feels so surreal; I've browsed these racks plenty of times before, day-dreaming about going to a dance with Adam. It seemed far-fetched then, just a little girl's hopeless pipedream, and yet here we are.

I sigh. "No, I can't decide!" I have it my head that the dress, *my whole look*, has to be perfect. As Adam's new girlfriend, all eyes are on me, and I feel like I need to live up to the expectations of what it means to be that girl. It's a lot of pressure; though he never asked me to be any kind of way, I don't want to let him down or give anyone a reason to question why he's with me. I keep imagining homecoming as my own Debutante Ball - my introduction as the new and improved Bee.

"How have the girls been? I haven't heard much about them lately," Mom asks, flipping through the racks.

"They're good." I hold up a purple sequin mid-length dress. "I haven't been hanging out with them much because of Adam, but Rochelle has Charlie now, and Stacey's busy with work."

"And Sara? How does she feel about Adam? Or your new friendship with Scarlett?"

"Fine, why?" I ask, wondering if she somehow knows about the fight Sara and I got into yesterday after I bailed on another homework session.

"Oh, just wondering... it can be hard when one of your friends suddenly has new people in their life."

"I'm sure she's fine, she knows how long I've liked Adam," I say, annoyed. The last thing I want to worry about is my friendship with Sara. I finally have exciting things happening in my life: a boyfriend, a new friend, a fashion show to get ready for, and I don't want to think about how the better things get for me, the less happy she seems. She used to be my biggest advocate, my ride-or-die, but lately, it feels like we are at odds, and I'm constantly tip-toeing around her bad energy.

"Okay," she says, holding up a dark green dress. "How about this one?"

"Oh, that is *so* pretty!" I squeal, rushing over, knowing that it's the one I've been looking for. "But is it too formal? I think a lot of girls wear short dresses to Homecoming."

"It's a very casual, long dress," she assures me. "Let's try it on."

When we sit down for dinner later at *Legal Seafoods*, I

finally let out a sigh of relief. "I'm really excited now." I look down at the green fabric that's peeking out from the white tissue paper. I'm going to try it on again the second we get home, with the black tassel earrings and suede strappy heels we got to go with it.

"You weren't excited before?" she asks, surprised.

"I'm just nervous. I feel like I'm headed into the Lion's den. I know Caroline and her minions will have their eyes on me. I had a dream last night that they locked me in the bathroom and told Adam I'd left with Connor."

She laughs. "Better not use the bathroom, then," but quickly adds, "Kidding!"

I sigh. "I just wish my friends were going, too."

"Rochelle will be there," she says encouragingly.

"Yeah, but we're going with completely different groups."

She nods. "Fair enough, but I bet you'll be pleasantly surprised by how amazing the night turns out to be."

The server drops off rolls, and we order our chowders and salads.

"What are your thoughts on sex?" I ask suddenly, when he walks away.

She drops her butter knife, looking completely thrown off. "At least wait until my salad comes before you spring *sex* on me." Recovering, she asks, "My thoughts?"

I nod. "We've never really talked about it, and I guess I'm wondering what you think about it, in general."

I've been waiting for "the talk" for a while now; my friends already had theirs, and even though I still cringe at the thought of it, I'm curious about where Mom stands. The other conversations seemed so forced and uncomfortable, and I was surprised to learn that they weren't even really talking but listening; hearing how their *parents* felt on the subject. And it's always the same: either *be careful* or *don't do it*. There doesn't seem to be a middle ground or any interest in discussion. I find it strange; on the one hand, you don't want to talk to your parents about that kind of thing, but how are you supposed to get the truth about it all, if not from your parents? Google searches are too broad or vague because as it turns out, the subject is seriously subjective. There doesn't seem to be a clear-cut answer to any of it.

Sex is a taboo topic, and yet, it's still one of the most important decisions we ever make, or so we're often told. There is us and them, the experienced and unexperienced, and I guess the unexperienced are just expected to figure it out for themselves.

She takes a bite, chewing slowly, trying to buy herself some time. I can almost see the wheels turning in her mind, feeling like she has to get this right. "Well," she says finally, "I guess, I'd say, sex, in general, can be complicated."

I meet her eyes, waiting for her to go on. "Meaning what?"

She takes a sip of water, still gathering her thoughts. "Okay, so, in many ways, it's really great, for obvious reasons: it feels good, and the intimacy can bring you closer to your partner. However, it's a very vulnerable thing to do with someone, and I think it's important to make sure that the person you decide to do it with is someone you deeply trust. It's difficult at your age to understand your feelings about these things because they are *big feelings,* and I think you can easily get it wrong."

"What happens if you get it wrong?"

"Well, that's a loaded question but base line, it might make you feel bad about yourself."

"So, are you saying that you shouldn't do it while you're young, like in high school?"

"No, I'm not saying that. I don't think there's a perfect age, everyone is different. I'm just saying that the decision shouldn't be made lightly because at your age, your feelings fluctuate, sometimes day-to-day."

"How old were you?" I ask.

"Sixteen," she says, more comfortable now.

"Oh, so, my age."

She nods. "Yes, but my situation was entirely different. I was taught abstinence. Sex before marriage was strictly forbidden in the environment I grew up in. So, then, when I did it anyway, I felt an incredible amount of shame from it, for years, really."

"Why?" I ask, intrigued. Mom rarely talks about the specifics of her childhood; I know she disagrees with the strict, religious aspects of my grandparents' home, but shame isn't something she's ever mentioned before.

"Yeah, I thought I'd done something very wrong: broken all the rules, turned myself into a certain type of girl, and yet, I still wanted to do it. No one told me that exploring your sexuality is actually a very normal thing to do, healthy, even. So, let me be clear - I'm *for* you exploring yourself in that way. I'd encourage you however, to be safe and think through the decisions you make. It's dicey when you're this young."

"So, do you still carry that shame with you now?"

She shakes her head. "No, but I spent many years stuck on it, not exactly sure why I felt the way I did."

"How did you work through it, then?"

"I started seeing Beth." Beth, her therapist, is someone she really admires and respects. "I felt kind of funny being a grown woman talking about things that had happened when I was a teenager, but she really helped me."

Our food comes, making the conversation even more laid-back. "Who was your first, then? Did you love him?"

"Dennis Blanchet. He was a nice boy," she says, smiling, clearly thinking of him now.

"What happened?"

"We dated in high school. Obviously, Grandma didn't

approve - he wasn't from the "right" kind of family, but I adored him. I thought we'd get married and start a family, but eventually, we broke up. He just sort of stopped loving me."

"What?! What do you mean he just *stopped*? Didn't you care?"

"Of course I cared! I was devastated. I felt so sure that my life would never be the same again, and I guess it never was because I changed after that, grew up a little more. But when you look back, you gain perspective. I loved him, but I never let myself be known to him, not really. I was young, I hardly knew myself, and it's like I was trying on different characteristics of a person I thought *he* might like. So, *yes*, I was sad by the loss of him, but he never really knew the real me, anyway." She looks at me thoughtfully. "I've had a few loves after him and for me, it was all a learning experience because when I met your father, I knew - he was a little bit of all of them, the perfect man for *me*."

"Would you have thought so if you hadn't dated the other boys?" I ask.

She thinks it over. "Yes, of course, but with every relationship I had, I came out of it a little more grown up and knowing more about myself."

"What if you're only sixteen and you feel like you've already met the person you want to be with?" I ask, feeling mopey. It's not lost on me that the two women I admire most, my mom and Mrs. Holmes, are saying variations of the same thing.

"My story isn't *your* story, Bee. I'll never tell you how to live your life; you're smart and strong and you can handle anything. You'll make mistakes, but you'll learn from them, too, and everything that's supposed to happen, will."

16

AFTER FIVE FRAZZLED HOURS, A TUBE OF CONCEALER, AND an ugly cry, I'm ready for the dance. The day hasn't been as picturesque as I hoped, but that's to be expected when you wake up on the morning of an important dance with a zit the size of Delaware on your chin. After the zit, it was the hives, and then just to make sure I felt as insecure as humanly possible, I walked into the curling iron and burned my arm. The reality, no matter how hard I try to deny it, is that I'm nervous, *consumed* with the what ifs. *What if I'm gassy? What if he hates my dress? What if he falls back in love with Caroline? What if I do get locked in the bathroom?*

Mom invited the whole neighborhood over for photos, and I expected all the moms, who have known me since I was in diapers, to gasp in delight, *Bee, you've grown into such a beautiful, mature woman, no wonder Adam dumped Caroline for you!*

But as I make my long-anticipated descent down the stairs, no one's even paying attention. That is, until Nia Khatri moves away from her spot by the window and I see Adam. Watching me. And that's when I realize I don't need the gasps from everyone else. All I need is him, looking at me, exactly like this. "You look beautiful," he whispers when he reaches me.

I look down, blushing. Mom and Sara transformed me into an Old Hollywood actress, and the way he's looking at me now makes the stress of the day worth it.

"Thanks! You look nice, too."

"Mom helped." He seems shy. We hadn't talked much today.

I smile, thinking that he could be wearing a trash bag and still be the most handsome boy in the room. "Where is she?" I ask, looking around.

As if the dance hasn't been enough to stress over, I'm anxious about seeing his family for the first time since we've become official. June is apparently thrilled about us, but I'm not worried about her; I'm nervous about his dad, Luke. I know he likes Caroline, and I have to find a way to make him think I'm the better person for Adam.

June spots me from the kitchen and storms in, pulling me in for a tight hug. "Brooke!

"You look gorgeous! This dress is incredible."

"Thanks. Mom found it, of course."

She smiles. "Of course."

Jenny and Jo run up, hugging my legs. "Oh, my goodness, you look like a princess."

"Wow, thanks," I say, waiting for Luke to follow them into the room. I've been going over what I might say to him, even going as far as Googling finance blogs so I'd be more versed in the things he's interested in. *The Dow is up today, huh?* or *Let's talk rate of returns.*

He finally walks in with Dad, talking about the weather. They are always talking about the weather. They've known each other since they were kids, but no one would ever mistake them for friends because frankly, two men could not be more different.

Where Dad is warm, Luke is a little cold. Where Dad is welcoming, Luke is closed off. Our families have stayed close over the years because of Mom's friendship with June and Kyle's friendship with Adam. The dads, it seems, just put up with each other.

"Our volunteer day is coming up, you kids excited?" Mom asks as she starts waving everyone into the living room for photos.

"Yeah," we mumble. Every December, we volunteer at our local soup kitchen together. I haven't said anything to Adam, but I'm especially excited for it this year. I imagine our families together, smiling for a picture that I'll post to Instagram with a caption like, *the family that volunteers together, stays together.*

"Just another thing you boys can add to your college resume. Admission offices eat that stuff up," Luke says, still looking down at his phone.

I'm trying to figure out a way to work *cash flow* into the conversation when Mom directs everyone to line up against the wall.

"Adam," Luke whispers, "where's Caroline?"

Adam and June stiffen beside me as my parents and Kyle pretend like they didn't hear. Mortified, I look down, picking at my freshly painted fingernails. Sara used a pale pink called *Let Me Bayou A Drink,* but I suddenly feel like biting them off. *Does he really not know about us?*

June breaks the silence. "Luke...Dear," she clears her throat, reminding me of my stern sixth-grade teacher Mrs. Collins. "Adam's not with Caroline anymore, remember? Brooke is his girlfriend now, and they're going to the dance together."

It's like I leave my body, floating above myself as I watch the rest of it unfold. Luke's eyebrows push together, looking from Adam to me and back again. He seems blind-sided, confused, and not at all happy with the news.

I'm embarrassed, *yes*, but I'm crushed, too. Adam worships his father. What does that say about his feelings for me if he didn't bother to tell him? What will it mean if he doesn't approve?

Finally, Luke's eyes settle on me. "Oh, that's right, I'm sorry about that. You look lovely, Brooke."

"Thanks," I say as Adam takes my hand, leading me to the wall for pictures. There's a tension in the room now, at least between our families, but we smile anyway, trying to pretend like that wasn't the most awkward thing ever.

When we're finally alone on our way to the dance, Adam apologizes. "I'm really sorry about that. I did tell him, I swear, but he's been stressed at work, and it must have slipped his mind."

"It's okay," I say, feeling like this couldn't have happened at a worse time, just before *his* dance. If I told him the truth, that I don't think he told his Dad about us at all, what would happen then? Would the rest of the night be tense? Would we fight? Without his attention, I'd be on my own without any of my friends to fall back on, like being at a party and only knowing the person who brought you. I can't risk him being mad at me tonight, even if that means pretending I'm fine.

"You sure?" he asks, pulling into the school parking lot.

I take a deep breath, letting it go. "Yeah, I'm sure."

He smiles, reaching over for my hand. "You excited?"

"Yeah, a little nervous, too."

"I'll be with you the whole time."

We park next to Kyle, watching as his date, Mandy, starts sneaking sips from a flask that's covered in pink rhinestones. "She's already drunk. Kyle's going to be babysitting her all night."

We wait for them outside, watching as she awkwardly climbs out of the passenger side door and shoves a piece of gum in her mouth. "Don't you look nice," she says to Adam, ignoring me. It stings.

I take Adam's hand, squeezing tight.

The transformation in the gym makes me gasp. It always smells faintly of sour feet but now it's more like a dreamland. There's a sheer sparkling tent covering the mostly dark room, the only light coming from strung up holiday lights surrounding the tent. People are already crowded around the DJ's booth, dancing to a remix of Jason Derulo's *Take You Dancing*.

I find myself smiling as we put our stuff down on a table. Despite not getting off to a great start, we're here, and this feels big.

"Come on." He pulls me toward the dance floor. "I've been dying to see those goofy moves of yours all day."

Eight songs later, the DJ takes a break. It's only then, when I'm sweaty from dancing and my jaw hurts from laughing, that I can admit to myself I'm having so much fun. We find Rochelle on the dance floor, the two of us greeting each other like long-lost sisters, and that's when I feel myself finally relax.

Adam sits at a table, pulling me down onto his lap while the boys and their dates cram in around us. It's a subtle move, something I know couples do together, but it still makes my heart pick up a few beats. I'm a girlfriend, claimed as someone's person, and it's not just anyone, it's Adam. My worries about the night feel far away now, as if I've been officially accepted as part of their group.

"No joke," Jonathan says, looking down at his crotch. "I just ripped my pants doing that split out there." The table erupts in laughter. "What am I supposed to do now?" He chuckles. "How much longer are we here?"

"Not too long, and then we can go to Jessie Morgan's rager," Andrew says eagerly.

My stomach tightens -and not for the first time- at the mention of the party. I agreed to go, even though I can't think of anything I'd like to do less. Jessie is one of Caroline's friends, and it would be like walking into enemy territory.

Out of nowhere, Mandy shoots up, wobbling back and forth. "I think I'm going to be sick," she announces, covering her mouth.

We all watch her for a moment, unsure of how serious she is, but when she starts dry heaving, I jump up and pull her to the bathroom. Once she's in front of the toilet, she starts throwing up.

"How much did you drink?" I ask, holding back her hair. The situation doesn't allow for much small talk but, I've never done this before. I assume I have to say *something*.

"I've been pre-gaming since four," she whines, heaving again. The tangy, vile smell rises up through the stall, and I pinch my nose closed with my other hand, thankful that I'm not the kind of person who gets sick at the sight of puke. No wonder she's sick. It looks like all she's eaten today is a banana.

"I think I'm done now." She stands back up. Mascara has pooled around her eyes, and her cheeks are streaked with tears. "I've gotta pee."

I walk out of the stall, shutting the door behind me. I feel sorry for her; it's not prom, but it's still her last Homecoming dance and when she looks back on this night, her memory will likely be of how drunk she was, if she remembers anything at all.

I start reapplying my lip gloss, listening to the familiar

voices of Caroline's friends Dina and Britt in the next stall over. "She probably thinks she looks so hot."

"Her green dress is hideous." They snicker, and I realize they're totally talking about me. "Wait until they announce it. Caroline already has it all set up."

Announce what?

I storm out of the bathroom, holding back my tears. Adam's waiting for me just outside the door. "Hey, you all right?"

I look away. I can't tell him. I don't want him to think I care about what anyone is saying about me. He thinks I'm this laid-back girl who's unconcerned with gossip or rumors. How can I tell him that I've been the opposite of that since we went public?

"Bee?" he says, pulling me in for a hug.

I lay my head against his chest, taking comfort in his closeness, barely registering that Mr. Cummings is on the microphone calling out people's names.

"I'm okay," I lie. "Just needed a breather." I want to tell him the truth, but I don't even know where to start. This last month has been such a whirlwind of emotions for me and while it's been incredible, I'm insecure about us, especially now after what happened with Luke.

"And this year's Homecoming king and queen are Adam Stanson and Caroline Conlon! This dance is yours!" Mr. Cummings announces.

Adam pulls back, horrified. "Bee... I... um... I had no idea."

The crowd starts clapping, looking around expectantly. Caroline practically skips to the center of the dance floor, waiting for him to join her so they can walk up together. *This is the worst thing that could have happened* I think as Adam scans the room.

"We can leave... I'll leave with you right now," he says without much conviction. He can't mean it. There are too many people watching, and he'd never make a scene that way.

I shake my head. "No, go ahead, it's just one dance."

Relieved, he kisses my cheek, breaking away to meet her. She winks at me before leaning into him, whispering something private. My rage hits suddenly. The heat surging inside me feels like it needs to bust out, attack. At the very least, I want to scream.

I clench my fists, looking on as they're crowned, but when Edwin McCain's *'I'll Be'* starts playing, and he wraps his arms around her, I step away, bumping into Rochelle and Charlie.

"Well, that was an unfortunate turn of events. You okay?" she asks.

"I'm okay, I just need some air." I storm out. The contrast between the gym and the hallway is so severe that my ears pinch together with a ringing sound. Except for a lone couple making out in the corner, I'm alone out here. After a beat, I realize it's Harper and Jeremy. *Great. Sara's going to be crushed.*

I need to get outside, I need fresh air, I need to cry. I make my way down the stairs, the song still echoing from behind the gym doors, *and tell me that we belong together.*

"Hey, Bee!" I hear from behind me, but my ears are still too tight to know who it is.

I spin around, hoping that it's Adam coming to whisk me away from this sorry mess of a night, but it's Tucker. "Where are you going?"

"Oh, Tucker, hey. I just needed to cool down. It's hot in there."

"Cool. I'll come with you," he says, leading me out.

The air is cold, and the sweat on my skin stiffens, my body unprepared for the change in temperature. I forgot it was only forty degrees earlier, Dad had been worried that I would be too cold.

"Here," he says, taking off his coat and placing it on my shoulders before I can say no. I know as a girlfriend, you shouldn't be wearing another boy's coat, but the lines start to blur when your actual boyfriend is passionately slow dancing with his ex-girlfriend in front of the entire school.

"So, how have you been? We haven't talked in a while," he asks, pulling out his vape pen. It makes me think of the brochure I recently read at my pediatrician's office saying that vaping was worse for you than smoking regular cigarettes. I wonder if he's seen them, too.

"I've been good. Busy, I guess. You?"

"Yeah, good, you know, we played a show the day after Thanksgiving, so that was pretty cool."

"Yeah? How did it go?"

"It was good. You should come to the next one, I think you'd like it."

I smile, uneasily, aware that he's flirting with me. I want to tell him that I'm with Adam, but it's obvious that he knows. There's an edge to his advances now, like I'm a challenge he's set for himself and as awful as it was inside, I want to be outside with *him* even less. "I'm feeling better. I should get back inside."

The doors open, Adam and Kyle stepping out. *Of course.*

"Bee?" Adam says, his eyes lingering on Tucker's coat.

"I just needed some air." I shrug off the coat and hand it back. I only accepted it to spite Adam, and we all know it.

Tucker drapes it over his arm. "Hey, Stanson, congrats on Homecoming King... you must be tickled pink."

I look down at Adam's clenched fists. It's not like Tucker's said anything outwardly horrible, but winning Homecoming King in his world would be right up there with Sperry boat shoes; definitely not something he'd consider cool.

But Adam doesn't care whether or not Tucker thinks he's cool. He's angry about the coat.

I've only seen him in a fight once, when he was twelve. He'd never been aggressive but when an older boy pushed Jimmy to the ground, Adam went after the kid until he ran away. I was terrified; still young enough to think that a small scuffle would lead to someone being murdered, but I was strangely impressed, too.

"Yo, we're about to leave, let's go back inside," Kyle says, pulling Adam back. They lock eyes, Kyle seeming to say things telepathically, and just as quickly as the tension appeared, it's gone. Adam shrugs once, taking my hand, and leads me back inside.

Once we're alone, he turns to me with a clear edge to his voice. "What was that about?"

"What?" I ask. It wasn't my proudest moment, but he's the one who was just locked in an embrace with Caroline. "What do you care? You were busy."

People start flying down the stairs, laughing, shouting, making plans for later. I'm filled with regret; our perfect night together is ruined, and the last person he danced with was Caroline.

He ignores them, looking at me, his face softening. "I didn't know that was going to happen! Obviously, I care that my girl-friend's outside, alone, with another guy! You were wearing his coat!"

Even in my rage, I want to smile because I love hearing him call me his girlfriend. *Grow up, Bee, you're having your first fight right now.* "Well, it didn't seem like you cared that much when you left me to go cuddle up with her." Then, seeing his face fall, I add, "that just really sucked, okay? I'm jealous. I didn't want to stick around to watch how perfect you look together."

I open my mouth to say more, but he cuts me off by leaning in for a kiss. "I'm sorry about everything. We're just having an off day. Want to start over? Let's bail on the party and go get tacos from Abuela's."

I take a breath, still reeling from the kiss. "Are you sure?"

"I'm sure." He moves in, planting a quick peck on my cheek before wrapping his arms around me.

Caroline's walking down the stairs as we make our way out of the school. In the chaos of the last few minutes, I haven't even considered the fact that she obviously found a way to rig the votes for the homecoming king and queen. That's what I overheard Dina and Britt talking about in the bathrooms. If she was willing to risk getting in trouble just to one-up me, what else is she willing to do? I chance a glance in her direction. If I could hear her thoughts, she'd be warning me. *This isn't over yet.*

Dear Journal,

Things have settled down after the fiasco of homecoming. Caroline seems to have backed off over the last few weeks, but she's like a lion waiting for her perfect chance to pounce. I don't know when it will be but I have to be ready for her. Sometimes I wonder if I'm cut out for this. Do I really want to go up against Caroline? But what choice do I have? If I give up — I lose Adam and let her win. I can't do that. I know he wants to be with me, I think he might even be in love with me. He hasn't said it yet though but I mean, he spent three hours on Sunday helping me build a gingerbread house... pretty sure you don't do that unless you're in love. Especially because the game was on and I knowww he was itching to watch it with Kyle. As if the Adam thing isn't enough to deal with, SARA has been coming for me almost daily. She's mad at me for telling her about Jeremy and Harper at homecoming - as if I'm the one who was making out with him! I was trying to be a good friend... you know, be honest with her, but does she see that? No. She won't say it but she's totally jealous about Adam and Scarlett too. It feels like I can do nothing right!! Rochelle and Stacey don't seem to care. Why does she?

17

I PICK UP MY THIRD TRAY OF CARROTS, SHOUTING TO MOM over the loud humming of the industrial dishwasher. "I have the last tray!" We've been working at the soup kitchen since six-thirty this morning, finally setting up for our last food service of the day. Breakfast and lunch went by in a blur, the minutes and hours blending together with all the chopping and stirring and cleaning.

I head out into the main lobby, recognizing some of the same faces from earlier. I have mostly kept my thoughts to myself, but I can't shake the question that has been hounding me all day - *how could this many people need food?*

Adam meets me at the door, looking around nervously.

"Hey Stranger!" I say, happy to have a moment with him. There hasn't been much time to chat - both of us were put to work as soon as we got here.

He takes the tray of carrots from me, his eyes fixed on the front door. "Look... I think—"

I follow his gaze just as the door opens and Caroline walks in. "What is *she* doing here?"

"She's volunteering... I'm sorry - I thought she was coming next week." He looks down at me guiltily. She's always volunteering. Last year, there was a write-up in the school newsletter about her clocking fifty-two volunteer hours. Jenica Myers called her a teenage Mother Teresa, a ridiculous exaggeration, obviously, since she was more like Prince Hans from Frozen. She raised the stakes by coming here today, and involving his family is below the belt.

"Whatever, it doesn't matter." I turn around, walking into the main dining room, relieved when he follows me in. "Did you know she was coming?"

"She *just* texted."

I have to fight the urge to ask him for more details. *Does she text you often? Why don't you ever talk about her?* There is still a big part of me that's too proud to ask. I want to appear like I don't care about her, but it's getting harder. And it feels like she's crossing a line by coming here today when our families are doing something together.

"I better get over there." I find my place next to Dad at the buffet table. Caroline walks in, scanning the room until her eyes fall on me. I don't know what I expect her to do, but it's not... smile. It tells me everything I need to know though - she *is* here on purpose. She finds Donna, the program director, and they talk for a moment before Donna points to the head of the table, where Luke is standing. Caroline happily makes her way over, and when Luke sees her, he lights up. "Caroline! Long time no see. We miss seeing you around the house."

Ouch.

I hoped to talk to Luke myself today, but there hasn't been time. Plus, he's always excusing himself to take a phone call.

I glance over again once the line starts moving. She's only just put on an apron but already, she's winning over the ladies in the line. *This is why she's the captain of the debate team,* I sulk. She can talk to anyone and like Adam, she has the ability to charm. It was another reason why everyone was so obsessed with them as a couple - the two of them were basically a big ball of charisma.

I thought *I* might be the unsung hero of the day, but my throat closed up during the breakfast service. I found I was too nervous to speak to anyone. I couldn't explain why, really - it's like I lost my voice when I realized what the bigger issue is. *These people are here because they are hungry.* I feel guilty for having what they don't, and I thought they'd find me ridiculous if I tried to relate to them in any way. Before Donna told us that Massachusetts has one of the highest hunger rates in the country, I thought today was important simply because it would look good on my college applications one day.

I watch as a vaguely familiar man shuffles down the line, breaking out in a smile when he sees Dad. "Eddie, hey!" Dad says, scooping up a piece of shepherd's pie and plopping it down on to his plate. "I saw your brother the other day."

Eddie's eyes widen, excited. "Is that right? He's been really busy getting the new business going. I'm awfully proud." He inches forward again, careful not to hold up the line, looking at me briefly and nodding before focusing his attention back on Dad. I know I've seen him somewhere before, but it could have been from earlier today. I take him in as discreetly as I can; with his ripped jeans and the old paint stained thermal, he looks like a man who doesn't have two pennies to rub together. My heart breaks a little, wondering where he'll go after he leaves here.

"I'll come find you in a few," Dad says, nodding to him.

Laughter comes from the front of the table, and when I look again, Caroline and Luke are chuckling about something together.

This. Sucks.

I scan the room for Adam, finding him in deep conversation with an older man. Despite my resolution to be annoyed, I soften at the sight. More than any of the other volunteers today, Adam has been the most engaged with everyone. I've caught him absorbed in so many conversations, offering them his full attention. Unlike Caroline, Adam's charm is different because it's genuine.

He catches me watching and smiles, quickly leaning back down and saying something that makes the man look up at me. He waves, I wave back, and he beams as he says something to Adam. Adam starts to laugh, and I find myself embarrassed to be the topic of a conversation that I'm not a part of.

When the last person goes through the line, a bell is rung, and someone from our assembly line lets out a loud whooping sound. Then all at once, everyone who's seated stands and starts clapping for us. *Us.*

The volunteers make a plate, sitting at one of the empty tables in the back. Adam sits by me, and I try to ignore the fact that Caroline is still hanging by Luke. *Why doesn't anyone else find this weird? Is Adam noticing this, too?*

"You okay?" he asks. I know he's referring to Caroline, but I still don't want to break the facade. I need to appear mature and unfazed. *I'm not jealous. I'm not jealous. I'm not jealous.*

I lean my head on his shoulder, blowing away a rogue piece of hair that slipped out of my ponytail. "Today was exhausting," I change the subject. "Why didn't I realize how important this is before now?"

"I know what you mean. We really do live a privileged life, so far away from the reality of how some people live."

I'm reminded suddenly of a lecture my history teacher, Mr. Kimball, gave last year on understanding current events. He explained that it's easier to understand something when you've actually experienced it, and I guess this is what he meant.

"You were great today... so natural with everyone. You could literally talk to anyone."

He shifts, smiling down at me. "Yeah? So were you."

"No... I barely spoke to anyone. I don't know why, but I felt so intimidated... like when I heard some of their stories and realized why they are actually coming here... I just like... froze up. I don't think I was thinking of them as real people before today. I know that sounds awful."

He kisses the top of my head. It's the first time he's shown me this kind of affection in front of our families and I love that it feels so natural, like it's almost not even worth noting. Doesn't hurt that Caroline definitely saw it too.

"You could never be awful. I'm glad we did this today. Together."

"Me, too. By the way, what did you say to that man earlier, when you pointed at me?"

He smirks and shrugs, feigning innocence. I poke him hard in the ribs, just where he's the most ticklish, and he squirms away, laughing. "Okay, okay. He told me to marry you as soon as I get the chance, that a girl like you is something to hold on to."

I raise my head, looking at him. "What did you say?"

"I said, *Jack, you don't even know her! She could be a lunatic for all you know!* But he just shrugged me off and smiled, saying, *I don't need to know her to see that sparkle.*"

I can't hold back my smile when I say, "That Jack is one smart guy!"

Dad starts telling a story, and I narrow in on Luke as he types away on his phone. Despite my determination to win him over, I don't really know him that well. People are always commenting about how similar he and Adam are but again, it doesn't seem like it to me. He isn't one of those dads that stands out for any reason - he is never the friendliest or the most embarrassing, he doesn't have a coin collection or wear an infamous grilling apron. He's always just sort of *there*.

But there *has* to be something special about him for Adam to hold him in such high esteem. Sons look up to their fathers, sure, but there is more to it than that for Adam. Like at some point, he decided he would do anything in his power to make his dad proud.

Later, after finishing the cleaning and putting away all the leftover food, our group stands in a circle, chatting in the middle of the room. The cafeteria is mostly empty now with the exception of a few stragglers finishing up their coffees.

I'm the only one who sees Luke when he comes back in, so I wave him over, hoping that he'll appreciate my assertiveness or at the very least, Caroline might take note.

He nods, glancing back down at his phone as he makes his way over to us. I turn away for a moment, but when I look back up again, he's walking head-first into one of the other volunteers carrying a large dessert tray.

The tray tumbles - cakes falling all over him.

The entire room stops, frozen by the scene as Dad runs over to help the person behind the trays. After a little commotion, I see that it's Eddie. He waves Dad off, stepping over the mess to where Luke is standing and holds out his hand. "I'm awfully sorry, Sir, I didn't see you standing there." But Luke's body language is all wrong - rigid and closed off, and I hold my breath, suddenly nervous about how this might play out.

Luke looks down at Eddie's hand, shaking his head. He motions to his suit, now covered in whipped cream, and says, "Do you have any idea how much this suit costs? " He lets the question hang in the air and Eddie looks confused, wondering, I think, if Luke is really waiting for an answer. But then he goes on, giving Eddie a quick once over, " No, you wouldn't."

I feel the blow in my bones, and it's not until this very

moment that I realize just how impacted I feel from my experience here today. Here, right before my eyes is the problem; Eddie is being judged based on his circumstance, by the way he looks, and in a different context, I was just doing the same thing to him. Instead of trying to understand his life, I pitied him for having less than me.

Eddie scratches his head. "I'm sorry, truly, I am. I'd be happy to cover the cost if it's ruined."

Luke actually laughs, and the sound echoes through the cafeteria. "Right. I won't hold my breath on that." He turns away.

"What happened?" June asks, breathless.

Luke smacks at his suit, trying to wipe away frosting. "I don't know! Bee called me over here, and then the next thing I know, I'm being mauled."

Wait... is he blaming me?

Adam steps in. "It's not Bee's fault..."

Caroline pops up out of nowhere. "How about we get some fresh air... outside?"

June nods. "That's a good idea."

After a few awkward moments, the Stanson's make their way out... with Caroline. This couldn't have worked out better for her.

Luke is waiting for us at Mom's car, and Adam is standing a few feet behind him, still looking at his feet. Luke's sulking, like he's being forced to wait for us, and the whole scene feels so backwards, so out of place, like Adam's the parent, urging his kid to explain himself. "I'm really sorry about that. I lost my temper."

Dad nods. "Eddie feels really bad about it. He's still inside if you want to talk to him."

Luke steps up closer, shaking his head. "Look, I'm sorry for *your* sake. I made a scene, and I'm sure it was embarrassing for you and your family, and that wasn't my intention, but I have nothing to say to *him*."

Mom straightens beside me, a tell-tale sign that she is *pissed* now, and with some regret, I realize that Adam knows it, too. How awful it must be for him to know that she's upset at his Dad right now. We can't even pretend like none of it happened because we were all there to see it.

It's quiet as Dad reaches into his pocket to pull out a business card. He's never had a great poker face, so I can see clearly the things he's feeling: anger, disappointment, but the thing that sticks out the most is that he doesn't seem at all surprised by Luke's behavior.

I glance at Kyle, but he doesn't seem surprised, either.

Dad hands Luke a card. "He wanted me to give you this, *his business card*, in case you wanted to take him up on the offer to replace the suit. That was Eddie McFadden, by the way, of *McFadden Development*. He owns this soup kitchen."

Luke's mouth falls open when he hears the name because *everyone* has heard of Eddie McFadden. He's easily one of the most successful businessmen in Massachusetts, and it must have been why I recognized him before. Luke looks down, grumbling something under his breath and for the first time, he looks remorseful about what happened. But I can't shake the feeling that his remorse is for the wrong reasons, and I can almost hear everyone else thinking the same.

Dear Journal,

Well, turns out, Christmas with a boyfriend is the BEST. We've basically been inseparable. He came over on Christmas Eve like he always does but for the first time ever, I went to HIS house on Christmas day for dinner. It was all very civilized and grown up and I FINALLY got a chance to spend some time with Luke... for a little while anyway, until he left for an "important" business call. But it was such a relief, especially after what happened at the soup kitchen. Luke can be funny if he wants to be. He might not like me as much as Caroline... yet but I'm hoping that I can win him over with my skiing skills during the Cove Family ski weekend. If anyone will appreciate athletism - it will be him. OMG also... Adam gave me the most beautiful black and gold ornament of a SEWING MACHINE. Can you even think of a more thoughtful gift? I made him a tie with navy-blue silk. It was way harder than I imagined it to be and basically had to put all my other projects on hold for all of December but still so worth it in the end because he was practically speechless. Said it was the coolest gift he's ever received. So basically BEST CHRISTMAS EVER.

18

WE'VE BEEN COMING UP TO VERMONT FOR THE COVE Family Ski Weekend since I was six. Our parents rent out an entire cul-de-sac of townhouses, and it's basically like a commune for three days: everyone, everywhere, doing what-ever. Jonathan's mom, Mrs. Walters' organizes the events for the weekend, kicking it off with her Night One Smorgasbord.

I'm helping Mom make a plate of loaded nachos for it while Dad, Kyle and Jimmy are hanging out on the couch. Dad's reading the same fishing book he started last year during the Cove Family Weekend, knowing full-well he won't finish it this year, either.

I've been periodically looking over at Kyle while he's tried his hardest to cover up the fact that he's been texting someone almost incessantly. It started just before Christmas. He's always had suitors, people freak over him just as much as they do over Adam, but so far, Kyle hasn't dated anyone seriously. I thought maybe it was just another one of his text flings until the other day, when I actually witnessed Kyle McGrath *giggle*. That's when I knew it was serious.

When he realizes I'm watching him, he frowns, sliding his phone back into his hoodie pocket. Then he looks at Jimmy. "Dude, I can't wait to get out there tomorrow. I say we go straight to the moguls."

"I'm in. I want to be out there first thing."

"Do you think we'll all ski together this year?" I ask, holding my breath as I add more shredded cheddar over the top of the nachos.

"That's going to be a negative," Kyle says.

"But..." I whine.

"Negativeee," he sings.

Jimmy shakes his head. "Bee, it's called bro-boarding for a reason."

I shouldn't be surprised. They never invite us to come along. They snowboard and act like they are more gnarly or whatever than us skiers, but I hoped this year would be different because Adam and I are together.

Kyle teases, "Don't tell me you're planning to force Adam down blue hills with you all day."

"Obviously not," I say defensively. "He can do whatever he wants."

Jimmy raises his eyebrows, looking over at Kyle. "Do we have a *Stage-Five* on our hands?"

I look up, confused, and they bust-out laughing. "A what?"

"You know, a *Stage-Five Clinger*," Jimmy says again with no explanation.

"Shut up, idiot!" I walk over and punch his arm, but it only eggs them on more.

"Guys, stop teasing her." Mom walks to the door, winking at me. "I'm sure Adam will want to ski with you too Brooke. You guys ready?"

"I'm not even worried about it." I lie, moping as I follow her to the door.

Dad puts down his book, meeting us. "Did you know that one of the biggest reported fish ever caught was a lemon shark in North Carolina?"

"Can't say that I did." Mom smiles.

We're one of the last to arrive at the Walters' rental. I'm instantly struck with the smell of food; the dining room table is covered with every dish imaginable, and my stomach tightens, thinking of all the people at *The Nurturing Bite*. I can't see large quantities of food anymore without remembering all the people who don't have what we do, but instead of feeling shame from it, I feel grateful. I changed a little after that day, and I started brainstorming ways I might be able to give back, in my own way. And with the help of Mrs. Holmes and our sewing class, we managed to make and donate over fifty hats before the holidays.

I walk by the food, headed toward Sara and Stacey, who are sitting on the floor in front of the fireplace. It would just be the three of us *Cove Girls* this year because Rochelle has family visiting from Florida.

"Hey, Hey!" Stacey says, pulling me down to them.

"What did I miss on the drive up?"

She smiles. "Missy Elliot."

"Ugh! I love Missy!"

I try to make eye contact with Sara, but she keeps her eyes focused on the fire. She's mad again because I broke tradition and drove up with Adam. "You still mad at me?... Because I did something really cool for us."

She looks over reluctantly, giving me a half smile. "What?"

"You know how you've always wanted to do one of those night-time gondola rides up to the summit to make s'mores around that outdoor fireplace thingy?"

"Yes...."

"Well, I bought three tickets to go up on Sunday after dinner! Just us three."

"Ohmygod! That's amazing, Bee, thank you! " she squeals. "I can't believe you did this!"

It's enough, for now at least, to clear the air between us. It was beginning to feel like I was in a relationship with Adam *and* Sara, only Sara didn't seem happy unless she was giving me a hard time about Adam. Or Scarlett.

"Speaking of food. Let's go make a plate."

I glance around the room again, just to make sure I didn't miss the Stansons coming in. I parted ways with Adam after our amazing drive together, but he's been MIA since, not even responding after I'd texted him a photo of the chocolate chip cookies I helped Mom bake.

Stacey scoops Caesar salad onto her plate. "I couldn't sleep last night, so I totally trolled Insta and you know that girl group in Cali that makes all those videos to Ariana Grande songs on Tik-Tok?"

We nod.

"I'm pretty sure that one of their parents, just like, bought a house and let them live in it for the sole purpose of making videos."

"Must be nice" Sara says, bitterly. "By the way, did you see my last video is up to a thousand views?"

"I think I've seen it at least six hundred times" I admit.

"And I'm the other four."

We laugh.

The front door opens and Adam walks in with his family, but right away, I can tell something is off. Their posture is all wrong - stiff and uncomfortable.

"I'll be right back." I tell the girls, making my way through the crowded room. He doesn't see me at first, but I watch him scanning through each group until our eyes finally meet. He lights up and my heart skips a beat, still surprised, even now, that in a room full of people, I'm the one he's looking for. He takes a step toward me, but too late because Cole Jackson walks up and drags him into a conversation about college. He nods politely, sneaking a look my way, as if to say, *what can you do.* So I smile and walk back to the dining room, just as June is coming out.

"Hi, Mrs. Stanson," I say.

"Oh, Brooke, hi, I didn't see you there." She pulls me in for a hug but it's half-hearted, nothing like the squeezes she usually gives. "How was the drive up?"

"It was good. Adam didn't go a hair over the speed limit," I joke because she spent fifteen minutes lecturing him on the dangers of speeding. He'd been such a good sport; letting her finish without interrupting even once.

"Excuse me a moment, Dear, I need to...um... I need to get some air. Let's make sure we spend some time together this weekend, okay?"

"I'd love that," I say as she turns away.

I go back to the girls, whose plates are now filled to the brim. I start mine, loading it up with the most random things: egg rolls, mac and cheese, potato skins, and shrimp cocktail. Just when I've added so much stuff that there isn't any space left, Adam comes up and wraps his arms around me.

"Mmm this looks good."

"Are you talking about the food or Bee?" Stacey teases.

"I guess they've moved on to the PDA portion of the relationship," Sara adds.

"Thanks for letting Bee drive up with me today." He winks, flashing them his smile, and I know that even *they* could never stay mad at those dimples.

Once the girls are back at their spot by the fireplace, I turn to Adam. "Is your Mom okay?"

His smile fades, making me feel like I've said the wrong thing. "Yeah, why do you ask?"

"No, nothing, she just seemed distracted a minute ago."

He looks around, worry written all over his face. "What did she say to you?"

I regret asking, so I try to change the subject. "She just wants to hang out with me this weekend. You know, girl stuff."

"Ok..." he hesitates, seeming unsure. "You sure? Because—"

Mrs. Walters stands, clearing her throat. "I just wanted to say how happy I am that we're all away for a ski weekend again. These little trips have meant so much to us, and I'm so grateful for this amazing community! So! Let's talk about this weekend. Tomorrow morning is open to do whatever you want: skiing, cross-country skiing, tubing, whatever, but in the evening, the adults are going downtown for a wine tasting! Teenagers are welcome to night ski, and the following day is race day. Any takers this year?"

I look up, scanning the room for Dad, my biggest ski supporter, hoping he'll stay quiet but before I even find him, he's shouting, "Bee!"

I blush, shaking my head as the room turns to look at me. "No, no. I don't think I'm racing this year," I croak, hating all of the attention. No one is more awkward than me when it comes to speaking in front of a crowd. Last year, during my oral presentation on Alexander Hamilton, Mrs. Witmeyer let me wrap up early when I couldn't get the word *freedom* out.

Suddenly, Adam chirps in, saying, "I, for one, would love to see you race, Bee!"

I suck in my breath, not sure whether I should hate him for contributing to my mortification or adore him for calling me out in a way that only a boyfriend could.

Jonathan jumps up. "Do it for the Cove!" Then he chants, "Bee, Bee, Bee."

Before I know what's happening, they've all joined in, shouting my name.

I find Luke in the crowd, knowing that this is my chance to win him over, to bring him over to Team Bee.

"Fine!" I shout, covering my face with my hands to hide my blush.

They cheer, and Mrs. Walters goes on. "After the races, we'll do a group ski followed by a big bonfire in the middle of the cul-de-sac. And for our final gathering, we've rented out the banquet room at *The Small Village* for dinner."

There's some whoops and whistling; you can feel the excitement in the air because we all know that memories are made on the Cove Family Ski Weekend.

19

THE NEXT DAY, AFTER SKIING THE MORNING WITH MOM and Dad, I meet Sara and Stacey in the lodge for lunch. We're going to ski the afternoon together too, much to the relief of the boys who convinced Adam to *bro-board*. It's fine. I reasoned that we both need time with our friends. Bonus points if it shows everyone I am not a Stage-Five-Clinger- which I learned, much to the amusement of everyone else, is someone who is completely obsessed. Not a far cry from reality.

We order hot dogs from the cafeteria, and for the first time in weeks, it feels like we're the *Cove Girls* again. Minus Rochelle. It's not like I haven't seen them, but sitting with Stacey and Sara now makes me realize just how absent from our group I've been. I miss them, and I make a promise to myself that I'll make more time for friends in the new year.

"So, I have to tell you something," Stacey says, looking at me.

I look up, waiting for her to go on. From the look on her face, it seems like she's about to say something major. *Is it Murder? Sex? Is she moving to Argentina?*

"I can tell your mind has gone to dark places, Bee," she chuckles, "but it's nothing bad... I think Leann O'Connell likes me."

"No, she definitely likes you," Sara adds.

My mouth falls open. Stacey's had a crush on her since seventh grade. She was to her what Adam is to me. "Ohmygod. This is so exciting!" I clap my hands together. I'm excited for her, but I can't help feeling left out. I'm definitely the last to know about it.

"I know. We've been texting a bunch. I don't want to get my hopes up or anything, but she says that she's liked me since last year's *Freshman Frolic*."

"What! Why did she wait so long to tell you?"

"Because people are stupid sometimes," Sara adds. "Before I forget," she looks at me, "I think Briana is definitely part of the ring. She was texting Caroline last night giving her updates on you and Adam."

"Why do you think that?" I ask, suddenly nervous. There have been rumors fueled by *Little Lucy* that Caroline has organized a network of spies to provide her with information on Adam and me. I know it's ridiculous, but ever since I heard about it, it seems like people *are* always watching us. I'm still nervous that someone will find out about what happened on the night of Halloween, and the idea of her digging around for information about us doesn't help.

"I walked behind her and saw Adam's name on one of the texts."

Stacey shrugs. "Could have been anything, though."

"Yeah but like, I think it's pretty unlikely she talking about what color his ski jacket is. The spy ring is real."

"That's like, so weird! But who cares? What do you even have to worry about?"

"Who knows what she's trying to dig up! I don't trust her."

When Stacey gets up to throw away her trash, I lean across the table, whispering, "You never said anything to anyone about the night of Musters, right?" It still bothers me. I know there isn't much Caroline could hold against me now, but if she found out about that kiss, I know she'd find a way to make me pay for it. Plus, I feel this underlying sense of guilt, that we were sneaking around before he was officially single, that we started things off the wrong way.

"No, never." She makes a face, clearly insulted that I even had to ask. "No one will ever know."

I take a breath, relaxing into my seat. It does seem pretty unlikely that anyone would ever find out. Unless someone saw us in the woods that night -which is not at all likely- the secret is safe with me, Adam, Kyle and Sara.

Later, we're sitting in the snow outside the summit base lodge when I see Adam come off the ski lift. My heart practically leaps from my chest; it was nice to catch up with the girls, but I'm ready to hang out with him again.

"Hey." He leans in for a kiss. His cheeks are chaffed red, but his eyes are glowing; he's high off the mountain air.

"Having fun?" I ask.

"A blast," he says, breathless, "I really missed you, though. I was thinking about you the whole time."

It's exactly what I wanted to hear. If I was braver, I'd tell him the thing that's been on my mind almost constantly over the last few weeks. *I love you. I love you so much.*

"Oh, come on, you guys have been back together for all of two seconds, and you've already gone all doe-eyed again. We've lost him, boys!" Jonathan complains.

Adam chuckles, pulling me down into the snow with him.

"You should have seen the jumps we hit on the mogul hill," Jimmy says to Sara.

"Nothing I haven't seen before," she replies, batting her eyelashes.

I look at Kyle, back on his phone a few feet away. "What's up with him?" I ask Adam, knowing that if anyone knows who he's been talking to, it'd be him.

"He's cool, but if I didn't know any better, I'd think he was having his own secret relationship."

I look at him, waiting for him to go on, but Jimmy jumps up, challenging Sara. "I'll race you to the bottom, winner has to buy everyone hot cocoa."

"Extra whipped cream." She stands, acting casual.

"What?" he asks.

"You'll need to know that I like extra whipped cream once I've beaten you."

We laugh, following them to the edge.

I look at Adam, trying to appear nervous. "I feel like you're going to be mad at me."

"What? Mad at you for what?"

I line up my skis and lift my poles. "For beating you to the bottom," I say, taking off, hearing his laugh from behind me.

"I'm coming for you, Bee!"

I'm counting on it.

After having a pizza dinner with all the Cove families, a big group of us kids get together to go night skiing. "Night skiing freaks me out," Sara says as we walk the small trail behind the cul-de-sac to get to the base lodge. "I feel like Bigfoot is going to pop right out of the woods."

Jimmy scoffs at her. "Yeah, you should be on the lookout for the *Loch Ness Monster,* too."

"Umm, this coming from the guy who cried at Musters?"

she dishes back, making everyone laugh. There was a rumor that someone found him crying in a corner of the hospital after he got separated from his group.

"That was a lie!" he barks, storming past us to walk ahead.

Briana turns around, looking from me to Adam and back again. She definitely seems like one of Caroline's cronies. I even saw her reading something on Little Lucy earlier.

Sara elbows me. "See."

"I don't get it," I whisper, not wanting Adam to hear me talking about Caroline. When I mentioned the underground ring to him a few weeks ago, he laughed like it was the funniest thing in the world, not even entertaining the idea that she would want to know what we are up to. "What would she even be saying?"

"I dunno, just keeping tabs on you," she says. "You can't trust Caroline. She's insidious."

"Whoa... big word."

She winks, clearly glad I commented on it. "Thanks... it was in the movie last night."

When we're getting our stuff on at the base, Adam comes up to me, whispering, "I have an idea."

I smile, knowing that whenever Adam Stanson says he has an idea, it's going to be a good one. But I play it cool, anyway. "Oh yeah?"

"Let's do one run with the group and then sneak away."

"Okay..." I say. "And go where?" Because I've become a little bit obsessed with making-out, I think of the empty rental, trying to calculate how much time we'd have alone if we got back there in thirty minutes. We could do a lot of kissing in an hour.

"Let's go to the summit lodge and get a deep-dished choco-late chip cookie."

Oh.

"Sounds good," I mutter, recovering quickly.

We follow the plan, going down the mountain with everyone, and when the coast is clear, we take a different trail down to the lift that leads up to the summit. When we're settled inside the restaurant and sitting by the fireplace, I realize I've been waiting for this moment all day. We order the deep-dish cookie and two hot cocoas.

I lean across the table. "Hey... about that playlist yesterday... how did you know all of my favorite songs?" On our drive to Vermont, he surprised me by queuing up a playlist called *Bee on Skis* with all my favorite songs. But not just recent favorites, some went as far back as middle school.

He takes a sip of his cocoa, smiling at me. "I know you."

"But Feel Again by One Republic? I don't think I've ever mentioned that one before."

He looks at me like I'm nuts. "It's on repeat when you sew!"

I laugh out loud. It's true, my sewing rituals are pretty set in stone. I like to listen to Feel Again while I chew on Mango flavored gum. "It's my amp song."

"Your what?"

"My amp song. You ever notice in the movies, whenever there's a big scene, a song starts playing in the background, and it connects you with what's happening?"

He laughs, nodding. "Yup, like at the end, when the love story is being put back together, and they're running through airports and stuff."

"Exactly! There's always some catchy song playing. It must be so romantic, having a love moment while your amp song is playing..."

He reaches over and takes my hand. "Okay, Bee. I can take a hint."

Luckily, I don't actually need him to make some outward display of affection to me because every day feels like a movie scene when I'm with him. "Let's play a round of questions..." My parents started this game years ago to encourage dinner conversation. We'd pick a person, then everyone would fire off a bunch of questions at them. It could be anything: something as simple as favorite color, or sometimes we'd get deep, like what do you think happens after you die. Adam and I have taken the game on as our own, asking each other things on our drives or sometimes when we're just hanging out on the couch. "What's your favorite memory of us?"

He doesn't skip a beat. "Probably the night you almost killed me in the McDonald's parking lot when I let you drive." I almost hit a parked car, *once,* and now he likes to bring it up whenever he has the chance. When he sees my face, he laughs. "No, you're a natural. What's yours?"

I knew mine before I even asked the question. "Definitely the night of the student/faculty game. I'll remember that night forever. Have you ever wanted something for so long that when it happens, it doesn't feel real?"

"I have." He nods, his face suggestive, like he knows exactly what I'm saying because he feels the same way.

"Okay. Here's a juicy one for you. What's the most jealous you've ever been?"

He thinks about it. "I was crazy jealous the night of the football game when Tucker interrupted us at the concession stand."

I laugh, grateful that those days of uncertainty are far behind us now. The waitress brings the cookie in a cast iron pan with a generous scoop of vanilla ice cream. We dive in, hitting spoons, fighting over who gets the better bite. "What about you?" he asks after I've won. "When were you the most jealous?"

I sigh, rolling my eyes. "That day at the *Willow Glen* when you and Caroline carved your names into the tree."

He stops chewing, looking at me seriously. "Really?"

"Ugh. Yeah. I was crushed. I think I was always holding out hope that she wasn't your forever girl, and I don't know... seeing your names on the tree made it feel more official somehow."

He's quiet, like he's thinking of that day now.

"But I just always felt like it was our spot, you know, maybe not *me and you* but ours, the *Cove Girls* and the boys. I can't even tell you how many times I imagined us putting our names up there together. You know the big heart, right at the bottom?"

He nods.

"Well, one day, I did it... I put our initials together and then, realizing it was too creepy, I scratched it out and made a heart."

"I always wondered who did that." He looks both regretful and nostalgic. He takes another bite, letting it sit in his mouth. "How about this? On the first day of spring, we'll go and add our initials together, properly."

"Deal."

"What are we going to do next year when I go to college?" he asks suddenly.

I nearly choke on my cocoa, surprised that he's finally bringing up college. I sort of settled on the fact that he just didn't want to discuss it and we'd figure it out when the time comes. I didn't want to push him into talking about something that stressed him out already.

"I don't know, isn't that really your choice?"

"My Dad told me yesterday that he spoke to the coach of Villanova last week and that they're going to offer me an early acceptance."

I startle, surprised. "Ohmygod! Congratulations!"

"Thanks," he says absently, taking a sip of water.

"Are you happy?"

He takes a deep breath. "I don't think I am. It doesn't feel right."

I wait for him to go on, and when he doesn't, I summon up the nerve to be honest. "I think you should go to Ecuador. Take the internship and go study something you're really interested in."

He holds my gaze, his face blank. "I told my dad about the internship, and he dismissed it right away. He said it would be foolish. And part of me hates him for that, you know? He's never asked what I want to do. Not once. It's like he doesn't care. But the other part of me doesn't want to let him down, like he's my dad and he's counting on me and how can I just choose to do something different? How can I choose to disappoint him?"

It breaks my heart to see him so lost and confused. Deciding what you do after high school is supposed to be exciting, *a next chapter*, it shouldn't be this stressful. It's not fair that he has to decide between what he wants and what his dad wants.

"How are you supposed to be sure about these things at seventeen?" he asks.

"You're not, you just need to do what feels right. At the end of the day, he can't make you do anything. If you decide not to go to Villanova, he'll get over it eventually."

"And what about us?" He moves his face closer to mine. "We'd be a plane ride away from each other either way."

I look away, gazing into the fire, trying to figure out how I really feel about it. I wish we hadn't waited so long to get together, I wish I wasn't younger than him, I wish we could stay like this forever. "It will suck," I say, knowing that no matter how I feel about it, he needs to be able to live his life without regrets. "But it's going to suck anyway, and you can't base your decision on us."

"Why not?"

"Because it's *your* future," I say, faltering. I need to stay strong for his sake, otherwise I'll cave and tell him to stay in Padstow until I graduate.

"But I want you to be in my future."

I break out in a full-on flush. He's making it hard to keep up this tough-girl act. "Whether it's South America or Pennsylvania or Boston, you'll still be away at school, *not with me*. Do you really think you'll want to stay together while I'm stuck at home for another two years?"

"Yes," he says like it's not even a question. "Bee, these have literally been the best few months of my life. Whether I'm miles away or close by, I want to stay together. I... I..."

I raise my eyebrows expectantly, feeling my heart quicken.

"I love you" he says. I've never heard him sound so sure of himself and if I didn't love him before, I definitely do now. "I really love you, and leaving for college won't change that. I promise. I don't want this to end. If I go away, the only option is for us to stay together and do it long distance. That's what I want. What do you want?"

"That's what I want, too."

He smiles, looking into the fire, and I see him for what he is, just a boy, baring it all to the girl he loves.

"Adam?" I say nervously.

His eyes meet mine slowly, and I say the thing I've been waiting my whole life to say. "I love you, too."

20

I STARTED RACING COMPETITIVELY WHEN I WAS EIGHT-years-old. Dad had noticed, I guess, that I was skiing a little faster than the kids my age and encouraged me to enter a race. So I did, and I won, thus beginning my short-lived career in competitive skiing. By eleven I had joined a ski team on a mountain in New Hampshire and Dad was driving me two-hours, twice a week for practice and races. I was good; improving every time I got out there, impressing a lot of the adults that were around and watching. It wasn't that I disliked it, *per se,* but once I began to do it competitively, skiing lost some of its magic for me. I love to ski, and if I'm being honest, I loved the attention I got from being good, but the drive to win wasn't in me. I quit just before high school, maybe breaking Dad's heart a little in the process, though he'd never admit that.

It's no wonder I wake up feeling nervous on the morning of the race. It's the race, *yes,* but it's also the fact that Adam Stanson loves me. Not only does he love me but he wants to stay together when he goes away to college. My twelve-year-old self would be absolutely freaking out. *He loves me!* He loves *me! We're in love!* The race, or more importantly, getting Luke to join *Team Bee,* is even more crucial now, especially if Adam isn't going to go to Villanova and study finance. I need Luke to think I'm a good idea before he decides I'm the reason why everything fell apart. *I need to win today's race.*

I roll out of bed, checking my phone, and there's already a text from Adam.

You ready Flash?

I smile, writing back, *I'm nervous.*

You'll do great! I can't wait to see you do your thing. I'll be right at the bottom, waiting for you! Good luck! I love you!

He loves me. He actually loves me. I jump up and down, letting my giddiness take over; it's a miracle I even slept at all with this much excitement. I actually feel like I could burst.

The girls would be over soon to French Braid my hair, so I rush to the shower, letting my mind wander over every detail of last night. The questions game, the college talk, the declaration of love, the gondola ride down the mountain, stopping to kiss on our way back to the cul-de-sac. It feels like I'm operating on a higher frequency; in a place that's reserved only for people who are in love. Like if I died right this second, I'm sure I'd be escorted to the section in heaven where loved people go. I've graduated from girldom into womanhood, and I've done it without even batting an eyelash. I'm basically a love warrior.

When I get back to my room, Sara and Stacey are sitting on my bed, talking. "And then she asked how my vaca has been, so like, what do you think *that* means?" Stacey asks.

"Leann?" I ask, and they nod.

"What do *you* mean, what does it mean? It's not, like, rocket science, she's asking you how your winter break has been."

"Yeah, yeah, *obviously,* but do you think she's just asking to, like, make conversation, or is she asking because he really wants to know?"

I flip my head over, running my fingers thru
hair while trying to hide my smile. I'm so grateful to
of the juvenile stuff and in the stage of love where you
totally, completely sure of everything. *Real love.*

Sara hands me a brush. "I don't know, Stace, you're over-
thinking it; she definitely likes you, you've known each other
for years, and she's never hit you up to be like, 'how's it going?'"

"Seriously, people don't just ask how you are unless they
like you," I add.

"Excellent point ladies, excellent points," Stacey says. "But
what do I do now?"

"Just answer her!" We say at the same time, laughing.

I change into a pair of leggings, a thermal long-sleeve and
hoodie, then I start slathering sun-block onto my face. The last
thing I need today is a sunburn.

"Sit here." Sara points to the floor and I do, handing her
back the brush. She brushes through once, making a part in the
center of my head and I close my eyes, enjoying the feeling of
her fingers working through my hair. There's nothing more
relaxing.

"I think I'm more nervous than I've ever been before." I
admit.

"Probably because Adam will be watching," Stacey says.

I nod. It would be too complicated to explain that I'm more
nervous about *Luke* watching. How can I tell them that it's how
I'm planning to finally win him over? I know it's ridiculous, but
I'm still convinced it's the only way.

"Adam told me he loved me last night," I say, almost
whispering.

Sara's fingers stop moving, and Stacey looks up. "Whoa."

"I know," I say, smiling again. "He said he wants to stay
together when he leaves for college."

"Ohmygod!" Stacey gasps.

The elastic snaps against Sara's fingers, but she says nothing. I wait for her to comment, but after a moment, she stands and looks at me. "This might be my best braid yet."

Nothing. I drop this bomb on her and... nothing?

It takes us less than five minutes to walk down to the base with my parents and Kyle, and as soon as we get out of the woods, I see the large crowd gathered at the bottom of the hill. Most of the *Cove Families* are already here, and I find myself surprised that this many people came to watch. *This is good. The more glory I receive, the more impressed he'll be.* I look around for the Stansons, but they aren't here yet.

Mrs. Walters comes over, chatting to Mom and me, and before I know what's happening, Dad is back and handing me my number. I look around once more, hoping to see Adam, but I can't find him. *Probably lost in the crowd.*

"Good luck, Babe, have fun," my parents say.

Kyle walks me to the lift, setting up my skis. "You've got this, Kid," he says with a quick hug and a tap on my helmet.

When I get off the lift, I ski over to the booth where the rest of the participants are waiting, taking the opportunity to check my phone to see if Adam's texted yet. *Still nothing.*

I look down at the crowd that's forming around the last flag. We're not terribly high up, but it's still too high to see anyone clearly; they're all just tiny specs, a big blurb of colored dots. Adam would definitely be there by now. *Waiting for me.*

"Brooke McGrath!" A lady in a florescent yellow coat calls. "You're up fourth in your group," she says, pointing to the line of girls forming in front of me. I take my spot, counting the others- ten of us altogether.

The horn blares, and the first skier takes off down the mountain, moving fast. I'd been too quick to assume this would be easy. I scope out the course - the flags are spread out in the first half of the hill, but toward the middle, the flags get closer together, marking the most difficult parts. I wish I'd prepared for this better.

The racer is almost at the end when one of her skis grazes a flag, making her lose balance and tumble forward. She's not seriously injured, but she's already lost too much time, there's no way she can win now.

The next girls go in succession, while I absently watch on, telling myself that there's no point in worrying now; whatever happens, happens. I go back to thinking about Adam. *Is he anxious to see me after last night? Is he talking me up to the others? Telling everyone that he loves me?*

"Move up, Hunny," the lady says, waving me forward.

I take a deep breath, moving the tips of my skis to the edge of the hill. *Focus.* The horn sounds, and I push off the mountain, picking up good speed as I pass the first flag. My mind goes clear, focusing only on the snow underneath my skis. I imagine myself as a machine - an old trick from my racing days - and as a ski machine, my only purpose is to get to the finish line as fast as possible. It helps my instincts take over. I push harder, make my skis tighter, and I skid around another flag. Then another. And another.

It doesn't even matter when I'm going through the most challenging part of the course; my body bends and leans in all the right ways, absorbing it all with ease. With one final thrust, I bend my knees, shifting my skis so that they are completely straight and push myself forward, bombing through the last flags and skidding to a stop.

The crowd erupts in cheers, and I pant as a race volunteer waves at me, ushering me over to the side.

"Great job," he says, beaming. If I wasn't sure on my time before, I am now; his face reveals it all.

"Thank you!" I say, still trying to catch my breath.

The whole Cove rushes over then, excited and eager to say

good job, and *that was amazing.* It's all very generous, the course wasn't *that* complicated, but I'm happy, anyway.

Kyle pulls me in for a hug. "Respect. You are an absolute ninja."

When the crowd breaks around me, I get out of my skis and finally ask Sara and Stacey the question that's been on my mind since we got here. "Where's Adam?"

Stacey looks around, like it only just occurred to her that he wasn't here. "I haven't seen him."

Jonathan walks over, high-fiving me. "Kudos, Bee, that was some serious shredding."

"Thanks," I say, pulling out my phone. Something must have happened; he's sick or fell back asleep or broke his arm. He wouldn't miss this. But I still have no new texts.

When Mom walks back over to give me a water, I ask if she's talked to June at all.

"No, why?"

"The Stansons aren't here."

She nods. "That *is* strange. I'll call June." She comes back a few minutes later, her face looking grim. "I just spoke with her. She said that Adam is at the rental."

I frown. "I don't get it."

"I don't know... she rushed me off the phone. I'm sure there's a reasonable explanation for all of this, try not to worry. Why don't you guys go hang out in the lodge until the winners are announced?"

But I am worried. How could he not show? What if he was regretting everything he said last night? What if he realized he didn't mean any of it?

I pass the time watching *YouTube* videos of prom proposals with the girls until a crowd forms at the bottom of the hill again. A woman gets on the microphone, making introductions before she starts announcing the winners.

She begins with age ten, working her way up by category. My stomach flips; it all feels like too much - the race, the pressure to win, Adam being MIA. I barely hear the names being called for second and third place. "And first place goes to Brooke McGrath with a time of thirty-three seconds. Folks, we have a new record in this category!"

The crowd cheers as I walk up to the DJ booth, but I'm barely aware of anything going on around me.

"Congratulations!" the announcer says, handing me a medal.

"Thank you so much!" I say, hardly believing it.

A photographer steps in front of us, snapping photos of the winners. I smile, feeling proud of myself, I just wish Adam *or* Luke had been there to see it.

While the rest of the Cove goes on the group ski, I decide to go back to the rental to nap. My nerves are shot from this morning. I know it's excitement from winning the race, but it's also the uneasiness I feel about Adam not being there. There has to be a perfectly reasonable explanation, but it doesn't stop my mind from being all over the place with worry.

A text comes in from Scarlett, congratulating me on the race. I don't even have enough energy to ask her how she knows already. Sara must have posted it. I silence my phone, knowing I'll be asleep the second I close my eyes.

I wake groggy, fighting the urge to roll over and go back to sleep, but someone is sitting at the bottom of the bed. *Am I dreaming?* I sit up, clearing my throat. "Adam?"

He stiffens before turning around to look at me. "Hey."

"Are you okay?" I ask.

He lets out a long sigh. "I missed your race."

I shrug, pull the blankets off, and crawl over to him. "What's going on?" I ask, laying my head on his shoulder.

"You won, didn't you?" He leans his head down so that it's resting on top of mine. It would be sweet if I didn't feel the weight of whatever is going on with him.

"Yeah."

"I'm really sorry, Bee."

"It's ok," I say. I can't say I'm disappointed about him not being there when something is so clearly wrong. "It's no big deal. Is everything okay? You're making me nervous."

He pulls back, searching my face before moving in for a kiss. His lips feel like a relief; whatever is going on with him, it isn't about me. "Will you lie with me?" he asks between kisses.

"I assume no one is here?" I ask.

He leans his face into my neck, breathing me in. "Everyone went on the group ski. They won't be back for a while."

I crawl back up to the top of the bed, opening the blanket for us. He kicks off his shoes and gets in, pulling me against his chest. I breathe him in, his perfect smell, trying to savor the feeling of lying next to him. This is a first for us; we've never had an opportunity to lie down in a bed together.

He exhales, then his breaths become rhythmic, rising and falling in a natural flow, making me feel sleepy again. He kisses the top of my head. "I love you, you know that, right?" he whispers.

I sink deeper into him, looking up at his face. "I love you, too," I say, but he's already drifting off to sleep.

My face is pressed against his stomach when I wake. I don't know what time it is, but the house is still quiet, so I know we're alone. I want to see his face, watch him sleep, but I don't want to wake him by moving around, so I slowly start peeling my body away from his until there's enough distance between us. I look up, but I'm too late; he's already looking at me. "Hey," he says, amused.

I lift myself up and stretch my arms above my head. "Hi."

"You're pretty cute when you sleep," he says, grabbing my hand and pulling me back down. "Except for the drooling. The drooling is gross."

I cover my face with my hands. "Please tell me I wasn't drooling."

He laughs. "I'm just kidding, but you were definitely snoring."

I push him away. "How long have you been awake?"

"Only a few minutes." His smiles fades. "Do you hate me?"

"What? No! How could you ask me that? Of course I don't hate you."

I reach up, brushing his cheek, trying to be reassuring.

"You killed it, though?"

I nod. "I killed it."

He laughs, tickling my stomach. "I knew you would. I really am sorry, though."

"Are you going to tell me what happened?"

He closes his eyes, groaning. "Something is going on with my parents."

I nod, and he goes on.

"They were fighting when I got back in last night, and then again this morning. And just before we were about to leave for the race earlier, my dad left, so my mom stormed out after him. Jenny and Jo were so upset about them fighting, and I just couldn't leave. I should have called you, but I was upset too. I think it's bad... they've never fought like this before. I'm sorry, I feel like such an asshole for not telling you what was going on."

"Don't worry about me," I say.

"They finally came back a few hours later, acting like none of it happened. It was the weirdest thing. Mom said that they had a disagreement and everything was fine, but I know she's lying... it's been strained between them lately."

"I'm sorry," I say, taking his hand. "That's stressful. If it makes you feel any better, my parents fight sometimes, too. Maybe it's just more heated than usual?"

He shrugs, clearly eager to talk about something else. "Was the crowd big?"

"Yeah, pretty good size."

He mopes. "I wish I saw."

"I'm sure someone recorded it."

He looks up at the ceiling, his mind clearly wandering back to his parents. I decide that he needs a distraction, something that will take his mind off of them. Without thinking too much about it, I hop on top of him, lifting my shirt off in the process. I wish I was wearing something sexier than a black sports bra, but he doesn't seem to mind.

His eyes practically pop out of his head.

"Is this okay?" I ask.

He opens his mouth to say something, but nothing comes out. I've surprised him into speechlessness. Adam Stanson is speechless. Because of me.

A sound comes from outside of the window, and he seems to register what it is before me because in the next moment, he's throwing us both off the bed, scrambling to right himself with a speed I would have thought was reserved for falcons. It's Mom's voice, I realize, or her laugh, more accurately. Now I understand his urgency.

He tosses me my shirt, helping me get it on. "Good?" he asks a moment later as he takes my hand and pulls me out of the bedroom. We stumble onto the couch, Adam snatching up the remote and flipping through the channels.

"No, no! Not this... this is *Fifty Shades of Grey*!" I shout.

"Oh, God." He scrambles, changing the channel until he finds a cooking show.

The front door opens a moment later. "Brooke?" Mom calls.

"In the TV room with Adam," I squeak.

My heart races, waiting for her to come in.

"Hey!" she says as Jimmy and Kyle run up behind her, making their way over to Adam.

"Yooo! You missed the most epic jumps!"

Adam sits up, clearing his throat. "We should go out again before dinner," he suggests, casually.

"I'm down!" Kyle says.

Put the artichoke hearts in a bowl and toss until just coated, the woman on the TV says brightly.

Mom walks over to us, her eyebrows touching. If I could have one time where she's absolutely clueless, I'd pick right now. *Oh god. Oh god. Oh god.*

"Brooke." She reaches down to touch my cheek. "Your face is *so* red, you must be wind burnt from the race!"

"Really? I hadn't noticed!" I squeak.

Adam makes a sound, something between a cough and laugh.

21

THE SMALL VILLAGE IS A LOCAL, DIVE RESTAURANT RIGHT in the center of town. It's homey, the kind of place that prides itself on tradition. It hasn't changed since the first time we ate here back when I was a kid. The lobby is littered with framed photos of local celebrities, and the only cups they've ever used are the tall red plastic ones with the Coca Cola logo on it. It wouldn't be a trip to Vermont if we didn't stop in for a basket of fried seafood and a piece of blueberry pie. Best in the state.

Sara grabs my hand as soon as I walk into our private banquet room. "Let's go to the bar," she says. "The bartender is making virgin daiquiris, and I'm feeling kinda crazy tonight!"

Stacey laughs.

I spot Adam sitting alone at one of the long tables. "I'm just going to go say hi to Adam really quick. I'll meet you over there."

Sara frowns, dropping my hand. "Just don't bail on us like you did last night."

I bite my tongue, failing to hide my annoyance. If she could just stop obsessing over me and Adam for three seconds, she'd realize something was going on with him. He spent the rest of the day in a bad mood, and I'm becoming more and more worried. "Will you just chill? Please? Even for five minutes?" I storm off, taking the seat next to him.

"I was just thinking about you." He wraps his arm around me.

"I'm always thinking about you," I say, then add, "I didn't see your jeep."

"I came with my parents."

I scan the room for them, finding June standing by the bar with the other moms while Luke is on the phone in the corner of the room. He's always on his phone.

"Any better?"

He shakes his head, still clearly upset. "They were fighting again before we got here."

I lean into him. "I'm sorry."

When Kyle, Jonathan and Jimmy walk over, Adam clears his throat, sitting up a little straighter in his seat.

"Who's dog died?" Jonathan asks, reaching out his fist to Adam. "Or is Bee talking about sewing again?"

Adam bumps it. "We're good."

They take a seat, just as Sara and Stacey walk back over carrying the daiquiris. Sara shoves one in front of me, and I get the sudden urge to dump it over her head. I'm so sick of her.

Sensing the tension, Stacey clears her throat. "So, what's the deal for after this?"

"Hm?" I say.

"The s'mores thing?"

With the race and the nap and trying to be there for Adam, I've completely forgotten about the gondola ride up to the summit. "Yup... I have to double-check the confirmation, but I think we leave at eight-forty-five."

"Sounds good."

When the boys start talking about basketball, I take out my phone. The appetizers come and go, and the conversations get louder around us. Some parents are getting tipsy, obvious from the high-pitched shrieks and belly laughs coming from their tables.

Adam puts on a brave face throughout dinner, laughing along to Jonathan's impersonations of Mr. Cummings and trying to seem interested in the conversation they're all having about their fantasy football league, but every once in a while, I catch him looking at his parents.

After dinner, Jonathan and Jimmy leave the table, looking strangely suspicious, but I can't focus on that for long because I notice Kyle's texting again. Finally, seeing my opportunity, I ask, "So, what's up, Kyle? Who do you keep texting?"

Adam looks up, too.

Kyle's about to say something when Jonathan rushes back over to the table.

"Yo, we just stole a bottle of vodka from the bartender. Let's go!"

Adam hesitates, glancing at his parents. "Yeah... let's go." He stands, pulling me up with him.

Sara looks over. "Whatever you guys are doing, we're doing!"

Jonathan pulls out his wallet and hands her some cash. "Go to the vending machine and get us some chasers. Let's all meet behind the restaurant in five."

"Ok, what's a chaser?" When his face falls, she adds, "Kidding.. but I'm keeping the change."

We sneak out of the room just as the blueberry pie is coming out.

When we step outside the restaurant, Adam lets out a breath. "It was suffocating in there."

"Yeah, forget about all that for now," I say, taking his hand.

The air is cold, and tiny snowflakes are starting to fall from the sky. Vermont already has a lot of snow on the ground, but this is the first it's snowed since we got here. We walk around the side of the building to the back where the boys are already waiting.

Stacey and Sara round the building a moment later, holding a *Sprite* in each hand.

"Finally!" Jonathan complains.

Sara gives him the finger.

We stand in a circle, our shoulders all touching. Jonathan takes the bottle of vodka from inside his coat and unscrews the top. "Can you open that Sprite for me?" he asks Stacey.

She nods, fumbling for a moment. In theory, we know what a chaser is; we've seen enough party movies to know that you need to "chase" down the hard liquor with something sweet, but we've never actually taken a shot of anything.

He sips the vodka, drinking the Sprite right after, passing the bottle to Jimmy who does the same. "Ahhh," he says, "it burns."

I swallow, my stomach feeling queasy. They aren't exactly selling me on this whole shot thing so far.

The bottle gets passed, and when it's Adam's turn, he surprises everyone by slugging it without a chaser. He's about to pass the bottle by me when I reach out to take it. "You sure?" he asks.

I nod. "Can I have that Sprite?"

"Ohhhh! Bee's about to get funny," Jonathan hollers.

Everyone laughs.

I touch the bottle to my lips, and an awful, chemical stench fills my nostrils. I wish someone had warned me to hold my breath. I tip it back, letting the liquid fill my mouth and then I realize, too late, that I've gulped too much. I pinch my eyes closed, too scared to swallow.

"Sip the Sprite," Adam says, motioning to the soda.

I swallow and it burns, but I take a huge sip of Sprite after, and it helps.

The boys laugh.

The bottle makes its way around the circle a few more times, and with each hand-off, it's like another layer of something is being stripped away from us. We're louder, more talkative, unconcerned that the temperature has dropped a few more degrees and the flakes are fatter now, falling harder.

The backdoor swings open just as Stacey's handing Sara the bottle. It's a server with a cigarette hanging out of her mouth. "Um... you guys shouldn't be back here," she says, eyeing the bottle.

"Sorry, sorry." We scramble, rushing away, running to the other side of the building and then further on to a parking lot behind an outlet store. It's closed for the night, and besides one randomly parked car, it's empty.

"Dudeeee. There's definitely people hooking up down there," Jonathan says, pointing to the car.

I suddenly feel tingly and start to laugh.

Adam smiles, slowly stepping toward me. "What's so funny, Bee?"

I step backward, making my way over to a wall. When my back is pressed against it, he hovers over me, a smile pulling at his lips. I feel a jolt of pride for having helped him out of his bad mood. This is exactly what he needed. "I feel a little funny," I admit. "I must be drunk."

His head tips back in a loud laugh. Then he leans down to kiss me; he tastes like the vodka and Sprite, but I find that I don't mind it as much coming from his mouth.

"Here we go again," Stacey yells, running by. Then I hear the distinct sound of a snowball hitting the back of Adam's coat.

He whips around, watching her run off. "It is *so* on!" he declares and everyone scatters, grabbing snow and forming balls with a familiar quickness.

We run up-and-down the parking lot, losing track of time, all the while inching closer to the parked car. It's obvious that people really are inside; music is playing faintly, and the windows are fogged.

Jimmy waves us over, bending down to start a huddle. "Operation sex-in-car, our mission is to infiltrate and scare."

We laugh, getting low and following him over.

He somersaults to the side of the car, Kyle inching behind him.

Jonathan, Stacey and Sara crawl to the other side while Adam and I hang back.

"I'm nervous," I say. "These poor people."

He laughs, pulling me against him as he lowers his head down to whisper into my ear. "Probably because you also like to hang out in the back seats of cars."

"Jeeps," I correct, and he laughs again.

Jimmy starts to count, his voice so low that only we can hear. "One, two, three."

They jump up and start banging on the windows.

The people inside the car scramble, moving all around the back seat. We all bust out laughing. Mission Complete.

"Let's go," I say, taking Adam's hand and pulling him in the direction of the restaurant. By now, our parents are definitely wondering where we are, and I need to get myself together before Mom figures out that I've been drinking.

But we don't get very far when Adam realizes that no one is following us.

I look back, and for some reason, everyone is still standing around the car, making no move to run away.

"What the hell?" I hear Kyle say, looking from Jonathan to Jimmy and then finally, to Adam.

"What is it?" Adam asks, dropping my hand and taking a few steps toward them.

I can tell that something is wrong from the expressions on their faces, but nothing is making sense. Why are they all looking at Adam?

Adam moves closer, but Kyle jumps forward, trying to push him away. "Let's just get out of here." Adam stops for half a second, considering, like maybe he knows he should listen to him. "Don't go over there, man!" Kyle pleads, but it's too late. Adam pushes by him and looks in the car.

I hold my breath.

It feels like a long time before he turns around again, his face ashen white, even in the darkness of night. It's the expression of someone who's just seen something very, very bad. But what? The door swings open, and Luke sticks his head out. For a moment, I'm filled with relief, until I see the woman in the back seat with him.

It takes me a second to process what I'm seeing. *Luke is in the back seat with a woman I don't recognize.*

"Adam?" someone shouts.

We all turn, bewildered, when we see June and Mom striding toward us.

Sara drops the bottle of vodka, and not even a coat of snow keeps it from shattering into a million pieces on the ground.

Adam snaps out of it, turning away from the car.

"What are you kids doing back here?" June asks, her arms folded across her chest. They aren't wearing coats, like they rushed out of the restaurant to find us. "What's wrong?"

"Mom, let's go back inside...we were just messing around," Adam says, trying to block her view.

But now she's intrigued and pushes by him.

She's confused at first until the truth of it smacks her square in the face. *Luke is in the back seat of a car with a woman,* I imagine her saying over and over again in her head.

I swear I see her world collapse. June, who is so composed and cheerful all the time looks like the life just got sucked out from under her. And it happened so fast.

"Mom?" Adam says, sounding so small.

Without another word, she turns around and walks away. My mom's voice echoes through the parking lot. "Everyone get back to the restaurant, NOW!"

I run over to Adam, grabbing his hand, but it takes me a full minute to summon the courage to look into his eyes. When I do, I see him, but he's not really there.

I'm woken by the sound of buzzing. It's my phone, I realize, somewhere in the couch. There's an infomercial playing on the TV; a woman with perfectly manicured finger nails is talking about essential oils with an enthusiasm that is hurting my head. *"Oh, that smells heavenly! To you folks at home, I'm not kidding ya, this stuff is amazing!"*

I stare at the screen, jumping when I realize I'm looking at the TV in my basement, *in Padstow.* The events of the last few hours come flooding back to me: the rush to get back to the rental, Mom whisking June into one of the bedrooms, the hushed sobs. It was a nightmare. Adam barely spoke a word to anyone until June came back out and announced that they were leaving. Mom said we were, too, so we all came back to our house while Dad stayed in Vermont to pack up the rental. We didn't get home until midnight.

I hear the muffled sound of a voice by the stairs, realizing that Adam isn't on the couch next to Kyle anymore.

I walk over, surprised to see him sitting on the bottom step... on the phone. When he sees me, he jumps, whispering *I gotta go* before hanging up.

My stomach sinks. "Who was that?"

He stands, still looking as miserably as before, only now there's are red rings around his eyes. Was he crying? "Just my mom checking in."

Relieved, I take his hand, guiding him back to the couch. "Are you all right?"

He nods. "I'm fine." Then he lies back down, tucking himself into the corner just like before.

Within seconds, his breathing is calm and even and I know he's asleep. My phone goes off again, and I drop to the floor, sticking my hands underneath the couch until I feel it. It lights up with a message from Sara. *Sara.* I'd completely forgotten about going up to the summit with them, not that she would have expected for me to go after what happened. Even she would understand that I need to be with him right now.

I pull the blanket over Adam's shoulders before sitting down again to go through my phone. I click on the home screen; thirty missed text messages, all from Sara. I scroll to the beginning, my heart picking up when I see that a few of the messages are long. Never a good sign.

The first ones are what I would have expected, lamenting about what happened, but they get increasingly hateful around eight-thirty when she starts to realize that we wouldn't be going up to the summit for s'mores. And by ten-thirty, she's downright mean. *Bad friend. Bitch. Only care about yourself.* The last one came in three minutes ago, saying that she doesn't want to be friends with me anymore.

My hands shake as I look down at the message. I wish I could say that I'm surprised, but the truth is, Sara has been awful to me since she found out about Adam. She's jealous, difficult, and needy, and I'm done with it, *done with her.* Before I can change my mind, I write back exactly what's been on my mind.

> *You're SO dramatic, Sara. For months, I've been taking all your BS but not anymore. YOU'RE WRONG. SO. WRONG. How can you not understand why I stayed with my bf when he literally CAUGHT HIS DAD CHEATING? If you think it was more important to stay with you and go up to the stupid summit for dumb s'mores, you're more delusional than I thought. I don't care anymore. I mean it. I'm done caring about what you think. If you were a good friend, you'd find a way to be happy for me but it's impossible because you're a HORRIBLE person. So, it's totally fine that you don't want to be friends with me because I DEFINITELY don't want to be friends with you!*

I wait, watching the text bubbles go off and on until there's nothing. For the first time in our friendship, I'm the one with the last word. I toss my phone, glancing at Adam again. Nothing else matters as long as I have him.

Dear Journal,

> *This has been the worst week in the history of all weeks. First, (obviously) the stuff with Adam's parents is level-5 HORRIBLE. All the details have been coming out about his year-long affair with his secretary at work (so typical). June's devastated, Adam's distant, and Jenny and Jo are confused about why their Daddy isn't sleeping at home right now. Adam is like a ghost of himself - he hasn't wanted to hang out all week. I mean*

I get it, the man he respects more than anyone has just totally ripped apart his family and I think if this was happening to me, I wouldn't want to hang out with anyone either. It's just that... I want to be there for him and it's hard considering he doesn't seem to want me to be. AND I have hardly seen him in school because the third quarter schedules just changed and I had to switch out of study hall to take a music class for more credits. So, I'm basically just following him around hoping that I can do something to make him feel better. It's not working. Then there's Sara and the fact that we aren't friends anymore. She's also been avoiding me - not that I care (that much) but you'd think she'd be cool for the sake of Rochelle and Stacey. But that's just not how she is. She always makes me feel like everything is my fault. What did I even do wrong? Get together my dream-boy? Make a new friend? She ALWAYS finds a way to make everything about her. I don't care anymore.

22

THE FIRST BLIZZARD OF THE SEASON ARRIVES, BRINGING IN three feet of snow, *a lot* even by New England standards. I was awake all night - not that I've been sleeping much lately - refreshing the Graves website until school was officially cancelled at five a.m. I fell back asleep until ten, only waking because my phone kept going off. Apparently, a plan had been hatched while I was out; Scarlett is coming to get me and we are going to Cherry Hill for her first ever day of sledding.

I climb into her passenger seat, gawking at her holographic one-piece snowsuit. "Ohmygod, you look so cool..." I snap my seat belt into place. "Do you mind if Kyle comes with us?"

"Of course!" she beams. "I feel like we're in the artic. I'm not a snow person."

Kyle gets into the back, nodding at her. "Scarlett."

She nods back. "Kyle."

I laugh. "Why so formal?" When neither of them respond, I go on, "Anyway, it's not like you moved here from Hawaii. It's snows in New York, too. How are you not used to it by now?"

She shrugs, pulling down the road. "It's different when you live in the city - we stay inside until it's safe to come out."

"Then why are we going to Cherry Hill?"

"Because I've never tried it before! Is Adam meeting us there?"

"Yeah." I look out the window, trying to ignore the butterflies in my stomach. I know he'll be there, but only because Kyle mentioned it at breakfast. I promptly picked up my phone Googling *how easy is it to fall out of love.* According to Dr. Steven Bridges, he is probably still in love with me, even if he hasn't said so all week.

Scarlett drives slowly through town, turning a five-minute drive into twenty-five, and Kyle basks in the opportunity to tease her. If I wasn't so lost in my own thoughts, I'd be happy that they are getting along.

When we finally pull onto the road that leads up to Cherry Hill, we find it's already packed, mostly with cars I recognize from school. "Looks like everyone decided to come today."

When I hop out, *Dev's Like a G6* is blasting from the top of the hill. *Poppin bottles in the ice, like a blizzard. When we drink we do it right, gettin' slizzard.*

Scarlett gawks. "Whoa, this is like *The Hangover* meets *Frosty the Snowman.* Is it always like this?" We look up, watching as Brett Andrews jumps onto a unicorn float and slides down the hill.

I shake my head, amazed. "Never."

When Adam sees us, he walks over. "Hey, snow bunny." He surprises me by leaning in for a kiss. "I missed you."

"Oh... hi. I missed you, too." He pulls back slightly, looking over my face, and I feel my first wave of relief. We're going to be okay.

Jonathan pushes by Adam, trying to get to Scarlett. "I don't know that we've officially met. I'm Jonathan."

She smiles. "Scarlett...Brooke's friend."

To the surprise of no one, he lifts her hand to his lips, planting a chaste kiss on top of her glove. "Why don't you ride down with me? Your sled is a little pathetic."

She chuckles. "Pathetic?"

He nods, motioning to his sled. "I call this guy here Hunter. He's like the *Aston Martin* of sleds. You'll feel like you're flying."

Kyle walks away, headed up the hill. "Come on, let's go."

"I think I'm more of a minivan kind of sledder, but thanks."

"Suit yourself, Stanson... let's move." He steps away, pointing to the top of the hill where a group of their friends are trying to get a canoe to balance on the slope.

"Do you mind if I go down with them?" he asks, already turning away.

Trying to hide my disappointment, I say, "Oh. Yeah. Totally cool. No problem."

He leans back over, kissing me quickly before following the boys up the hill. I pretend I'm fine because pretending has become somewhat of the norm these days. If I let myself feel my actual feelings, then I'd have to admit that it *feels* like something is wrong between us.

"Forget them," Scarlett says, seeing my disappointment. "Show me the ropes."

An hour later, after we've made our way up-and-down the hill about a dozen times, we sit in the snow and people watch. The hill started to group off by grade sometime after the canoe ride, and the seniors are now naturally dominating the top section with Adam at the center of it all. He hasn't looked back in my direction once. I know because I've hardly stopped watching him.

Scarlett starts talking about the fashion show, and I zone out, alternating my attention between Adam and the Cove

Girls. *How did things get to this point?* I wonder. A month ago, I was on top of the world. I had the Cove Girls, a new best friend, a fashion show to plan for, and an amazing boyfriend. But now, I have one friend and an absent boyfriend. Rochelle and Stacey made a point to say that they aren't choosing sides, but how can they not? In one way or another, they'd always be choosing, and right now, it feels like they chose Sara.

"How's your look coming?" she asks.

"What?"

She laughs, giving me a look like *are you serious?* "The fashion show?"

"Oh..." I blush. "I'm actually really behind." It's an understatement. I was supposed to have my jeans finished by now, but with everything going on, I'm not even close.

We're distracted from the conversation when Jonathan starts calling the boys down to help him with a pizza float that's big enough to fit half the basketball team.

A group of them come barreling down, each grabbing a corner to drag it back up. At the top, there's some discussion, then Adam, Kyle, Andrew and Jonathan position themselves on the float. But just before they're about to push off, Caroline and Dina hop on, Caroline neatly placing herself right behind Adam, with her legs dangling on either side of him.

I stiffen, waiting for him to move, but then they're sliding down the hill, her face up against his back. They hit a bump, and Jonathan falls, making the float spin until it finally stops at the bottom. Caroline rolls off first, falling onto the ground, and reaches her hands up for Adam to help.

I hold my breath, praying that he doesn't help her, but it's no use because he leans down, taking both of her hands and pulling her to stand. Then, instead of walking away, he stays, laughing with her about something I can almost guarantee is not funny.

I feel Scarlett's gaze on me. In fact, I think everyone on the hill turns to see my reaction.

"I hate her," I say, standing. This was intentional, calculated, and downright bitchy. Who makes that kind of move on someone else's boyfriend? "I've seen enough. Are you ready to go?"

Scarlett stands, gathering our sleds. "Yeah, let's get out of here. That was a cheap move, and she knows it."

"Yeah it was, but what's his excuse? Besides the fact that he was just chumming it up with his ex-girlfriend in front of the entire school, he hasn't spoken to me since we got here."

As if on cue, he runs up behind us, calling my name. "Hey! You leaving?"

Like you care.

"Yeah," I say, feeling angry at him for the first time in our relationship. It's not enough that he's practically ignored me all week, but now he's going to humiliate me with Caroline? *No.*

"Okay. Is everything all right?" he asks.

"Fine," I say, turning away.

He grabs my hand, pulling me back around. "Can I take you out to dinner tonight? Just us two?"

"Oh," I say, surprised. *Hold steady, Bee, don't let him off too easy.* "Um... I..." *Oh god, not his dimples.* "Yeah, that sounds nice."

"Cool. And look, I'm sorry that things have been weird between us lately. I promise, it will be better."

"Okay. I'll see you tonight then?"

He leans in, kissing me before running back over to the boys. All relationships go through ups and downs, right? Right?

"You look beautiful," Adam says when he picks me up for our date. I spent an inordinate amount of time getting ready; painting my nails and straightening my hair, I even caved and put on my red cashmere heart sweater that I've been saving for Valentine's Day. I wanted to knock him off his feet, remind him of what we had, show him that we are in love, even if the last week has proved otherwise.

"Thanks, so do you."

He smiles. "Burgers from Patty's?"

"Yes!"

The restaurant is busy, not even a snow storm keeping people inside their houses for long. Patty's is usually a mecca for teenagers on account of the inexpensive burgers and pinball machines, but tonight, it seems like we are surrounded by mostly young families. After a short wait, we're seated in one of the booths in the back.

"So, what kind of weird concoction are you getting this time?" he asks.

I laugh, looking over the menu. I prefer to experiment with my cheeseburger combinations while he always goes for *The Classic*, no surprises. "*The Bleu Burger* - bacon, lettuce, tomato, and blue cheese. Essentially, heaven in a bite."

"I thought your *Dream Cream* combo was heaven in a bite?"

"Okay ... fine. This is second best."

He makes a face, disagreeing. "Whatever you say."

We order our burgers, cheese fries, two cherry cokes, and a Strawbizzle, a strawberry shake to share.

"So," I say, hesitating, as I try to find a way to ease into the topic of his family. It feels like the right thing to bring up but more than that - I want him to feel like he can trust me. "How's it going at home?"

He shrugs, his expression turning to disdain, and I know at once that I messed up by asking. Of course he wouldn't want to talk about it - he was probably hoping to take his mind off of everything.

He looks relieved when the cheese fries get dropped off. He digs in right away, acting like he's forgotten about my question. "Fries are good tonight."

I nod, taking one from the middle of the stack, saturated with that fake, yellow nacho cheese that tastes so good. *Let's try this again.* "What's everyone up to tonight?"

"Jesse Morgan is having a party."

"Oh yeah? Do you want to go?" I ask, holding my breath. We've been to exactly one party together, and we left early because we both agreed that it was more fun to watch a movie, alone.

"Maybe."

I let out a breath, not showing my disappointment. Maybe a party would be a good distraction for him. *For us.*

Our waitress, a girl I recognize as being a senior from last year sets down our burgers. "Do you need anything else, Hun?" she asks Adam, practically swooning. It's strange, I think, when anyone under the age of sixty-five uses the word "hun" - it's like it should be reserved only for grandmas.

"I'm good, thanks," he says, looking at me.

"Me, too."

Once she's gone, I know what to say to make him smile. "Do people flirt with you a lot?"

He chokes on his burger. "What?"

"Didn't you notice the way that girl just looked at you when she dropped off our food? She was totally gawking!"

"No," he says, scanning the restaurant, "I didn't notice. How could I notice anyone else when I'm with the girl of my dreams right now?"

I blush, deliriously happy with that level of a compliment. You don't call someone your dream girl if you're trying to pull away. I toss a fry at him, trying to play it cool. "Oh, what a line! You're just trying to change the subject."

He laughs, taking a bite of his burger. "Maybe."

"But seriously, I'm just curious, does it happen a lot?"

He shrugs, trying to ignore the question. "Do people flirt with *you?*"

"No, never," I say firmly.

He laughs. "That's not true! You're just oblivious to all the attention you get."

"No way, I'd know."

"Bee, you have *no* idea, you just don't know when someone's flirting."

"I knew when Tucker was flirting," I tease. And then it's his turn to throw a fry at me. He finishes his burger, signaling to mine, and I push my plate across the table for him. "Go ahead, but this makes you a weirdo too."

"If you're a bird, I'm a bird."

"Oh, this is just too rich. Now he's quoting *The Notebook?*"

He takes a bite, nodding. "Wow, pretty good. Anyway, you were a hot topic in the locker room last year. I heard you got asked out by Frankie Philips *and* Brandon Detmier."

I raise my eyebrows in surprise. "Locker room talk?"

"You think girls are the only ones who gossip? The boy's locker room is like a cesspool of information - I wouldn't be surprised if *Little Lucy* was actually like," he taps his face, thinking, "James Moroney."

I throw my head back with a laugh. "That *might* be true, but I cannot believe what you just managed to do here."

"What?"

"Completely ignore my original question."

He laughs, holding out his hands in defense. "Ok listen, sure, sometimes people flirt with me, but I revert back to my original statement - I'm not really paying attention because I'm already with the person I want."

"Such a charmer," I say because that's exactly how I feel: *charmed*. "What?"

"Nothing." He dips his finger into the milkshake and pokes my nose.

"You did not just do that," I say as it starts to drip down onto my lips.

He leans over the table, and in one fell swoop, he licks it off.

I shriek, wiping my nose as he sits back down. "Ohmygod. You just licked my nose!"

"You want me to do it again?"

"Yes," I blurt.

Our gazes lock, and I think we have the same realization - it's been too long since we kissed.

"Do you want to go back to your house and watch a movie?" he asks.

"I thought you wanted to go to the party?"

He shakes his head. "Nah, that will be lame... let's go watch that new Adam Sandler flick on Netflix."

"My parents are at a dinner party. They won't be back until late."

"You should have started with that," he says, scanning the restaurant for our waitress. He goes to say something but stops short, his face falling.

I follow his gaze, panicked when I see that Caroline and Dina are headed straight for our table. I don't have a chance to say anything before they're right in front of us, smiling at him.

"Hey, you," Caroline says.

For a moment, he's stunned into silence, his eyes just fixed on hers. Her calmness is unnerving; it's as if she's not aware that it's weird to come up to us like this.

"Hey," he says finally, clearing his throat. "What's up?"

"Sorry I didn't get a chance to call you back," she says, batting her eyelashes. "I was exhausted after Cherry Hill and decided to take a nap."

"Yeah, um," he looks at me, "no worries."

She goes on talking, but I find myself zoned out, focusing only on the way he's watching her, the way he's so focused on every word that's coming out of her mouth, and suddenly, it hits me. He's not interested, *he's nervous*, unsure of where this conversation is going. But why would he be worried unless he has something to hide?

"Anyway, we've got to go, but I'll call you later," she says. "I promise." She puts her hand on his shoulder as she walks by. It's just a subtle touch, but it speaks volumes of comfort, familiarity, and years of history together.

When they're gone, I stand. "I have to go to the bathroom," I say, wanting to be far away.

He grabs my hand. "Hey, that was intentional. I can explain."

I snatch my hand back, running to the bathroom and locking myself into a stall. *How is this happening right now? Why did I just sit there while she made me look like an idiot, again? Why was he looking at her like that?* I pull out my phone, hovering over Sara's name because she's the only one who would know what to do right now. But just as I'm about to send the call, the door swings open, and Caroline steps into the bathroom, alone.

Without thinking I push the door open, startling her. "What the hell was that all about?" I ask. She steps back, faltering. "What? Not so confident when you don't have one of your minions with you?"

I wait for her to respond, but she stands there, stunned. "You came over tonight to try to make me look like an idiot, right? But what you don't understand is that you're the one who looks desperate. Just let him go."

She regains her composure then. "Your make-up is smudged."

"Trust me, that's the last thing I care about right now."

"You should," she interrupts. "Because you're a hot mess." She steps away to wash her hands, looking at me through the mirror. "I'll admit, you just threw me off. I didn't think you had the guts to confront me, but you've obviously gained a little confidence since stealing Adam away. That's good. You'll need that confidence in the coming weeks once everyone figures out what kind of girl you are."

What does that even mean?

"This game you're playing is pointless."

She laughs, turning to face me. "That's what *I* thought, too. But then he called me after he found his dad cheating. He was *so* upset. I guess he just needed to talk to someone that knows him the best, you know? Someone he could really trust."

My mind flashes to him sitting on my basement stairs. He said he was talking to his mom. Did he lie? Did he really call her?

"You must have known that you were only temporary, right?"

"What are you talking about?"

"You and Adam. You didn't really think that this little thing between you two would last, did you? You're a rebound, Bee. Everyone has them. You were always just a distraction, he told me himself."

I step away, sucking in my breath. The pressure is building behind my eyes, but I won't let her see me cry. *Don't cry. Don't cry. Don't cry.*

She twists her face into what can only be described as fake sympathy. "Oh, you poor thing, you totally thought it was serious. Here, let me get you a paper towel. You look like you're going to cry."

"Why can't you let him go?"

"Oh, I have let him go. This isn't about him anymore, it's about you. You humiliated me, and I won't stop until he's broken up with you, too. Then maybe you'll know how it feels to have someone meddle in your relationship."

I pull open the door and run out of the restaurant, not stopping until I'm out front, unable to quiet my brain. *Is she telling the truth? Am I a rebound? I can't be! He told me he loved me!"*

"Hey," Adam walks up, "are you all right?"

"I just need to get home," I say, walking to his car.

He follows me silently, neither of us speaking until we pull up outside of my house.

"That sounded worse than it actually is," he says.

"Remember when I found you sitting on the stairs the night we came home from Vermont? You said it was your mom checking in on you, but was that really Caroline?"

He nods, slowly. "Ye, yes."

"Adam!" I yell, startling him. "You lied to me?"

"Yeah, but it's not what you think... I need to explain. I-"

I interrupt him. "Are you kidding me right now? She just made me look like an absolute idiot back there! Am I just a rebound for you?"

"What! *No*, listen, she did that because she's jealous of you."

A loud, guttural sound barks out of my mouth. "And now you're defending her? I have to get out of here!" I pull on the handle but he reaches for me. "Wait. Just let me explain."

"How could you call *her* to vent about what happened with your dad? You haven't even talked to *me* about it!"

"I didn't call her... she found out about it from someone and called *me*."

"How often do you guys talk on the phone?"

"Not often." He looks up at me and seeing my expression, he caves. "I don't know, a couple times a week."

I gasp, turning way. I'm disappointed, angry, confused. I want to scream, I want to cry.

"I told you before - sometimes she's sad, and I just feel bad. Especially because of the way we ended. I mean, I cheated on her, Bee. I didn't want it to end that way."

"Oh, so this is my fault?"

"No... it's not your fault. I've just had a hard time cutting her off. I don't know how to explain it. She's not a bad person... her feelings are just hurt."

I laugh, wiping away the tears that have started falling against my will. Saying Caroline isn't a bad person is like saying Christmas is in July. It's just not true. I feel so stupid, so naive, and I hate that he's defending her. "Did it ever occur to you that it might bother me? That I might not want you comforting your ex-girlfriend?"

He tries to touch my shoulder, but I shrug him off. "You always seemed so cool about everything. Even when Caroline was straight-up bitchy, you didn't seem to care. I didn't think it mattered that much."

I think of all the times over the last few months, few years, that Caroline's made me want to crawl under a rock. I was so determined to keep Adam in the dark about my feelings, about how much it bothered me. It's almost laughable how much that backfired.

"She's a horrible person, Adam. You have no idea how awful she's been to me."

He's quiet for a while. "She's not horrible, Bee, she's upset. There's a difference."

So I tell him the truth, and he throws it back in my face. "It's so messed up that you're defending her."

My phone goes off. *Stacey.* I let it go to voicemail, but as soon as I do, a text comes through. *You need to call me right now.* I'm about to shut it down completely when she sends the one emoji that stops me in my tracks: the green pepper. I know right away that it's a non-bloody emergency. It's bad though - one step down from death bad.

"I'll be right back." I step out before he can respond. Whatever it is, it's bad. She'd never use the green pepper unnecessarily; we swore an oath to each other to use our language with honor.

She answers on the first ring. "Where are you?"

"Home, why? What's going on?"

"Have you been on *Little Lucy* yet?"

My stomach drops to my feet, the feeling of dread taking over. "No... why?"

She pauses, whispering to someone in the background. "Okay, Bee, listen, don't freak out."

"What is it?"

"There's a new post on *Little Lucy,* and it's about you and Adam, about what happened at Musters on Halloween night."

"What?" I say, confused. "What do you mean?"

"It's a letter... written by Caroline."

My body slides to the ground, and I thrust my head between my knees, forcing myself to take a deep breath. "What does it say?"

She hesitates. "It's about your first kiss... at Musters."

My heart beats against my chest. "I don't get it, no one knew. It was me, Adam, Kyle and Sara." *Sara.* "Ohmygod, did Sara do this?"

Another pause. "It was an accident. She told Nina and Nina told Caroline."

I'm quiet.

"Bee? She feels really bad. This all got out of hand."

"I have to go." I hang up, pulling open Little Lucy.

Dear Graves Student Body,

I have decided that I am going to resign as your trusted President. It has been the greatest of privileges to serve you - I am honored and deeply humbled that you trusted me with such a task for the last year and a half. I must admit - it pains me deeply, but I have to prioritize my mental health. As you all know, my recent break-up has been devastating. I pride myself on being strong, but I've recently uncovered the truth about Adam's unfaithfulness on the night of Halloween at Muster's. Adam and Brooke McGrath were caught kissing and the truth, I've learned, is that they were secretly hooking up for months before he broke up with me. I'm deeply hurt. I have lost all faith in humanity and I need time to recover. Unfortunately, because my resignation is coming so late in the year, I will have to cancel our senior camping trip, which cannot go on without me because I used my father's connection to organize it all. I know how much you were all looking forward to it but my nerves, you must understand, are too shot. Thank you for understanding.

Caroline Conlon

I read it three times before I realize that Adam is standing next to me.

"What is it?" he asks.

"Do you still think she's a good person?" I hand him my phone, watching as confusion takes over his features. At the very least, I know he's not in on it. You can't fake this kind of shock.

"I don't know what to say - I don't know how she found out."

"Sara."

He nods. "My dad is going to kill me... with everything going on at home, he's going to be super disappointed about this."

I snap. "Are you serious right now?"

He looks up, confused. "What?"

"You're worried about *your* dad? About how your stupid dad is going to take this? What about the fact that there is a very good chance the entire school is going to come for me on Monday?"

"That's not what I meant... I *am* worried about you, too, but this stuff with my parents is bigger than this." He holds up my phone.

"And whose fault is that? Adam - *he's* the one that's jeopardized your family's precious reputation! Not me! Not you! *Him!*"

He shakes his head. "You still don't get it... he said you wouldn't understand."

I suck in my breath, shocked. There, the proof that Luke doesn't approve of me. "Still don't understand what?"

He steps away, shaking his head.

"Say it!" I scream.

"That you're not serious enough to understand how important image is to my future." He could have slapped me across the face, and those words still would have hurt more.

"Is this why you've been ignoring me all week? Why you've been putting distance between us since we got back from Vermont? Because your dad has been telling you that we're not right for each other?"

When he says nothing, I go on. "If you loved me like you said, you'd lean on me, you'd confide in me about how you've been feeling, but you're pulling away, I can feel it. What did I do wrong? You trust Caroline but not me?"

"I didn't tell Caroline anything, you're wrong about that!"

"But not about your dad?"

He looks down at his hands. "Bee, what do you want me to say? Everything is getting messed up. I should go, I really need to go." He moves to go back to his car, but I step in front of him. "No! Tell me what's going on!"

He falters, stopping to meet my eyes. He's right in front of me, but he feels so far away. "I don't know... I don't know. There just isn't much of a point to this anymore, is there? I'll be at Villanova next year, and you'll be here. We'll never see each other and probably won't even talk much. I don't need any more distractions while I focus on school and basketball. I need to do the right thing, now more than ever." Spoken right from Luke's mouth.

I shake my head. "Ohmygod, Adam! Listen to yourself! This isn't you talking, it's *him*! You're doing what *he* wants. What about what you said to me? You told me that you loved me, that we have to stay together, no matter how far apart we are." I pause. "I could respect your decision so much more if I knew it was what you wanted, but instead, you're going to do everything he wants because you're too much of a coward to say no."

He scowls, his face twisting in anger. "You have no idea

what I want!" he yells. "I don't care if you think I'm a coward, I know I have the right intentions. It's not just about him, it's about doing the right thing."

"For who?"

"For everyone!" He shouts, then quieter, he mutters, "He's my *dad*, Bee. There's too much pressure, I'm under too my pressure. I don't want to let him down."

"Even though he doesn't care if he's letting you down?" *Has he already forgotten that we just caught him cheating?*

He's quiet for a long minute. "You don't know him." And then he's gone.

23

On Monday morning, I'm trying to come up with an excuse to skip school when Kyle knocks on my door. I've spent the whole weekend in isolation; holding out hope that I'd hear from Adam which, of course, never happened. So I locked myself away from the world and wallowed, alone in my bedroom. I heard the whispers outside my door. Naturally, Mom and Dad were worried, but Kyle must have eventually told them what was going on because they stopped trying to come in. I can't face them yet, can't face anyone, really. I want to hide away until it's time to leave for college.

"You ok, kid?" he asks, stepping in and sitting down next to me on the bed.

For a moment, I try to pretend like I'm okay, but the pity in his eyes is enough to make fresh tears fall down my cheeks. I spent the last two days alternating between crying and pacing, trying to decide whether things are bad or really, really bad. I know what's in store for me today because I saw it happen to Harlow Frank. It was brilliant, actually - the way Caroline pinned the camping trip being cancelled on me. Maybe people wouldn't have cared about their break-up, but she made it seem like the world is ending - and it's my fault.

"My life is over, Kyle!"

"I know it sucks but look at me."

I lift my eyes to meet his, succumbing to more tears.

"It will blow over, sooner than you even realize. Something will come up like it always does, and you'll be old news."

"It's true, though," I say, feeling ashamed. I can't even claim I'm the victim of fake rumors because some of it is true. We did kiss when he was still with her.

"It doesn't matter... it's still only going to be interesting for a little while. Right now, just focus on appearing like it doesn't bother you. If you walk into school today and play the part of the victim, they'll eat you alive. You have to rise above it, even if it's killing you. If they think you don't care, it loses its effect and the story goes away sooner." He hands me a tissue. "You can cry more when you get home, but for now, you have to buck up."

"What if I take a leave of absence? I can claim to have mono and be out for the next month."

He shakes his head. "No. You can face anything, Bee, especially some nonsense that was posted on *Little Lucy*."

"What if Caroline wants to fight me?"

He laughs. "Then I give you permission to knock her square out."

I manage a smile. "I wish this day was already over."

He checks his phone. "In about eight hours, the worst of it will be behind you."

"Ok..." I say, standing, looking at myself in the mirror. I don't know how it's possible to be both bloated and sunken in, but I guess that's what happens when your life is falling apart. "What am I supposed to do about this?"

He laughs out loud. "I'd start by plunging your face into a bucket of ice water."

Kyle's pep-talk gets me out of the house, but I still spend most of the morning with my head down. I'm expecting an army of angry teenagers to throw tomatoes at my face, but by third period, I've only received a handful of dirty looks. Scarlett tells me another post went live about Adam, comparing him to his dad, but I refuse to read it. It makes me feel uneasy.

When the first lunch bell rings, I rush to the bathroom, dreading the cafeteria. If anything is going to happen, it will be there, with all the grades massed together. I could chicken out, hide out in here for the rest of the year, but Kyle's speech won't stop ringing in my ears. *You can do anything.*

A couple deep breaths later, I'm hovering outside the lunch room doors, realizing too late that it was a mistake to linger in the bathroom. Now I'd have to walk in alone, when everyone else is already seated.

Here goes nothing.

The door bangs closed behind me, inviting everyone to look up, and I'm paralyzed by their stares. I feel like I'm stepping out onto a stage, starring in a show that I've forgotten all the lines for. My mouth goes dry, and my heart starts thudding too fast against my chest; I want to be strong, but I feel like I'm an inch tall. I can't do this. I'm not cut out for this kind of thing. I'm about to turn around, but then I see the Cove Girls rushing toward me.

"You ready?" Rochelle asks, taking my hand while Stacey and Sara cram into the other side of me. If I weren't in such a state of shock, I'd burst into tears from the relief; I need them, now more than I ever have before.

It's by pure bad luck that Caroline and Adam are both seated at the seniors' table, thankfully on opposite ends. But I can't think about that, not now, when the entire lunch room is staring at me. I force myself to focus on getting to the table. *Five steps, then three, then one.*

"She's back," Stacey says once we're seated. "That wasn't *so* horrible."

The volume level picks up around us, and I settle into my seat, letting out a long breath. "Was everyone watching?"

Rochelle nods. "Um, yeah, the next time you're the focus of a controversial *Little Lucy* post, I highly recommend you not entering the lunch room alone. Where have you been for the last forty-eight hours? We've been trying to call you!"

"I shut my phone off, but thanks for being there for me today," I say, letting my eyes scan past Rochelle and Stacey, purposely avoiding Sara. I look down at my hands, my heart still beating hard against my chest. I'm still so mad at her. Just because she showed up for me just now doesn't excuse what she did or how she's treated me these last few months.

Sara pushes a paper lined sandwich into my line of vision.

When I look up, her eyes are glossy. "It's peanut butter and fluff." The tears start falling from her eyes. "I'm really sorry, Bee."

I struggle to find words. It's never easy to see one of your friends cry, but I'm not the one who made a mistake.

"Ok so..." Stacey says, saving me. "We called a 911 Cove Girls Session yesterday." The last one we had was in the seventh grade after Rochelle got borderline addicted to stealing gum from the corner store. We established these meetings with the intention of providing brutal honesty when one of us was doing something wrong.

When I don't say anything, Rochelle clears her throat. "We want you to know that we," she points from her to Stacey, "are one hundred percent not okay with how Sara's been acting. We spent the better part of an hour reminding her that embedded in the doctrine of our Cove Girls friendships, this kind of behavior is bad enough to deem a forced removal."

I look up then, my eyes raking over the three of them, settling on Sara. "A forced removal?"

Sara nods, wiping away more tears. "I've been horrible. I know it now. I've just been so jealous. Of you and Adam. Of you and Scarlett. I let it eat away at me. I told Nina your secret and then she told Caroline. It's all my fault," she sobs, "all of it."

Quiet settles over the table. I still don't know what to say. While I'm relieved to hear Sara's apology, my life still feels like it's been turned upside down.

Sara hands me her phone, already open to the notes app. When I look confused, she explains. "It's a draft of the letter I've written to *Little Lucy* explaining my part in all of this. I know it doesn't excuse everything, but at the very least, everyone will understand that Caroline isn't some victim. They'll know that she was trying to bring you down for months. The underground ring was real. It wasn't as dramatic as that, but she's been totally digging around, trying to find something to smear your name." She chokes up again. "She obviously couldn't find anything... until I told Nina your secret."

I scan over the letter and in typical Sara fashion, it's cut-throat, only this time, it's directed at herself. It's dramatic enough that even I'm not thinking about the Halloween kiss anymore.

"I'm sorry, Bee. I don't expect you to forgive me, but I really am sorry. I'll never let my jealousy stand in the way of your happiness again."

I take a deep breath, thinking. Despite everything, I want to forgive her. The last few months have been so uncharacteristic of her and her usual loyalty, and I know deep down that she is sorry. For the first time in months, it feels like a weight has been lifted from my shoulders. "I forgive you."

More tears fall from her eyes as she comes around the table to give me a hug. "Cove Girls for life?" she whispers.

I smile. "For life."

After school, I'm standing outside with Scarlett, reading the latest Little Lucy post about Tucker and Jamie Elson hooking up in the art studio. Between that and Sara's letter, my kiss with Adam seems like old news.

"Sara came up to me just now and apologized," she says, looking somewhat stunned. "She invited me to her house tomorrow after school with you guys."

I look up from my phone, smiling. "I think she's making the rounds. She apologized to me too."

"You okay?" she asks, sensing my uneasiness.

"I'm all right, but I haven't talked to Adam. I don't know where things stand between us. I was hoping he'd find me today, but he's barely looked at me."

"Bee."

"I didn't expect for things to be perfect right away, but now that everyone knows about the kiss, I just feel like-"

"Bee... listen, don't freak out, but Adam is looking at you. Right now."

I look up, my eyes scanning the parking lot until they find him, leaning up against his jeep. "Ok," I whisper, "what should I do?"

She pulls me in for a hug. "Just go talk to him and then call me the minute you're done."

I nod, making my way over to him. Part of me wants to run and jump into his arms, tell him that I love him and that I never want to fight again, but I force myself to play it cool, trying not to show any emotion. This conversation is the last obstacle I need to get through in order for my life to feel normal again. I'll tell him the truth, that it's okay that we're not perfect. *Thank-you, Dr. Steven Bridges.*

"Hey," He moves forward to give me a hug.

I wrap my arms around him, breathing in his smells. I could melt into him, that's how safe I finally feel. *We're going to be okay.*

He pulls back too soon, and now that we're close, I see how tired he is. Another flicker of hope runs through me, knowing he's had a difficult few days, too.

"You all right?" he asks. "After what happened at lunch?"

I nod. "I'm fine." All said and done, it wasn't too bad at all. I'd definitely built it up in my head.

"Can I drive you home?"

Once we're in his car, he takes a deep breath and pulls out, not saying anything for a few minutes while we wait in traffic. I look out the window, trying to distract myself by watching a group of freshmen boys play with a remote-controlled car.

"Look, I owe you an apology," he says finally. "I don't even know what to say, I'm just sorry about it all. All of my parents' stuff has really gotten to me, and I guess I just sort of shut down." He runs a hand through his hair. "And I'm sorry about Caroline. Obviously, I was wrong about her."

I'm relieved when he turns down Summit Street because it means he's taking the long way home.

"There was nothing going on between me and Caroline while we were together. I guess I was feeling guilty about the cheating thing, that's probably why I kept talking to her. I don't know... as much as I wanted that relationship to be over, I didn't want it to end *that* way, so I was just dealing with it the best way I knew how."

Relieved, I reach over and grab his hand. "I'm sorry, too."

He flinches, surprised by my touch, but instead of

welcoming me in, he pulls away. "You don't have anything to be sorry for." He turns down another road.

"I'm sorry I called you out about the stuff with your dad. I know it's complicated."

"I get it," he says, cutting me off. "Thanks."

We fall back into an awkward silence, and I get this overwhelming feeling that something is wrong, that this conversation is headed in a direction I'm not prepared for.

"How's your family?" I ask, needing to break the silence. The not knowing is the worst part. But at the same time, I'm trying to draw it out, make it last.

He sighs. "It's just a mess."

Without thinking, I reach back over and place my hand on his shoulder, trying to be reassuring, but he tenses up again.

I look out the window. "I'm beginning to think this conversation isn't going the way I thought it would."

As if he's grateful for the opening, he says, "I don't want to hurt you, Bee."

My stomach flips, my heart picking up a beat. "You won't." My voice is unsteady, shaky.

"The thing is...I will, I know I will... I'll be gone next year, and I'll find a way to mess it up, and I just don't want to hurt you. I couldn't stand it if I hurt you." Realization hits me hard. It feels like the wind gets knocked right out of me - he's trying to break up with me right now. A million things rush into my head; *can I stop it? Can I say no? Do I have a choice? Can I change his mind?*

Before I have time to make sense of anything, he's pulling up in front of my house. In my daze, I didn't even realize what direction he was headed in. I want to shout, *No! Don't do this!* But I can't find my words.

I look out the window, only catching every other word now, *college,* and *pointless,* and *saving ourselves the trouble.* Bon

Iver's *Skinny Love* starts to play and I think, *this song will always remind me of this moment.* I never imagined us ending. Despite everything, I thought this was forever.

I snap of out my daze, suddenly ready to fight for us. "No... we're different. *I'm* different, you said that. What happened? What changed? You were so sure of us before, why aren't you now?"

"I don't know, Bee.... I've had more time to think it all through. This was never a good idea, we both knew that. In the end, someone was always going to get hurt, and I couldn't bare it if we became more attached to each other and then I hurt you more."

"More attached than this? We love each other! We're in love!"

His expression is pained, but there's something else there, too: a desperation I've never seen in him before. It's not just that his mind is set - he wants me to believe it, too. He *needs* to convince me that this is the right thing to do. "I don't want to hurt you."

I scoff. "You can't say you don't want to hurt me as you're hurting me, Adam, that's not how this works."

He puts the jeep in park, and I finally look him in the eyes. "You're wrong. You're making a mistake."

He looks at me miserably. "I'm trying to do the right thing."

"You told me you loved me, you said everything makes more sense when we're together. You said those things to me. If you've changed your mind, just say it." My voice cracks. "Have you changed your mind?"

"It's not that simple, Brooke."

The sound of my name feels like a knife to the heart. Already, he's distancing himself from me. "Don't!" I yell. "Do not say my name right now."

He jumps, surprised, and then I start crying, tears pouring

down my face. He tries to take my hand, but I shove him away. "You're ruining everything," I sob.

"I'm protecting you," he whispers. "You'll see, this will be better for you in the end."

I cackle through my tears. "How? How will this be better for me?"

When my head starts throbbing, I'm reminded of the last time I felt this sad, when I was thirteen and we had to put our golden retriever, Nikki, down. Adam was there that morning. My parents brought her to the vet, leaving the three of us home alone, but Kyle stormed up to his room so it was just me and Adam. He followed me around until I finally cracked and started crying. He came to me, wrapping his arms around me and holding tight while I sobbed into his chest. He smelled like fabric softener. I'd forgotten about it until now.

I bury my face in my hands. "I don't need your protection, I just want to be with you. I've always wanted to be with you."

We lock eyes, and I see that he's crying now, too.

I study his face. I took the closeness for granted, I realize it now that it's not mine any more. I would have cherished it more if I'd known I wouldn't have it forever.

Before I lose my nerve, I lean over and put my lips on his. He doesn't do anything at first, but after a moment, he's kissing me back.

Somewhere in the back of my mind, I'm urging myself to remember every single sensation: the taste of it, the smells, the pressure of our faces against each other. I touch the back of his neck, pulling him closer, wanting it to last forever. I don't know how long we sit there, but at some point, his tears start to mix with mine. *This is our last kiss.* The realization makes me physically sick. How often do people know when their lips are touching for the last time?

At some point, we pull apart, just slightly, with our foreheads still pressed together. It's just silence, but I guess there's nothing left to say. I sit up, my hand lingering on the handle, giving him one last chance to change his mind, but he keeps his gaze down at his hands.

"I love you," I choke, and then I step out into a new world.

Dear Journal,

Four weeks. It's been four weeks since we broke up. I don't even know where the time went... it's like I've been stuck in the Upside Down; living, not living... it hasn't even mattered, not to me anyway. I've been this broken, empty version of myself that I didn't even know existed, like I left myself behind when I stepped out of his jeep and away from him for the last time. I didn't even believe it was happening at first but when it hit me, I stopped caring about everything - family, friends, sewing, school, food. I wanted to stay in my bed and sleep forever but then there was my parents and Kyle and the Cove Girls and Scarlett who were here and despite their being totally freaked out, they didn't push me and it helped. So, here I am, four weeks later and I've decided to write it all down and get on with my life because that's all I can do now. I'm sad and pissed-off and not at all happy. I wish I could look back on what we had and be grateful for the time we did share but I'm not. I wish it never happened. Mom says that anger is a normal feeling during grief which seems ridiculous because no one died but it's real, these feelings I have are more real to me than anything else right now. I'm just so mad. I'm mad at myself and I'm mad at him and I'm mad at love. Why is love even a thing? Why should it exist if it can be taken away? What's the point? My heart actually feels broken and that's not me being dramatic. It literally hurts inside my chest. You know what else makes me mad? He hasn't tried to get in touch with me, not even one time. He talked to Caroline (behind my back) the entire time we were together because he wanted to be there for her but when it came to me, he dropped me like I was nothing. It's because he lied, he lied about it all. He never loved me, you don't do this to people you love and I was just so stupid, believing him. I'm mad about life too. I see all these people carrying on with their lives. There's still school and tests and other things that feel totally unnecessary now. I skipped the sophomore semi. The Cove Girls already had dates and I couldn't bear to be their loser-ish plus one. I thought maybe I would catch up on my Working Woman project but then I just moped around having fomo and refreshed my Instagram stories a hundred million times. Then when I realized just how behind I was, I told Scarlett I was going to drop out of the fashion show. But when I showed up to class a few days later, they surprised me by pooling together their time to help ME. I burst into tears, right there in the middle of class. Then everyone came up and gave me in a group hug. Even Mrs. Holmes. So, I decided I'm going to snap out of it. If not for my sake, then for the sake of the people who really care about me.

24

I'm sitting in the kitchen, eating a bowl of oatmeal with cinnamon-sugared apples when Kyle walks in acting strangely, acting *nervous*. Kyle, by definition, is not the kind of person who gets nervous. He's too sure of himself for that kind of thing, so anytime he's nervous, I become nervous, too.

He peeks inside my bowl, then goes around the kitchen island to scoop some for himself. *Bad sign, he hates oatmeal.* "I need to talk to you about something."

I suck in my breath, forcing the oatmeal into the back of my throat and coughing until I can swallow it down with a sip of almond milk. Then I smile up at him, hoping he can't see that I'm scared to death about what he's about to say. I've been expecting a conversation about Adam for weeks now, but they've been acting like he's *Voldemort* from *Harry Potter, the one who must not be named.* I know they're worried that I'd sink back into a depression at the slightest mention of him, but I'm eager to show them I'm fine enough to talk about him without bursting into tears. *Now.* "What's up?"

"Well... I've..." he stutters, his cheeks turning a deep shade of red. "I've sort of been seeing someone."

Oh. I hide my surprise and disappointment. It's not that I want to hear about how well Adam's been doing without me, but after almost two months, I'd welcome any kind of news.

Kyle waits, watching me carefully, and I decide not to harbor on my disappointment and instead relish in his embarrassment since it's probably a once-in-a-lifetime opportunity. "Well, well, well, I never thought I'd live to see the day," I say, finishing up my bowl. "Who's the unlucky sucker who got stuck with you?"

He tries to smile, but his nerves really do seem to have a handle on him. "That's the thing, and before I say who it is, I just want you to know that I really, really like her and obviously wouldn't be telling you this unless it was serious." He opens the refrigerator - I suspect to buy time because he closes it without taking anything out and comes back to where I'm sitting.

"It's serious... you know, and I want you to know that before I tell you who it is."

"Okay," I say, walking over to the sink to rinse out my bowl, silently making a list of people it might be. *Shanel Myers. Mia Anderson. Lily, the French foreign exchange student. Caroline. Oh God, is it Caroline?*

"Well... it's...um," he says, circling his spoon in the bowl, stalling.

I suddenly feel like I'm going to be sick. *What if it is Caroline? What if he's in love with Caroline?* "Spit it out Romeo, you're freaking me out."

"It's Scarlett," he says, slowly raising his eyes to meet mine. "I was going to say something before, but all the stuff with Adam happened, and I don't know... it just felt weird."

"Oh," I say, genuinely surprised. "So that's who you were

texting in Vermont." I slowly start putting the pieces together: the text messages, the smiles, the teasing. When I really think about it, it makes so much sense. They are perfect for each other. He's the ying to her yang, and I can totally see how it works.

He nods, opening his mouth to say something but closes it again.

"I'm happy for you," I push him lightly, and he cracks a real smile. "She's way cooler than you, you know."

He nods, pulling me in for a noogie. "She *is* cooler than me." Then he adds, "You're sure it's cool?"

I laugh. "After the way Adam and I got together, I'm not sure that I'd have a right to complain, even if I didn't support this courtship."

He cringes. "Ugh... courtship? *Bee*, no."

"But you really like her?"

He smiles. "Yeah, I do." I get the feeling he's still getting used to the idea himself. "She's different from anyone I know... she, like, makes me want to try new things."

I put my hand against his forehead like I'm worried for his health. "Kyle? Is that really you?"

He swats me away and walks over to the trash, dumping his uneaten bowl of oatmeal. "That was nasty, by the way."

I look around the kitchen, hesitating to say what's on my mind. I want to ask about Adam. I feel like I'm ready, even if everyone else is still teetering around the subject. The absence of him is felt in this house, and I'm sorry for that, sorry that I'm the reason everything had to change. I know they don't blame me, but I wonder if in the end, they think our relationship was a bad idea. "What's going on with you and Adam, like, are you guys, okay? I'd feel awful if your friendship was weird because of me."

He raises his eyebrows, weary, like he's not sure whether it's a good idea to go on.

I smile. "Kyle, I'm fine, I swear."

"Things were a little weird for a few weeks, but we're cool," he admits. "We're not going to stop being friends, if that's what you're worried about."

"I was worried about that."

He nods. "He's not going to come over to hang out right now, that would be a little awkward, I think, but it's still all good. Plus, I've been spending a lot of time with Scarlett, so it's been a good buffer."

"Well, good. I'm glad to hear it."

"You going to the game later?"

I nod. "Yeah, I'll be there."

"Cool."

I smile, an idea popping into my head. "So, does Scarlett know that you're breaking the news to me right now?"

He nods, a smile spreading across his face. "She's freaking out."

"Should we mess with her?" I say, clapping my hands together and doing my best mad scientist laugh. "Pretend that I freaked when I heard the news?"

"Yes, Bee, yes we should."

While Nina is looking for a parking spot, I scan the lot for Adam's jeep, a habit I've picked up since the *Great Depression*. It's the phrase the Cove Girls so lovingly coined after my breakup with Adam.

I've had a fair amount of success in avoiding him. He only surprised me a few times in the hallways at school and when we share the same lunch period, but now that the weather is getting warmer, I'm worried there would be more opportunities for us to run in to each other. I don't plan on hiding out for the rest of the year, but I know seeing him all the time wouldn't be good, either.

We park and walk over to the bleachers where we spot Scarlett and Kyle sitting halfway up. Before we mount the stairs, Stacey grabs my arm. "I'm going to meet Leann."

Sara rolls her eyes. "One."

Rochelle smiles. "And I'm going to find Charlie."

"Andddd two," Sara says. "A new record." She links her arm in mine, leading us up. "Thank God you're single, otherwise I would be standing by myself right now."

"Well, I'm glad it worked out for someone," I say, shuffling by a group of junior girls to get to Scarlett and Kyle.

"Hey Sister!" Scarlett beams, pulling me in for a hug. "We can call each other that now, right?"

I laugh. "Definitely... *sister!*"

Kyle stands by, stiff, still looking a little uncomfortable in his new role as a boyfriend.

"Well, you two are as cute as a button. Have you figured out what your couples' costume will be for Halloween next year?"

Scarlett laughs out loud, implying they've totally already talked about it. "Bonnie and Clyde, naturally." She leans into Kyle, and he wraps his arm around her waist, cracking his first smile. "Or The Joker and Harley Quinn."

We laugh, just as the crowd starts cheering for Tanya Russo, the captain of the field hockey team. When the whistle blows, we sit, and Scarlett tells us she was just accepted into the fashion design program at one of her top pick schools, *Rhode Island School of Design.* "Oh, my God, Scarlett! Congratulations! This is so major."

"Thanks, I'm pretty pumped about it."

"Didn't you just get accepted into Roger Williams, Kyle?" Sara asks suspiciously.

He nods, trying to act like he's oblivious to the fact that both schools are located in the same state.

Scarlett beams. "We'd only be thirty minutes from each other!"

"Wow, that would be amazing."

"Let's not get ahead of ourselves," he says, but I can tell that he's already made up his mind or, at the very least, wouldn't need much more convincing.

"I'm seriously so pumped for you both, congrats."

Behind us, someone yells, "Yeah, right, Stanson," and I freeze before turning slowly until I see him standing four rows up. His eyes meet mine right away, like he was expecting me to turn around. I whip my head back to the field, reminding myself that I can't avoid him completely. It's a small school, a small town, a small world, and he's still Kyle's best friend. I might even be invited to his wedding one day.

Sara gives me a sympathetic look. "We need a distraction," she says as Connor, James, and Johnny walk up onto the platform. She smiles, looking back at me before calling down. "Connor! Come sit with us!"

They run up, pushing in with us, Connor smiling right at me. "Bee! I've been looking for you everywhere." He sits next to me, leaving no space between us. "So." He wraps his arm around my shoulder and pulls me against him. "How's it going? I miss seeing you around."

"I miss seeing you, too! But I've been all right. You?"

"Not bad. Besides baseball, I've just been thinking about ways I might convince you to let me take you out."

I laugh out loud. "Lie your head right here," he points to his shoulder with his other hand, "and I'll tell you what I've come up with so far."

"Connor, you're a shameless flirt!" I laugh again but he just smiles, waving me on.

I indulge him and he rubs the top of my head like I'm a baby that needs soothing. It's all so ridiculous and funny, and Sara was right; it's the perfect distraction. "So, what do you say?" He asks after naming five very specific ways he's thought about asking me out.

"Maybe."

He jumps up and screams. "She said maybe!!!!!"

The crowd around us responds with cheers and boos, and I pull him back down, enjoying myself too much to care that he's embarrassing me.

Jonathan shouts down. "Yo, Kyle! Make space for us, we're coming down."

I freeze again, not daring to turn around because I know, *without knowing*, that Adam is with him. I hold my breath, watching as he slides into our row, his eyes fixed on mine. He stops right in front of me and I blush, unsure of what's about to happen. He bends down, picking up a lip gloss that must have fallen out of my bag. "You dropped your *Magnolia Shimmer*."

"Thanks." When I take it, he walks away, sitting on the other side of Kyle. I swallow, trying to collect myself. A memory pops into my head of the time he was going through my make-up bag, teasing me about the names. "*Magnolia Shimmer*," he read, laughing. "*It sounds like a Lifetime movie.*"

"I want candy," Sara announces, pulling me away.

I follow her out of our row, wondering if Adam's only intention by coming down here was to stop Connor and me from flirting. I'd be lying if I said I didn't take a little pleasure in knowing that Adam was probably watching us, but to actually interject himself between us was going too far; he forfeited his right to care who I talked to when he broke up with me.

"Thanks," I say to Sara once we're off the bleachers.

"That was intense." We sit on one of the picnic tables by the concession stand, far enough away from the bleachers that I can't even make out any of their faces. "You ripped the Band-Aid off," she says, holding up her hand for a high-five. "It will only get easier from here on out."

"I hope you're right."

She gets up. "I'm going to get some candy, be back in a flash."

"Get me some Twizzlers!" I yell.

A few minutes later, I'm scrolling through my phone when I look up and see Caroline and Dina walking toward me. Caroline rarely crosses my mind these days; funny how heartbreak can put things into perspective. I know now that she's not worth any of my time. Plus, she got what she wanted in the end.

"Look who it is," she says, a smug look on her face. I'm surprised by how angry she seems; we haven't so much as looked at each other in weeks. "Are you sitting here all alone, looking for someone else's boyfriend to steal?"

I stand, walking over so that I'm right in front of her. "I'm glad you came over actually because I wanted to apologize."

Her smile fades. I've caught her off.

"What I did was wrong, and I understand if you hate me, but I just wanted you to know that I *am* sorry."

She hesitates, looking a little relieved. Maybe she realizes that this fight is not worth it, was never worth it. We could go on blaming each other forever, or we could agree that we both got caught up in a boy.

Dina smiles beside her, clearly not ready to throw in the towel. She wants us to hate each other, I can see it written all over her face. "Were you sorry when you kissed her boyfriend?"

Caroline, unfortunately, takes the bait. "No, she wasn't, so save your apologies for someone else. You can't be the hero now after ruining my relationship."

"I didn't ruin your relationship. What Adam and I did at Muster's was wrong, but we both know that you were breaking up, anyway."

Rage flashes in her eyes, and she lifts her hand. "You don't know what you're talking about!"

"And" I say, determined to go on. "We both did things that we shouldn't have. Trying to get the school to hate me was a low-blow, and you know it."

"You deserved it."

"No, actually, I didn't. I never had some grand plan to steal him from you. I was honestly just as surprised as anyone else when I realized he liked me. I get why you were upset, but you went too far. You've never liked me, never even given me a chance, and this was your opportunity to take things to the next level. People break-up all the time, you just couldn't stand that it was me."

Her face softens for a moment before rage takes over again. *She's going to hit me. She's totally going to hit me.*

"Hey," Sara yells, pushing through the circle of people that have formed around us. "What are you doing!?" She looks at Caroline's hand.

Caroline hesitates, slowly lowering her arm back down beside her body. "This isn't over," she says, stepping back.

"It *is* over," I say plainly. "There's nothing more to talk about... I'm not even with Adam anymore, so what's the point of dragging this out? It's over, Caroline."

Sara steps up beside me. "Besides, can you imagine what the admissions office at UCLA would say if they knew that Caroline Conlon was bullying an underclassman?"

"Shut up, Sara, you wouldn't dare."

Sara nods. "I think it would be fair, considering you wrote that post after what I told Nina."

Caroline rolls her eyes, trying to appear like she's not rattled by the idea, but it's clear that Sara's struck a chord. "Whatever," she says, turning around and walking off.

The crowd breaks up around us, and Sara turns to me. "Was Caroline just about to busta cap in your ass? What happened?"

I laugh. "It doesn't matter anymore. It really is over now."

I sit back down, adrenaline still surging through me but I'm relieved. I've had this dark cloud hanging over my head, and now it's gone. I made a mistake, I took responsibility for it, and I can finally breathe easy knowing I did my best to make it right.

As we walk back to Nina's car, I fall behind the girls, looking up at the bleachers and noticing that there's only one person still up there. Adam. He's lost in his thoughts, not focusing on anything in particular. By now, he's definitely heard about what happened between Caroline and me, and I wonder if that's what he's thinking about.

It's like he can feel someone watching because he lifts his head and looks over, standing like he's about to come down, and as much as I want to run to him, I don't. He waits, looking, I think, for some kind encouragement; a wave or a nod, anything that says I need him. But I don't need him - *I want him.* I still want him as much as I ever did and what's more - I think he wants me too. I can see it in his eyes. The yearning. But I won't go to him. If he wants me, he'll have to prove it.

25

ONE WEEK OUT FROM THE FASHION SHOW AND IT'S JUST chaos. The sewing room, our projects, and the untamed emotions of eleven teenagers are like zoo animals being released into the wild. We're stretched thin but still determined to make the show a success. And on the upside, *for me, anyway,* I found I'm capable of crying over something other than Adam. Small victories.

I'm happy with my look; my high-rise mom jeans are finally done, and they're perfect. It was an aggressive undertaking. I seriously overestimated my abilities in taking on a project that big, but with the help of Mrs. Holmes and the rest of the class, I got it done. The only thing I have left to finish is the tote that Sara will carry while walking the runway.

"Oh, my God," I say, slapping my hand against my forehead.

Everyone in class stops, looking over at me. We've grown used to each other's outbursts lately; Ricky just finished one of his own when he discovered that the pockets to his pencil skirt were crooked.

"What is it?" he shouts, his face twisting in a way that makes me think he might burst into tears. "I can't take any more bad news."

I examine my tote in disbelief. "I put my zipper in upside down," I say, throwing it across the room.

Scarlett takes the pins from her mouth and begins stabbing them into a helpless mannequin. "This is a disaster."

Bobby surrenders his scissors. "Why is this so hard?!"

Mrs. Holmes laughs, walking over to us. I know she's about to give us one of her pep-talks because we've heard a lot of them lately. "Did you really think it was going to be easy?" She lets the question hang in the air, her eyes scanning over our defeated faces. "Let me guess... you thought because you *liked* to sew, it wouldn't feel like work?"

I swallow. *That's exactly what I thought.*

She nods. "Let me tell you something - this industry can be *brutal*. It's competitive, cut-throat, subjective, it's fast paced, it's always changing, and it will swallow you up whole if you allow it to. Just because you love what you're doing doesn't mean it won't be hard."

"But it feels like we're drowning here," Scarlett says, stabbing the poor mannequin again.

"Well, yeah, you're just starting out. Instead of focusing on the things you're *not* doing right, think about all the things you've accomplished so far. You started from scratch with nothing, and now we're days away from hosting a fashion show! *A fashion show!* That's a big deal. You've proven that your creativity knows no bounds. You can hold a piece of polyester in your hand and transform it into whatever you want. You're badasses! *Warriors.* If the world ends tomorrow and we have to take off for Mars, they'll take seamstresses right next to doctors and gardeners." That makes us smile. "Trust me on this, the harder it feels now, the more you'll appreciate it later."

We sit there, wide-eyed and speechless, caught up in her words. It's like in a sports movie when they're about to lose the game and the coach comes in at the eleventh hour to turn around the morale. All it takes is the belief that you can do it.

She picks up my tote, handing it back to me. "You're all incredibly talented, and I know that this is the very, very beginning of beautiful careers for you. Whether you go on to have your own line or become a buyer for someone else, or I don't know, open your own Etsy shop and sell knitted beanie hats for infants, you can do it. I'm honored, *truly honored,* to have been here at the start."

Ricky stands, starting a slow clap, and before I know it, we're all standing. I don't even care that this is the corniest scene ever, I'm so inspired.

"You're my hero!" Bobby yells, whistling.

She laughs. "One more week... you can do this. *We* can do this."

The loud speaker chimes, and we sit back down, motivated, ready to finish these projects strong.

Principal Cummings clears his throat, something he insists on doing every single time he goes on the speaker. "Graves Nation, it is I, your loyal leader."

Crickets... eye rolls.

"I have a few very exciting announcements. First, please join me in congratulating our very own Adam Stanson on his acceptance to Villanova on a full-ride athletic scholarship."

I stiffen, looking up at the speaker. "Adam... do you think you could bring home a cheese-steak for me at Thanksgiving? Ha-ha-ha. Kidding. *Kind of!* Anyway, we're all very proud... congratulations Adam. Go Wildcats!"

When the speaker clicks off, I feel everyone's eyes on me. They know how difficult these last few months have been because they went through it with me, even picking up the slack on my projects when I fell behind during *The Great Depression.*

"Whatever, he's not even that good-looking," Bobby says finally, breaking the silence.

We bust out laughing, even Mrs. Holmes.

Ricky shakes his head. "Why are they even congratulating him like this? Justine Miller got accepted into *Harvard. Harvard.* On an academic scholarship. Why didn't they announce hers?"

"The patriarchy lives!" Scarlett says and then, trying to change the subject, she looks around. "Anyone want to come over Friday night to watch *The Devil Wears Prada?* Maybe it will give us an extra boost of inspiration."

I zone out, thinking about the announcement. I shouldn't be surprised that he's going to Villanova, but I am. I guess part of me, despite everything, hoped that he would accept the internship and go to South America.

"Brooke?" Mrs. Holmes says, looking at me with an amused expression on her face.

"Did you hear what Principal Cummings just said?"

"No... sorry... what?" I look up, confused when I realize everyone is looking at me again.

"You just won Vice President."

"What?" I had put my name in on a whim after hearing Chelsea Whitmire complain about how busy they always are. I felt like it was exactly what I needed in the coming months - something to keep me busy. But I never expected to win Vice President.

"Girl, you the VP!!!!" Bobby shouts and then everyone jumps up again and starts clapping.

"I can't believe it."

"Congratulations," Mrs. Holmes says, walking over and pulling me in for a hug.

Scarlett turns around to face me. "Graves Junior class VP, next stop is the white house."

"What do I do now?" I whisper to Scarlett a few minutes later, once we've settled back into our work.

She laughs. "He said, *in a very official voice*, that all class officers should meet in the office after school."

I smile, still trying to process. *Vice President. Wow.*

"You're still going to the basketball banquet tonight, right?" she asks.

I nod, my stomach tightening. I've been dreading it for days. "Yeah, I'm going."

My parents are waiting for me when I come through the door after school.

"Congratulations!!" they shout, pulling me in for a hug.

"How did you even know?" I drop my backpack, noticing Kyle and Scarlett sitting at the kitchen island with cheesy smiles on their faces. "Never mind." Scarlett, much like Adam, has seamlessly molded right into our family life. My parents love her, I love her, and I have a gnawing suspicion that Kyle does, too.

"So, how was the meeting?" Mom asks, following me into the kitchen. Kyle's already dressed for the banquet, wearing khakis and a white button down with that embarrassing basketball tie that he wears every year.

"Really?" I say, pointing at the tie. "You're still wearing that?"

When Mom turns her back, he holds up his middle finger. "It's called *Fash-un*, Karen, look it up."

"Come on, tell us about the meeting!" Mom says again.

"I'm still a little bit in shock, but I'm excited. We're going to start meeting after school on Tuesday and Thursdays to discuss the agenda."

Kyle smiles. "The agenda, wow... sounds pretty serious."

I throw one of Mom's banana muffins at him. "Hater."

"Hey, enough," she warns, looking at us both.

Dad walks in to the kitchen, looking at his watch. "Better get going, Troops, don't want to be late."

Mom touches a hand to my shoulder. "Bee, I thought maybe you and I could drive together?"

I nod. "Sure, I'm just going to change really quick. I'll be right down."

In the car, she turns up Adele's *Send My Love,* and we start singing along thematically, hitting all the notes obnoxiously. She has a strict *Adele only* policy in her car.

My mind starts to wander to Adam, as it often does when I listen to the lyrics of most songs these days. As if she can hear my thoughts, she lowers the volume and waits. She doesn't have to say anything for me to know it's time we talk. I've held her at arms-length through my whole breakup knowing she has the capability to make me feel the things that I've been trying to avoid, but maybe I'm ready now. "I guess I'm wondering if it will always hurt this much. I've been trying to get over it, you know, move on, but it's so hard."

She nods. "The pain won't last forever, no."

"Sometimes I wish I could take it all back, all of it. Why would anyone want to experience love if it can be taken away? It's so unfair." I pause, looking out the window. "Do you think it was a mistake?"

She doesn't say anything right away, waiting until she's stopped at a red light to look at me. "No, what you shared was a good thing."

I scoff. "But what was the point?"

She thinks it over. "I guess I think we experience these things so that we can learn from them. You can learn a lot from having your heart broken."

"Like not to fall in love with your brother's best friend?"

She smiles. "You can't understand this yet, not when your heart is still so raw, but heartbreak is a major life event, almost like a rite of passage. You're not the same after it happens, and that's a good thing. You don't ever want to get yourself stuck being the same person. Growth only happens when you experience things. Especially, the hard things."

The tears start falling. "But why would I want to experience this? It sucks, Mom! It just hurts so much."

She turns into the lot, parking, then looks at me for a beat before pulling me in for a hug. "I know it does, *I know,* and one of the hardest parts is that it won't go away overnight. But I promise that you'll get through this, just let yourself feel it."

"What if it doesn't *feel* like it's really over?"

She pulls back, examining my face. "Maybe it's not. Or maybe you need closure, or maybe there are other things that are at play right now that you have no control over. It's hard, I know, when your future feels uncertain, but there's not much you can do but try and live for this moment."

"I am better, you know. It doesn't seem like it right now, but I am."

She nods in understanding, and her smile gives me so much comfort. "Of course you are. You're so strong, Bee, and I'm incredibly proud of you."

More tears.

Once I've settled down a bit, I look at myself in the mirror. "Great, now I'm all swollen and blotchy."

She chuckles, tucking a piece of loose hair behind my ear. "You're beautiful."

I check the time; the banquet starts in five minutes, and I can picture all the Booster Moms working in the small kitchen inside, preparing the pasta and meatballs. "Will you give me a few minutes? I'll be in soon."

She nods. "Take your time." She kisses my forehead, looks over my face again, and steps out.

I take a deep breath before guzzling half a bottle of water. I hate that with each moment, it's getting easier to live without him. Part of me wants to hold on to the pain because it's the only thing keeping me connected to him now.

I step outside of the car, walking to the front of the hall when I pause, remembering the bunker I used to play in behind the building. It's not a real bunker, it's actually just an old empty shed, but I used to sneak away from the banquets and hang out with the other younger siblings. On a whim, I decide to see if it's still out there.

I walk around the side of the building, past the trash barrels and the piles of broken down cardboard boxes, thinking about their first banquet four years ago. I was in the seventh grade, and I spent most of the night standing in front of a photo collage one of the moms had put together of all the players. I was trying to decide who my favorite boys were, who might be the funniest or the smartest or the most romantic. I told myself that Adam didn't count anymore, he would never be my number one again; he'd just started with Caroline, and I felt betrayed. I needed someone new, so I picked Jake Lyons, one of the senior captains. He didn't look like the kind of boy who would break an unspoken pact to save himself for me. But in a split-second decision, I ripped Adam's photo right off of the board and put it in my pocket. It was ridiculous to think there was ever anyone else.

A few more steps and the bunker comes into view. The

grass is still wet from the rain earlier, so I pull off my flats and walk toward the shed, not even sure what I'm hoping to see.

"Bee," I hear from behind me.

Adam.

For a moment, I consider running; I could do it, I could avoid him completely, even if it did make me look like a coward. But then he says my name again, his steps getting closer.

I turn slowly, watching him make his way over, wearing the tie that I made him for Christmas. He catches me looking at it and touches it self-consciously.

"What are you doing?" he asks.

My throat feels dry as I say, "What?"

His face lights up with a smile. I haven't seen a real smile from him in so long. "What are you doing back here with your shoes off?"

I look down at my wet feet, specks of grass sticking to my skin. "Oh... I wanted to see if the bunker was still out here."

"The bunker?"

"The shed," I point. "We used to call it our bunker." It's still standing, but just barely. It looks like it might fall over with the next gust of wind. For some reason, it makes me sad, like with its collapse, I have to let go of another part of my childhood. I guess I'm pretty sentimental these days. "What are *you* doing out here?"

"I followed you," he blushes, searching my face. "Have you been crying?"

I step back, shaking my head as my throat catches. I can't tell him the truth - that it feels like I haven't *stopped* crying since we broke up. "My allergies are bad this time of year."

He holds my gaze, skeptical. "Bee, look."

"Congrats... officially on Villanova," I say, changing the

subject. "It must be really exciting to finally know what you're doing next year."

He runs his hand through his hair, looking uncertain. "Yeah, thanks. I guess it does, and congrats to you, too, on VP. That's pretty cool. You never mentioned student council before."

"I put my name in on a whim."

"That's a pretty lucky whim." He smiles. I can tell he's proud, and I'm pleased, even though I don't want to be.

I shift back and forth, the grass making a squishy sound under my feet. "How's your family?"

"Yeah, good. Mom's better. She misses you, the girls too."

I'm happy to hear it. "I miss them, too." My throat catches again. "And your Dad?"

"He's not great. He was hanging around for a while, telling us that he was going to change, but then Mom found out that he was still talking to his girlfriend, so now she's leaving him, and I think his girlfriend left him, too."

"Wow."

"Yeah." He lets out a long breath. "You were right."

"About what?" *About his dad. About us. About everything.*

He holds my gaze, moments ticking by like he's hesitant to say it. "About everything." Another long breath. "I let my Dad get in my head. I just wanted him back, you know? That version of him that stayed up late to shoot hoops with me. And I don't know... after Vermont, he was around again. He was at the house, and we were hanging out - watching games together, laughing like the old times. I thought, okay, he made a mistake, and now he's trying to make things right. I trusted him. So when he started talking about *us* and Villanova, I thought maybe he *is* right. Maybe we're too young to have these kinds of feeling for each other. Maybe I should give his plan a try. He's my dad, right? He wouldn't try to manipulate me - he's just looking out. But then Mom caught him again, and I realized exactly what was going on. He's only been looking out for himself. This whole time."

"I'm sorry," I blurt because I am. I can't imagine realizing that about my own dad. I was wrong about a lot of things, but I didn't want to be right about Luke.

"*I'm* sorry. I've been such an idiot. I miss you. I miss you so much - I... I messed up. I really messed up."

"It's...okay?" I'm taken aback. I've thought about this moment so many times in the last few months, but I never imagined it happening like this; barefoot with grass sticking to my legs. I guess part of me knew -on some level- that he would realize it eventually. But I didn't expect him to admit it so freely now.

"It's not okay." He moves forward. "I'm sorry for the way I treated you before - I feel bad about it every single day. I was scared... I'm still a little scared because when I'm with you, you make me feel... *everything*."

"What's wrong with that?"

"Nothing! Nothing... it's just...God... this sounds so corny but... you inspire me to go after what I want. Like, I was ready to just go on doing what was expected of me until you called me out on it. And I don't know... I guess for a while, it was easier to just play it safe, but you come through, encouraging me to be...." he looks around, helpless, "me."

"Wow." I let out a breath, overwhelmed, surprised, ecstatic. I should have worn a better dress.

"Do you think I'm losing my mind?"

"No."

"No?"

"No."

He smiles. "After everything I just said... that's all you've got?"

"Yes." I spin on my heels, hiding my smile. I have to get out of here. No matter how excited I am right now, I'm going to make him work a little harder for my attention this time around. He may be Adam Stanson and everything, but I'm Brooke McGrath.

26

I SLAM MY PHONE DOWN ON ONE OF THE RUNWAY PROPS. "I'm screwed. I'm totally screwed," I pant, looking at Scarlett with panic in my eyes. The show is starting in less than thirty minutes, and Sara just bailed as my model.

"What happened?"

"Sara's sick! Ohmygod. Ohmygod. Ohmygod."

Scarlett turns to me, putting her hands on my shoulders. She's already dressed in her faux black leather construction uniform, looking like a sexy cat-woman. I, on the other hand, look like Cinderella after that spell wore off. I have been working all morning, trying to get ready for the show. I wasn't planning on having to walk the runway!

"You have to wear the look yourself. It fits you the best, anyway."

I shake my head. "I can't go out there, you know I can't. I'll fall flat on my face. There has to be another way." My knees wobble just thinking about being in front of all those people. I can't do it, I just can't.

Ricky chuckles, adjusting the skirt on his model, Ruby. It's bright red with the names of brave women throughout history stitched on top: *Mary Wollstonecraft, Rosa Parks, Malala Yousafzai.* "Babe, if you fall wearing sneakers, you have bigger problems than that." He points to the stage.

I look back at Scarlett, whose hands are still firmly planted on my shoulders. "You can do this, Brooke. You can do anything for sixty seconds." I hold her gaze for a beat, pulling back when I realize that as much as I don't want to, I don't have a choice. But maybe it won't be so bad. There are a lot of things I've been discovering about myself these days - mainly my strength - and just how much I'm capable of doing. "Okay, I'll do it."

She squeaks, pulling me in for a hug. "Let's get you dressed."

Once I'm dressed and ready, Mrs. Holmes comes up behind us asking if we're ready. There was no pep-talk today, but we don't need it this time. All she says is, "you've got this," before opening the curtain and walking out onto the stage.

"Okay, get into your spots," Max Bingham, the stage manager, directs. He was the one who transformed the stage, making it look like a scene right out of *West Side Story.*

Mrs. Holmes makes an introduction, something about *exceptional young people* and *evolution of fashion* and before I know it, the curtain is opening and she's saying, "without further ado, I present you with *The Working Woman.*"

Beyonce's *Run the World* clicks on. Max looks at the first model, Sam, nods, "go," and she's off, the first look of the night, strutting like she does this every day. She's wearing a short, tight hot pink halter dress with a white lab coat and stethoscope hanging from around her neck.

Mrs. Holmes commentates. "This is Sam. Sam is a Urologist. She does not conform to formality and instead chooses to express herself through her favorite color, pink."

I smile, thinking of the other night at George's, when the

class met to write the descriptions for each of our looks. I haven't laughed that hard in months. We were going for honest but ironic, fierce but funny. I think we nailed it.

Sam makes it to the end of the stage, curtsies, and walks back while the audience starts clapping along to the song. *Who run the world? Girls.*

Sam does a final hair flip and steps off the stage. "This look was created by Amber. Thank you, Amber."

Bobby's model, Stassi, is next, wearing a blush-pink coverall jumpsuit with feminist patches stitched on. They read *Feminist AF* and *Unladylike.* "This is Stassi. Stassi is a mechanic. She spends her days under the hood of your car but at night, she advocates for the NOW. She enjoys the simple things in life - equal pay opportunities, longer maternity leaves, and quiet Sunday mornings."

"Why are so many people here?" I whisper to Scarlett. Now that the curtain is drawn open, it's obvious that the auditorium is packed. I expected maybe thirty people, not a filled assembly.

My eyes rake through the first few rows, trying not to be disappointed when I don't see Adam. He'd been texting me for weeks, asking to talk, to hang out, then he moved on to duck-face selfies and absurd questions like, *if I had to choose boogers or ear wax to eat for breakfast every day for the rest of my life, which would I choose?* He followed me in the hallways, even getting written up by the hall monitor one day for lingering outside my classroom. He sent flowers, balloons, dropped off about a year's supply of Twizzlers. He even left a box out front one day filled with retro, hot pink fabric with a note that said it was his grandmothers. I hadn't responded to any of it. I was determined to make him sweat.

"I have no idea, it's like New York Fashion Week! " She squeezes my hand. "It's thrilling."

Scarlett straightens her back as Stassi heads off the stage.

"Wish me luck." The audience gasps as soon as she struts out. She's made for this kind of thing. There's lots of clapping and hair tossing, but I'm hardly paying attention. *I'm next. Oh God, I'm next!*

"Brooke?" Scarlett says, back in front of me now. She's glowing, breathing heavy like she just finished running a marathon. And in a way, she did.

"Yeah?"

She pushes me forward. "You're up!"

This is it, *my* moment. I thought my moment was Adam, I thought he was the greatest thing to ever happen to me, but it's actually right now. It's getting to be a part of something that's bigger than either of us. If I learned anything this year, it's that I can do things that are hard, that I'm capable and strong. So, I'll do this for me, not for Adam or the Cove Girls or Mrs. Holmes. *For me.* I might fall, but I'll get back up, ideally without a sprained ankle.

When I open my eyes, I'm at the corner of the stage - the bright lights blinding me for a moment. Before I can take a step forward, Kyle's voice fill the auditorium. "Yeaaaaaaah Bee," he shouts. The song switches to Taylor Swift's, *The Man* and I start moving, looking for the designated X's on the floor that Max marked to map out our route.

Mrs. Holmes voice urges me on. "This is Brooke. Brooke is a stay-at-home mom. She has many jobs; she is a master culinarian, a domestic CEO, a doctor, surgeon, a chauffeur, administrative assistant, and a life coach. She is *everything.*"

I stop on the X at the midway point, put my hands on my hips like Scarlett just did, and smile at the crowd. There, in the front row is Mom, beaming with tears in her eyes. I keep moving, stopping again at the last X, getting ready for my grand finale. *Snacks.* I reach into my tote, pulling out fun-sized packs of chips and cookies, pausing for a moment before tossing them out into the audience. It was Sara's idea. She said it would be a nice touch, and she was right. The audience goes wild over it.

"Oh, my God!" Scarlett and Ricky say, pulling me in for a hug. "You did it!"

"*We* did it!" I shriek. "I can't believe we pulled this off!"

Ricky waves his hands around his face. "We're amazing!"

After the last model walks, Mrs. Holmes calls us out onto the stage one last time for a bow. I'm not intimated this time, too jazzed up with adrenaline. We stand in a wide line with our arms draped over each other: smiling, laughing, crying.

Mrs. Holmes waits until there is a lull in the applause. "I would just like to personally say thank you to all of my amazing students, who have made me so proud this year. Bravo!"

She steps down and we rush over, pulling her in a group hug. Then she goes back up to the podium. "And to you, our family and friends who have supported us all year long, we couldn't have done it without you!" The lights flash to the audience, and the room lights up like a Christmas tree. My eyes are drawn to the lone person standing in the back of the room. *Adam.* A proud smile is practically tattooed on his face.

I'm pulled into another group hug, and when I look back again, he's gone.

The curtain closes, and we all look around at each other before letting out a big whooping scream. This is the coolest thing I've ever been a part of, and I'm proud of myself and my friends. Mrs. Holmes was right; the payoff is sweet.

I'm sitting with the rest of the class after the show. The adrenaline stayed long after the post-congratulations and the clean-up, and we are just savoring the feeling of having done something so major. Mrs. Holmes full-on cried, saying it was one of her proudest moments ever.

"After the third hair flip, I thought she pulled her neck." Ricky laughs as he recalls Scarlet's runway walk.

She holds her hand to her neck. "I might have, actually."

We bust out laughing. Everything is funny right now.

"Excuse me," we hear from the side of the stage.

When I turn, I'm surprised to see Isabelle, the girl from the concession stand last fall standing there. When she sees that I recognize her, she relaxes and walks over.

I stand to greet her. "Hey, long time no see."

She tucks her hair behind her ears, peeking at the rest of the kids behind me. "I saw the show. It was really cool."

"Thanks! Do you want to sit down?"

"No... um... I've been sent on a mission."

My head jerks back. "A mission?"

She nods, smiling now, motioning to the envelope in her hand. "I've been sent to deliver an invitation."

By now, the rest of the class is standing and walking over, circling Isabelle like a bunch of hungry lions. "Do you accept?" she asks.

I hesitate, but only for a second. "I accept."

She hands me the envelope. "This message will self-destruct in fifteen seconds."

I laugh, looking down at my name written in bold blue bubble letters

"Girl... if you don't open that right now, I will," Ricky nudges.

With my heart fluttering, I rip it open, reading out loud, *Please, read to Feel Again by One Republic.*

Ohmygod. My movie moment.

Scarlett pulls out her phone, hands shaking. "I got it!"

"Read it out loud!!" Amber shouts. "Please."

Dear Bee,

I'm sorry. I'm sorry for everything. I'm sorry for bailing on you. I'm sorry that I left you hanging. I tried really hard to convince myself that I didn't deserve you, that I would end up hurting you. I let myself be swayed and that's no excuse for how I treated you but I was scared. I'm still a little scared of how much I care about you.

I know I'm leaving in the fall but it's true what I told you at the summit lodge - I want to stay together because I want to stay together forever. If you'll have me. You're amazing – you're kind and smart and sweet and creative and goofy and sexy. You're everything, Bee. MY everything. It's always been you and it always will be. You're the best person I've ever known and you mean the world to me. I'm serious.

I can't predict the future and I can't guarantee that it will be easy but I want to try. No matter what happens you'll always have my heart. I love you, take me back?

Adam

PS. I'll be at the Willow Glen, waiting for you. I'll wait for you forever.

"Hol-lee-shit," Ricky shouts.

I look up, stunned, wiping away the tears that are falling down my cheeks. "What do I do?"

"Go!" Scarlett yells.

"Go?"

"Go!" they all shout at once.

"Can someone drive me?"

It's amazing how fast you can get somewhere with the support of ten fashionistas. I make it to the reservoir within minutes.

When I see Adam's jeep parked in one of the usual spots, I dart into the woods, running way faster than I ever thought possible. I run like my life depends on it, or at the very least, like my *love life* depends on it.

I find him standing under our tree, looking out at the water. I'm suddenly struck with the desire to go back to that day almost two years ago when everything changed between us. I'd tell my fifteen-year-old self that everything would be okay. That high school would be fine, that I wouldn't get hazed, that nothing exciting would even happen until I was sixteen and my actual dreams came true when Adam Stanson became my boyfriend. *Yes, that Adam Stanson.*

I'd tell her, that despite having him, it isn't easy, it's actually really complicated. But on the other side of all the drama, I'll be running, at full speed, into the exact spot where it all began. To meet him, to start over or start for the first time, it doesn't matter. The only thing that matters is that we're together.

A stick snaps under my feet as I take a step forward, the sound making him look in my direction. He lets out a sigh and walks over, reaching out his hand. "Bee."

I reach for him, but when our hands touch, I keel over, coughing. "Sorry," I pant, "I ran in."

"You hate running."

When I've caught my breath, I stand on my tip toes, tilting my head up, waiting for him to meet me halfway. "I'd run for you."

And then finally... his lips are on mine.

After a while, he pulls away. "I know I'm a little late." He reaches into his pocket and pulls out the Swiss army knife that Luke gave him for his tenth birthday.

"Please don't ruin this moment by killing me."

He laughs, leading me over to sit beneath the willow tree. "Sorry it took me so long." He starts carving, and when he's finished, it's perfect. It says, *Adam + Bee*.

I lean into him, resting my head against his chest. "After all this time, I can't believe I'm back here with Adam Stanson."

He leans down, kissing the top of my head. "There's no place I'd rather *Bee*."

EPILOGUE

To: BEEfashionfun@gmail.com
From: A.Stanson@gmail.com
Subject line: Hola from Ecuador

Hola my beautiful baby Bee hive. I miss you already. I listened to that playlist you made me at least thirty times on the flight over. I must have looked pretty mopey because the lady next to me took my hand and said, *you'll be okay.* At least, I think that's what she said. My room is cool, I have a pretty sweet view of the town I'm living in. It's so different from home. The family I'm living with seem nice too, they've nicknamed me muscle-man-boy and Clara, the mom, says she's going to teach me to cook. So maybe I'll be culinary master by the time I'm home. Thanks for the bathing suit, by the way. Is that why you snuck back into my room? How's home? I know it's only been like, twelve hours, but I already miss it. Mom said you had dinner with them yesterday. That was nice. I'm jealous. I have to be honest, Bee. I'm nervous. Now that I'm here, it just seems so **crazy.** But you make me feel like I can do anything.

But what about this stationary? You really expect me to use stickers? Okay... I'll use the stickers. I love you. I love you so much. I'll see you in a year.

Adam

ACKNOWLEDGMENTS

When I first started writing this book, I was two months postpartum with my second child and I thought, on many levels, that the creative part of myself would be caged for years to come. But then I was vacationing on Cape Cod with my family and an idea popped into my head. Something about pickle juice and dream boys and instead of ignoring it, I decided to write it down. And I fell in love. With the characters, with the process, with having something for myself, outside of being a mother. And I knew inherently that I had begun something that would change my life. That I wouldn't be able to come back from it. The only reason this happened was because I took a chance on something that would cost me nothing and just... started. So, if you're wondering how to start, it's just that, to start.

Molly Czarnecki. Thank you for reading every single version of this thing. No one on this planet has been as invested in this as you and without you're support it would have been very lonely for me. Your critiques have helped shape this book. *You* have helped shape this book. Your pep-talks kept me going and I'm so grateful for your friendship. Thank you.

I'll always be grateful to Parker Peevyhouse for giving me my first professional critique. Your advice was so important to this story and without it, I may have gone in a totally different direction. Thank you.

Jenn Hanson-DePaula, the world's best book coach. You

have been my north star during the post-writing phase of this project. Knowing you were in my corner, helping me through this has made all the difference. Thank you!

My editor, Borbala Branch, for loving this story as much as I do and for making me feel like I had something special. My designer, Sarah Battistelli for meeting with me one day and letting me go on and on about Adam and Bee and from that, creating such a beautiful cover. From day one, you made me feel like we were in this together and I'm so grateful.

To my first readers - my mom, Tanya, Liz, Chelsie, Cambria, Maura, Ada and Meg. You gave me the confidence to keep going, to revise harder, to make it the best it can be.

To my critique partners - Chelsie Prince and Kaitlyn Blackman, but more importantly, my "writer" friends. Getting to know you has been the best. You've been such a sounding board for me and I feel lucky to have met you at the beginning of our careers.

My parents and Karl. For being exactly who you are and believing in me every step of the way. To my girls - who have forever changed my life. I'm pretty proud of what I've accomplished with this book but I'll forever be the proudest of being your mom. Thank you for choosing me.

And to my guy. I'm so glad that I had the guts all those years ago to make the first move, because what we've created together is beautiful. I think you believed in me before I believed in me. You offered this project so much unyielding support, that I could never doubt myself for long. So, thanks, and I guess after everything, I can admit that you're right, most of my swoon-inspiration did come from you because you make me feel like I'm living in a romance novel every day.

Made in United States
North Haven, CT
11 March 2022

16996365R00186